"If it were up to me, you wouldn't have a job. You weren't my idea."

"And yet, here I am." His lips curved, but there was no humor in his eyes. "Whether I remain isn't up to you. It's up to Ms. Wright, and from what I've seen and heard, she's on the side of signing my checks."

Right. She was just another job for him, wasn't she? Just another paycheck. Why couldn't she remember that? "You're just always there. Here. Everywhere. I feel like I need to put a bell around your neck."

"You can try," he countered. "I get it, Peyton. You're used to being in control. You like your nice, organized little world as tidy and compact as possible. I'm an intruder. But here's something you need to know about me." He moved in, close enough she could feel his breath against her face, feel the warmth of his body radiating against hers. "I don't quit."

Dear Reader,

When we wrote the first collection of Blackwell books, we laughingly wondered if there was another group of stories to tell. Turns out, there was. Being able to return to Falcon Creek, Montana, with four of my best friends felt like lightning striking twice (in that good way). The proof is in these books.

The Harrison-Blackwell sisters are unique in that they're all different, but they all share the same big heart. Family is, and always will be, what's most important to them. Writing about the eldest sister, Peyton, was both a pleasure and a challenge. A pleasure because I got to watch this career-obsessed woman discover that she really can have everything she wants, and a challenge because she's carried a secret for a very long time. A secret that has damaged the close relationship she's had with her sisters.

She's not in any condition to fall in love... which means it's the perfect time. Not only does she find herself falling head over heels for her bodyguard, Matteo Santos, but also his adorable six-year-old son. Ah, love. It just puts everyone where they're supposed to be, doesn't it?

Here's to the Blackwell family...past and present. And all the love they bring to the world.

Anna J

HEARTWARMING

Montana Dreams

—

Anna J. Stewart

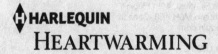

HARLEQUIN
HEARTWARMING

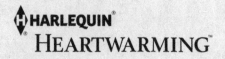

HARLEQUIN®
HEARTWARMING™

PLEASE RECYCLE
THIS PRODUCT IS RECYCLABLE

ISBN-13: 978-1-335-88989-8

Recycling programs
for this product may
not exist in your area.

Montana Dreams

Copyright © 2020 by Anna J. Stewart

This edition published by arrangement with Harlequin Books S.A.

For questions and comments about the quality of this book,
please contact us at CustomerService@Harlequin.com.

Harlequin Enterprises ULC
22 Adelaide St. West, 40th Floor
Toronto, Ontario M5H 4E3, Canada
www.Harlequin.com

Printed in U.S.A.

Bestselling author **Anna J. Stewart** is living her dream writing romances for Harlequin's Romantic Suspense and Heartwarming lines. In between bouts of binge-watching her favorite TV shows and movies, she puts fingers to keyboard and loses herself in endless stories of happily-ever-after. Anna lives in Northern California, where she tries to wrangle two rapscallion cats named Rosie and Sherlock, possibly the most fiendish felines known to humankind.

Books by Anna J. Stewart

Harlequin Romantic Suspense

Honor Bound

Reunited with the P.I.
More Than a Lawman
Gone in the Night
Guarding His Midnight Witness

Harlequin Heartwarming

Return of the Blackwell Brothers

The Rancher's Homecoming

Butterfly Harbor Stories

Recipe for Redemption
A Dad for Charlie
Always the Hero
Holiday Kisses
Safe in His Arms
The Firefighter's Thanksgiving Wish
A Match Made Perfect

Visit the Author Profile page at
Harlequin.com for more titles.

For Melinda, Amy, Carol and Cari—my very own
Blackwell sisters.

And Kathryn Lye, editor and
romance writer–wrangler extraordinaire.

PROLOGUE

"YOU MISS HIM."

Peyton Harrison ducked her chin to hide the sad smile spreading across her lips.

The gentle hand on her shoulder was, as always, one of comfort and understanding. A hand that had guided and supported her most of her eighteen years. A hand that had never once wavered or abandoned her. A hand that was always there when she'd needed it. A hand that with one gentle squeeze offered her the comfort she hadn't realized she'd needed.

Rudy Harrison, navy admiral and stepfather extraordinaire. From the moment he'd married their mother more than ten years before, he'd been their rock. Solid. Understanding. Loving. Most of all, he'd been present if not a bit... overprotective. The word made Peyton's lips twitch. There was very little Rudy Harrison wouldn't do for his girls.

He also had the uncanny ability to know when one of them was in trouble or hurting.

Amid the celebratory laughter and cheers, beneath the swirling streamers and bouncing balloons and *Congratulations, Peyton* cloth banner stretched across the backyard, he knew today, the day she'd graduated high school, not only opened doors to her future but also turned an overly bright spotlight on her past. And the man—the father—who wasn't there.

She reached up, placed her hand over her stepfather's gentle one and gave it a squeeze, buying herself an extra moment before facing him. "Not really," she lied, then let out an uneasy laugh at Rudy's chiding expression. "It's silly, I know." The tears no longer burned at the thought of Thomas Blackwell, the man who had walked away from his wife and children when Peyton was only six. But the longing... She didn't understand it. After all this time, all these years, how could she still miss him?

"It's not silly, and you know it." Rudy moved closer, slipped his arm around Peyton's shoulders and drew her in. Peyton closed her eyes, leaned into him. "Of course you'd want him to be here, Peyton. He's your father."

"He is," Peyton said softly. "But he's not my dad." She felt the surprise shift through Rudy and, even without looking at his face, knew she'd caught him off guard. She shifted slightly, looked out at the smattering of family and friends who had come to her graduation party. They were a colorful blur of activity and happiness against the backdrop of the four young women meandering around the backyard, toasting with their sparkling cider and taking turns with her graduation cap and honor cords.

Georgie, Amanda and Lily, her teenage triplet sisters, along with their little sister Fiona, could always, no matter what, lift her spirits. There was studious, analytical, science-minded Georgie with her book smarts and wry, observational attitude, and headstrong, fiercely protective, animal-lover Amanda. There was Lily, who, despite the childhood injury that left her with dexterity issues, dived headfirst into whatever adventure she could find. And then there was Fee. Fiona. Peyton's heart squeezed as the sound of her youngest sister's laughter rang through the party. Fee was love and kindness personified. Okay, Peyton might be a bit biased when it came to

Fiona. She had, in a lot of ways, been Peyton's own kid, what with their mother having five rambunctious girls all under the age of seven to care for once their father was gone.

But then Rudy had come and everything had…settled.

Everything except Peyton's heart, which still longed for the father she remembered. The father who had taken her on horseback-riding trips and taught her about the moon and the stars. The father who had one day been there and the next wasn't.

"I think today's hard on your mom, too."

Rudy's not-so-gentle suggestion that Peyton and her mother might have something important to discuss on this day had Peyton rolling her eyes. She might be on the brink of adulthood, but some topics—like her increasingly strained relationship with her mother— brought out the less mature aspects of Peyton's personality.

"You should talk to her."

Peyton pinched her lips tight and lifted her head from her stepfather's chest.

"Peyton…" Rudy shook his head and sighed. "I know this is a topic that's always been—"

"Off-limits." Peyton winced at the sharpness in her tone. "I've never been allowed to talk about him. Except…"

"Except to your mother or me. I know." He gave her another squeeze. "But you haven't talked about him much. With her."

Peyton winced. How did she explain? How could she even try when she didn't understand it herself? She knew the particulars—the details, as it were. Thomas Blackwell, instead of retiring from the service when he'd promised, had reupped and gone back overseas, leaving Susan pregnant with baby girl number five. Susan divorced him and, shortly after Fiona was born, married Rudy Harrison. End of story. At least as far as Susan was concerned.

Peyton was the only sister who remembered their real father, the only sister who knew they were not Harrisons but Blackwells by birth. She'd kept her mother's secret. A secret that had built a wall between mother and daughter brick by brick, year by year. A wall Peyton wasn't sure could ever be scaled.

"You know…"

Peyton took a deep breath. She knew that tone. Rudy—Dad—always started one of his *I think this how you should address this situation* lectures with *You know.*

"You know how quickly life can change, Peyton. In the blink of an eye you can lose someone. Lose the opportunity you thought would always be there. In the military, we're prepared for it. Or at least as prepared as we can be. You don't want to be someone who lives with regrets. Not when you're going out there and getting started with your life. Peyton." He took hold of her arms and turned her to face him, ducking a bit to catch her gaze. "Leave the baggage and the hurt feelings here. Don't take them with you. Your mother loves you so much. It breaks her heart to think she's hurt you in some way."

In some way? Peyton very nearly rolled her eyes again. That was part of the problem, wasn't it? Her mother had never understood the toll that secret—that lie—had taken on Peyton. To know she was keeping a secret—a huge secret—from the people she loved the most.

"Go talk to her," Rudy urged. "Consider that your graduation present to me."

Peyton grinned at his teasing. "I'm the one graduating, remember? I'm supposed to get the gifts."

"That's right. You are." He turned her around

and gave her a gentle push. Much, Peyton thought, as he had whenever she'd had to do something she didn't want to do. Because she knew he was watching, because she knew he was right, she mingled and weaved her way through her guests, issuing promises of cake-cutting and gift-opening soon, and avoiding her sisters' curious gazes as she got two glasses of iced tea.

Susan Harrison, military wife and mother of five, sat on the wooden bench she and Rudy had found in an old antiques shop shortly after they'd married. It was her favorite spot outside the house, in the middle of the lush garden she tended, surrounded by the flora and fauna of San Diego. Late spring and early summer provided explosions of color to accompany any celebration, enough, for a while at least, to push cares and concerns away. Or maybe just lock them in silence.

"Thought you could use a refill." Peyton held out the cold glass. Her mother blinked foggy green eyes at her and, for a moment, Peyton wondered if her mother had been somewhere else entirely.

"Thank you, Peyton. That's lovely." She

scooted down a bit and patted the bench. "Join me?"

Peyton sat, sparing a quick glance back to the porch where Rudy stood, arms crossed over his chest, eyes pinned on them. He offered her a quick smile and nod of approval before he headed back into the house, the sound of the screen door slamming behind him oddly comforting.

"I can't believe my girl's all grown up." Susan's voice was so soft. "High school graduate, all ready to head off for college. The house is going to be so empty without you."

"Empty with those four?" Peyton laughed as Lily and Amanda teased Georgie with one of Amanda's rescue kittens. Georgie, as usual, was determined to keep an emotional distance, but Peyton could see the longing in her sister's eyes when it came to the furry little creature. "You won't even miss me."

"Yes," Susan said and finally looked at Peyton. "Yes, I will." She lifted a hand, brushing her fingers against Peyton's cheek. "I'm so proud of you, Peyton. More than I can ever say. You're going to do amazing things with your life. I just know it."

Peyton could only smile. There was so

much pushing in on her, so many questions, so many… "Just promise not to let Amanda and Lily fight to the death over my room."

"I'll do my best," Susan managed with a small laugh. "Peyton—"

"Do you miss him?" The question leapt out of her mouth before she could stop it. Over ten years she'd been wanting to ask. Ten years she'd wondered. "Do you miss him at all?"

Susan blinked, her eyes shifting briefly to the house as if knowing Rudy had something to do with the question. But instead of anger or irritation as Peyton expected, Susan's eyes filled with tears.

"I miss him every single time I look at you girls. He was my first love, Peyton. The man I honestly thought I'd spend the rest of my life with. He gave me everything I could ever want. He gave me all of you." And yet, there was sadness, even in the explanation. "And then…he couldn't give me anything." She took a long drink of tea and settled back on the bench. "Hindsight, along with Rudy," she added with a flash of a smile, "tell me I was wrong to ever ask you to keep my secret. Our secret. But I needed to forget, Peyton. I needed to start over. It was selfish, I suppose, expecting you to do the same. But the idea of them having so many questions, all the time, about a man who was never going to be part of their lives…a man who broke my heart…" She shook her head. "I did what I needed to do, Peyton. I'm only sorry it hurt you. Thomas could not be a part of our lives, not even the memory of him. Not without causing far too much pain."

"They still don't know," Peyton whispered, shifting her own gaze to her sisters. Her crazy, loud, annoying, obnoxious, amazing sisters. Sisters she loved so much she almost ached.

"No," Susan said. "They don't. And they'll never have cause to. I suppose I'm still selfish, making that choice for both of us, but that's how it has to be. Nothing good will ever come of them knowing. Rudy is their father. In every single way that matters. Surely you see that?"

"Of course I do." Peyton swallowed the resentment, along with the disappointment that her mother hadn't changed her mind after all these years. "My feelings about our real father have nothing to do with Dad. With Rudy. But, Mom." She turned on the bench and grabbed her mother's hand. "The truth is going to come out some day. Wouldn't it be better coming from you?"

"It wouldn't be better coming from anyone."

Peyton saw it then, in her mother's eyes. All over her face. Susan Harrison was not going to change her mind. She wasn't going to tell her other daughters the truth. And she wasn't going to release Peyton from her promise, either. Peyton didn't believe in omens, but she did believe in honesty and the truth. And she knew, no matter how many plans someone made, the truth always found a way of getting out.

"I can barely remember what he looks like," Peyton whispered. "It's like he's this ghost in my mind. But I remember that he was kind and he loved me. He loved all of us."

"Yes, he did. But he loved the service more." Susan covered Peyton's hand with her own. "I can't fault him for that. But he chose them, Peyton. Not us. And I won't disrupt any more lives over it. Can you forgive me for that? For making you a party to this?" She inclined her head, met Peyton's tear-glazed gaze with her own. "Can you please forgive me?"

Rudy had said not to take the pain with her, to leave it behind. This was her chance.

To move on. To move beyond the resentment she'd held on to all these years. She could remember her father on her own. She didn't need her sisters for that. It would be her secret, just as it always had been. And in the meantime, she could give her mother the one thing—the only thing—she'd ever asked of Peyton.

"I forgive you, Mom." She scooted closer, rested her hand on her mother's shoulder and blinked back the tears. "I forgive you."

CHAPTER ONE

"MY DINNER RESERVATION is for seven o'clock." Peyton Harrison clicked her compact shut and, from the back of the Lincoln Town Car, looked out the windshield as the car veered toward the turnoff to the 101. "It would be faster to just stay on—"

"Yes, ma'am." The comment didn't come from her driver but from the man sitting in the passenger seat diagonally across from her.

Peyton bit back a sigh and tried not to stare daggers into the back of Matteo Rossi's head. A head covered in thick, glossy, black hair. It irritated her how often, in the last three weeks, she'd had the urge to run her fingers through that hair even as he lurked. Lurked. Followed. Hovered.

"An escort really wasn't nec…" She trailed off when Matteo turned and locked obsidian, sharp eyes on her. He didn't say a word. His expression never flickered. He just looked at her. What was he thinking when he did that? "Right." She offered a half smile and sank back in the corner of the seat. "You have a job to do."

"Yes, ma'am."

Needing a distraction, Peyton flipped open her bag and stuffed her compact inside. She was the senior vice president of a Fortune 500 technology company. She closed deals worth millions, sometimes billions of dollars and quicker than most people drank a cup of coffee. She didn't let irritating, overbearing men doing their job get to her. Besides, Peyton chewed on the inside of her cheek, he seemed to take a bit of pleasure in knowing he irritated her. "Don't you ever get tired of ordering people around?"

She caught it, a quick twitch of his lips when he said something to her driver, pointing out the window.

"I don't order, ma'am. I strongly suggest."

Seemed everyone *strongly suggested* these days. Her sisters had strongly suggested she throw herself full bore into the tilt-a-whirl family fray that had descended on them a little over two months ago. Her stepfather strongly suggested—albeit in his usual loving, generational-gap way—that it was time for her to look beyond her career and consider getting married and settling down. Most recently her bosses at Electryone Technologies strongly suggested (translation: decided for her) that she be assigned a bodyguard for the foreseeable future.

Frustration prickled at her like needles on her skin. For a woman who had made her mark in the business world, she seemed to have very little control of her life. The stress headache she'd managed to keep at bay now pulsed, and she squeezed her eyes shut in an effort to will it away.

It wasn't unheard of for the powers that be of million-dollar companies, when the need arose, to provide protection to their higher-ups. Peyton was well aware she could be difficult to work with and for, at times, but she'd always prided herself on being fair. Had she made enemies? Probably. No one achieved significant success without making a few. But Peyton wasn't convinced a few disturbing letters merited hiring a former Marine turned professional bodyguard.

Especially a bodyguard who had the unnerving tendency to distract her merely by stepping into her line of sight.

Peyton blew out a breath, fanned her face to stop the heat from rising in her cheeks. When she reached for the power-window button, Matteo looked at her again. "We're almost there, Ms. Harrison. Please keep the window closed."

Irritation slipped free, and Peyton rolled her eyes. "Unless it's bulletproof glass—" The very idea of anyone taking a shot at her made her feel like she'd been trapped in one of those TV thrillers she was addicted to.

Matteo didn't blink. Just gave her that look until she raised the window once more, then he turned back around.

Having grown up with four younger sisters, the urge to stick her tongue out at him was reflex, but she covered quickly by licking her lips when he glanced back. "Carlos, how are those grandchildren of yours?" Peyton asked her longtime driver.

"Light of my life, miss." Carlos, as bald as the sun was hot, and as calm as the ocean on a moonless night, shot her a smile in the rearview mirror. "Esmie just finished kindergarten, and Louis started walking. At top speed, mind you. You know how those toddlers are, miss. Jet packs in their diapers."

"In more ways than one." Peyton managed with a smile before turning her attention out her tinted window. She knew exactly how toddlers were, having helped raise her four younger sisters. Over the years, they hadn't exactly become less rambunctious, though.

Lily's recent runaway-bride impression had landed her, and subsequently Amanda, on a ranch in—wait for it—Montana, of all places. *Rambunctious* was definitely at the top of Peyton's list of descriptors for the triplets.

Even as her lips quirked, that ache in her chest throbbed. She missed her sisters so much. Granted, the last few years had been mostly phone and video calls, but Lily's almost-wedding had brought the girls together for the first time in forever. But now… Tears burned the back of her throat. She blinked them away and continued to stare out the window. At least they'd stopped freezing her out and were returning her calls. Hopefully, the emails she'd sent them had partially explained her side of things.

Not that there was any excuse for having lied to them about their real father all these years. How could there be when, years before, she'd told her mother what would happen if the truth was ever revealed. She'd let herself believe Susan Harrison was right—that it would never come out.

But it had. In the worst possible way, from a stranger. And Peyton had been dropped right in the middle of her sisters' anger.

It had only been after Amanda revealed to them her struggle with endometriosis that the barriers keeping Peyton away from her sisters began to crumble. They weren't completely back on track; there was still anger and resentment and definite feelings of betrayal for what Peyton had done, but they'd come together in support of Amanda as she considered her treatment options. She'd make that decision with a good man at her side. A man who wanted a future with Amanda regardless of her inability to have children.

How much easier things might have been on all of them if Peyton hadn't been keeping the truth about their real father from them. But a promise was a promise. No matter how much she'd disagreed with her mother, she'd kept her word. In the end, that decision had nearly cost Peyton the most important people in her life: her sisters.

What if… She swallowed hard, forcing herself to finish the thought.

What if they never really forgave her?

Enough of that, she ordered herself. It was just a bumpy patch. The sisters had had problems before; they'd have them again. They were talking, and for now, that would have to be enough.

Peyton glanced down at her designer pumps and A-line skirt in the same deep red as her silk blouse. The very idea of her sisters slogging around on a Montana ranch almost lightened her mood. She couldn't imagine them reconnecting with their long-lost father's roots through horses, mud and cattle calls. It made about as much sense as Peyton's life did these days—right down to Peyton hiring a professional matchmaker to find her the ideal husband.

Trying to push thoughts of her siblings aside, Peyton smoothed a forcibly steady hand down her stomach and wished for the evening to already be over. Her first few arranged dates with potential suitors had gone well enough. None of the successful self-made, practical men had been bad per se. They were looking for the same thing she was: a friendly relationship that would benefit their professional status, and in one case, get his mother off his back. Peyton smirked, recalling her date's frustrated alcohol-fueled tirade over a controlling, albeit well-meaning, parent. Thankfully she'd avoided that complication.

She supposed her own paternal experiences were going to cause some issues, as well. As difficult as the issues she'd had with abandonment thanks to her real father, Rudy Harrison had more than made up for Thomas Blackwell's shortcomings. That said…the fallout from the family secret finally coming to light was still happening.

Hopefully distance—and time—would help heal that wound. Her sisters were spread out across the country now. Georgie was up to her nose in whatever medical research she was conducting, while Fiona…well, Fiona was a people person and mostly stayed in her comfort zone of waitressing. Amanda wasn't too far away in San Diego, running her pet-supply business. The very idea Lily had upended her life and was going to marry rancher Conner Hannah and stay in Montana struck Peyton as another of Lily's leap first, look second dives into the unknown. A horse trainer. Lily was going to be a horse trainer and live on a ranch with a cowboy and his mother.

Stop the world, I want to get off.

Peyton was happy to stay right where she was, in the heart of Silicon Valley, California, far enough away where she could pretend everything with her sisters was just fine.

Always unflappable, Rudy hadn't missed a beat once the truth came out. If anything, his determination to see his girls happily settled had only intensified. Peyton had no doubt his focus had a lot more to do with losing their mother, but they'd each had to find a way through their grief. This was their father's.

It was a result of Rudy's determined insistence regarding her single status that Peyton had hired a professional matchmaker known for success. Because that's what one did when one needed—no, when one *wanted*—a husband without all the trappings and hassles of courtship and romance. Romance had never been on Peyton's list of priorities. It didn't make sense to move it to the top now.

As Carlos took a left, Matteo shifted around again. "I called ahead to make certain you were seated close to the bar so I can stay within earshot. I didn't think you'd appreciate another earwig interrupting your dinner."

Peyton's lips twitched. "I think we learned that lesson the last time." When the device had popped out of her ear while she was having dessert, her poor date ran from the restaurant, accusing her of corporate espionage.

"Mr. Rossi." Carlos glanced into his side mirror. "Have you noticed the gray sedan behind us to the left?"

"Yes." Matteo didn't blink as Peyton shifted in her seat to look behind them. "And I've made note of the license plate. I already have someone looking into it."

"Someone's following us?" Peyton's heart thudded so hard she could barely hear the traffic. "Why didn't you say anything?"

"What would I have said?" Matteo asked. "It would have robbed you of a relaxing drive into town."

Peyton gaped, earning an actual smile from Matteo. When his phone chimed, relief surged through her. She really didn't need him smiling at her. Not now. Not at any time. When she saw a frown mar his brow, however, she gave him a break. "Problem?"

"My ex. She's having some…issues with our son." He flinched, slipped his phone back into his jacket pocket. "It's fine."

"Take the call if you want to."

"I don't *want* to, but I will. Later. I'll call Gino as soon as I've got you back home and in for the night. If he's still awake."

Guilt pressed in on Peyton. She knew how tenuous a child's relationship could be with a parent. She didn't like the idea of being an obstacle in someone else's. "How old is he again?"

"He just turned six."

"Fun age." Carlos pulled into the designated drop-off.

"Something I'd like to know firsthand," Matteo said. "He's lived in Tokyo for the past two years with his mother and her new husband. Closest I get to fun is when we play video games together online. Are you ready?"

"Yes." Recognizing the change of subject for what it was—avoidance—she didn't press further.

"Out this door, please." Matteo motioned to the passenger door. "And wait for me to open it." He climbed out, closed the door, then shrugged, readjusted and buttoned his jacket.

She knew, from previous ventures out, that he was carrying a gun. She hadn't had cause to see it in use. She hoped she never would.

When Matteo opened her door, he moved around, held out his hand and aided her onto the sidewalk. "Stay close, Carlos. Parking lot across the street. First floor. I'll call when we're ready."

"Yes, sir."

"I bet you enjoy that," Peyton said as they walked toward Toscanini's, an elegant Italian restaurant known for its goat-cheese risotto and private reserve wine room. "Having people call you sir."

"Not particularly." He inclined his head.

"I meant since you were in the military and would have called others sir. Kind of a reversal of positions. Right?"

"Not really." He flashed a quick smile, then, with his hand lightly on her back, his eyes darting constantly, he guided her through the open double doors of thick oak.

The smell of roasted garlic and long-simmering tomato sauce hit her the second she stepped inside. Beautiful Italian marble floors, ivy-covered archways and the very subtle sounds of opera submersed her immediately in one of her favorite cultures.

"Ms. Harrison, how lovely to see you again." The short, rotund woman with a silver-and-black braid reached out her arms to embrace her. "We are pleased to have you back."

"Thank you, Rosa." She returned the embrace. "I'm meeting someone for dinner. Gabriel Shurley. Has he arrived yet?"

"Yes, yes. But…" Rosa glanced at Matteo "…you have two gentlemen with you tonight?"

"I'm just observing," Matteo offered. "I called earlier today about a special table for Ms. Harrison."

"Of course, of course." Rosa nodded. "We have it all arranged. Ms. Harrison, if you'd like to follow me?"

"See you on the other side," Peyton teased, surprising both herself and Matteo, given his expression.

"Yes, ma'am. Why don't you introduce me to your date first?"

"How about you judge him from a distance?" She planted a hand on his chest and tried to ignore the tingle that danced across her palm. "Honestly, Matteo. It'll be fine. Don't scare off another one."

"It wasn't my fault date number three had a guilty conscience."

"It might have helped if you didn't look like you wanted to pitch him through a window. Wait in the bar. I'll let you know when I'm done. Please." She pushed back when he made a move forward. "When all is said and done, you do work for me, and I'd prefer not to have Gabriel ask questions about why I have a bodyguard."

"All right." Something odd flickered in his eyes, something that sent a surge of warmth sliding through her body. Something that had her turning away and heading toward her date before she gave it any more thought. Rosa gestured to her table and, as Peyton approached, her date rose from his chair.

"Gabriel, how nice to meet you." She offered her hand.

"Peyton. You're stunning."

Peyton offered a smile, noting that his expression didn't shift as he walked around to pull out her chair. Once she was settled, she glanced to her right and found Matteo on the other side of an opening half-obscured by lush greenery. He gave her a quick nod to let her know he was fine with the arrangement.

"It's nice to finally meet you in person." Gabriel took his seat again and, after adjusting his diamond-studded cuff links, reached out and covered her hand with his. The tarnished watch on his wrist struck her as odd. Old-fashioned. Especially compared to the ostentatious cuff links. "Mr. Josiah assured me this evening would be well worth my time."

Peyton shifted her hand free and opened her menu. "Mr. Josiah is very enthusiastic about his matches." And about his success rate. He was already grumbling that his ratios were dropping because of her—what had he called them?—*eccentricities.* A polite way of calling her a challenging client. "Have you eaten here before?"

"No." He straightened his tie, the blue and red stripes clean and polished against the stark blue of his suit. He was handsome, she supposed. Blond, blue-eyed, with a physique that spoke more of sitting behind a desk than working out in a gym. It was understandable. From what she'd read about him, he worked nearly fourteen hours a day as a VP at an investment company.

"Well, I can recommend just about everything. The pasta carbonara is exceptional, as is the pumpkin gnocchi, which they only have from mid-October to Thanksgiving. What kind of wine do you prefer?"

"I was going to suggest a red."

Test number one presented itself right on schedule. "Would you mind if I chose?"

He shifted in his chair, glanced around, then seemed to force a smile. "Of course not."

He minded. Peyton smiled again, shifting him into her No column. As much as she didn't need a spark, she wanted a partner who wasn't afraid of an argument or standing up for what he wanted. Nor did she care for the undercurrent of irritation and resentment she could already feel pulsing across the table.

She ordered the wine, but she anticipated drinking most of it herself once it was poured out and Gabriel appeared less than impressed. She nearly asked the waiter to send a glass over to Matteo, who, she knew after only a few weeks, would approve heartily of her choice.

Not that they'd had much occasion to drink together. But they had discussed various restaurant locations as options for her dates.

"Now that we're alone." Gabriel leaned his arms on the table as their waiter disappeared with their orders. "I wanted to ask you about the new design of solar panels your company has devised."

"New solar panels?" Peyton blinked, a knot of tension tightening in her stomach.

"The ones Crossroads Industries presented to you? Olwen, I think it's called?" Gabriel's eyes lit up at the name, which started warning bells chiming in Peyton's head. "Named after the Celtic goddess of the sun. Clever."

Whatever crumb of promise remained for a positive end to the date turned to dust. "We have a number of projects going on at the moment." She sat back in her chair, glancing to where Matteo sat tapping a finger against the side of his club soda glass. She knew he never drank alcohol while on duty. "But I'm not at liberty to discuss any of them."

"Yes, of course." Gabriel ducked his head, seemingly contrite, and Peyton relaxed. "I thought perhaps the technology was something we might have in common. Something we could have a discussion about. So, small talk it is." His lips twitched into a smile that didn't reach his eyes. "Do you follow sports at all?"

MATTEO ROSSI HAD never put so much energy into not smiling. He'd been doing that a lot lately, purposely struggling to keep a straight face as Peyton Harrison pushed through each date. These ridiculous outings of hers would be entertaining if he didn't feel as if he was caught in a torturous reality show. Whoever this matchmaking Mr. Josiah was needed to reconsider his career goals.

He shifted slightly, watching Peyton settle in her chair and fold her hands in her lap. Her crossed legs and jutted chin told Matteo one thing: she'd already ended the date. Gabriel Shurley. Strike seven.

Matteo sipped his club soda and set a countdown as to when he could have Carlos pick them up.

The large shadow loomed a moment, long enough to have Matteo looking to his left as a tall, elderly gentleman lowered himself onto the barstool beside him. The restaurant was crowded, as was the bar. The man removed his well-worn cowboy hat, which looked as if it had seen as many hot Midwestern summers as its owner.

"Evening," the man said and motioned to the bartender. "Hope you don't mind. I didn't want to intrude on the happy couple over there."

Matteo glanced across the bar to where a

young couple with empty seats on either side of them were utterly immersed in one another. Matteo could see the faintest hint of a bulge in the man's jacket pocket, about the size of a ring box. The way the same man kept scrubbing his palms against his thighs had Matteo cringing in sympathy. Poor guy needed to be put out of his misery. "I doubt they would have noticed your presence," Matteo said. He leaned back in his chair, keeping Peyton in sight. "Are you waiting for someone?"

"Mmm-hmm." The man nodded and accepted the glass of whiskey he'd asked for, which he downed in one impressive gulp. "My granddaughter. Might need another of these." He gestured for a refill. "Nerves don't usually get the best of me, but our family situation is a bit…well, complicated. Elias Blackwell." He offered his hand.

"Matteo Rossi." Matteo shook the man's hand but barely took his eyes off Peyton. He knew her signals by now. She was content with her dining companion. Not ecstatic and certainly not enamored, but she'd see the dinner through because that was what was expected. And if he'd learned anything about her in the past three weeks, it was that Peyton Harrison always did what was expected. And she saw everything through to the end.

"Am I interrupting something?" Elias leaned over, a twinkle in his eye as he pointed discreetly at Peyton and her dinner date. "Or are you waiting for her to realize she has about as much chemistry with that pressed suit as I do with the queen of England?"

Matteo chuckled. "Professional interest." He had the feeling that if the man heard Matteo was there as Peyton's personal protection, it would only illicit uncomfortable questions. "I'm her get-out-of-jail card," he added and earned a sharp laugh from Elias. "Just waiting for the signal."

When his phone buzzed again, Matteo stifled a sigh and flipped it screen-up on the bar. His son's face was showing on the screen and had Matteo on alert.

"That your boy?" Elias glanced down.

"Yes." Gino rarely called him, and when he did, it was usually to tell Matteo how lonely he was being cooped up in the Tokyo apartment with only the nanny for company.

"If you need to take it, I can keep an eye on your…professional interest."

Matteo cringed. "I really shouldn't—"

"Talk to your boy," Elias said. "Trust me. You never know when you might not get another chance." He patted Matteo's arm. "Go on. The sooner you take it, the sooner you'll be back. Stay in sight. I'll signal you if she needs you."

Guilt battled against obligation. He'd always told Gino he'd be there when he called. Even if he was working. He had to keep that promise, especially since it was a promise that had never been kept for him. "Thanks. I'll be quick." He picked up the phone just before the voice mail clicked on. "Gino? Hey, buddy. What's going on?"

"Mom said she'd call you."

"She did. I'm sorry, G, but I'm working." He walked around the bar toward the front door where the reception was better. "Everything okay?"

"I want to come live with you," Gino announced. "Why can't I come live with you?"

Matteo's heart splintered. "I'd love for you to, G, but we've talked about this. Your mom—"

"Mom doesn't want me anymore." Gino's breath hitched, and it was all Matteo could do not to reach through the phone and hug him.

"That's not true, G. She loves—"

"She's having a new baby."

Matteo winced. Well, wasn't that just great. "G, your mother loves you. Nothing, not even a new baby, is going to change that." Matteo's heart pounded in his chest. Of all times for this to come down. He was so close to that promotion— a promotion that would finally give him enough money that he could challenge Sylvia's full-time custody in court. Getting distracted while on assignment like this wasn't going to do him any good. "I'm sure your mom wants you to stay with her, bud. I'll talk to her as soon as I can."

The silence on the other end of the line had Matteo thinking they'd been disconnected.

"Don't you want me, either?"

"Gino, no. Of course I do, buddy." Matteo leaned against the wall and squeezed his eyes shut. "You know that's not true. I would love to have you with me all the time, but we can't just—"

"That's okay. Never mind."

Even half a world away, Matteo heard the tears in his son's voice. "G, I will mind. I hear you, and I'm going to talk to your mom, and we'll work this out. Maybe she'll let you come out for a bit when school's out. That's only a couple of weeks, right?"

"Yeah. Okay. I need to go now. Bye, Dad."

"G, wait—" But it was too late. The line went dead.

Matteo took a deep breath and banged his head back against the wall, even as a flash of red shot across his eyeline. Peyton. She was on the move.

Matteo started over to the bar, to where Peyton was headed, her laser-beam focus on his empty seat. He swore, pocketed his phone and dodged through a large party on their way to being seated. She must have sent a signal he'd missed. Something had gone wrong, and she was looking for her backup.

When Matteo finally got back to his seat, he had the apology and explanation poised behind tense lips. "Ms. Harrison, I'm sorry. I had to take a—" It took an instant for him to realize he wasn't the target of her attention. She was standing in front of Elias Blackwell, hands on those curvy hips of hers, impatient fingers tapping against the fabric even as her hair swirled around her shoulders. "Do you two…" He glanced at Elias, who was holding on to his second whiskey glass, an amused grin on his face. "Do you two know each other?"

"After a fashion," Peyton said without taking her eyes off Elias. "Matteo Rossi, meet—" now she smirked and in that instant, Matteo saw the resemblance "—my grandfather."

CHAPTER TWO

"IF THAT AIN'T music to an old man's ears." Elias Blackwell offered a hand to Matteo along with a sly smile that had Peyton gnashing her teeth. She'd always taken meticulous care to keep her private and personal lives separate. She did not need this invasion. Not now. Not ever.

"Do you know," Peyton's grandfather continued when Matteo returned the greeting, "one day I've got my life and ranch full of five grandsons and their expanding families, and the next, I've got five granddaughters to add to the mix. Best and biggest surprise of my life, I can tell you. Pleased to meet you, son."

"Matteo Rossi," Matteo supplied easily before glancing over to Peyton's table. "You scare off another one?"

"No, I did not scare off another..." She turned and followed his gaze and found her table was empty. "Darn it." She closed her eyes, a flush creeping into her cheeks. "Mr. Josiah is going to strangle me."

"I definitely wouldn't ask for a refund." Matteo's unexpected grin had Peyton's stomach taking a funny little leap.

"I guess that means you can join me for dinner, then." Big E rose from his stool. "We'll just take that table of yours, shall we?"

For a big man, Peyton thought, he sure did move fast. Even if she'd wanted to protest, she didn't have time. She folded her arms across her chest.

The humor died in Matteo's eyes. "We can leave anytime you want. Just say the word."

"What makes you think I want to leave?" She didn't like the idea he could read her so well.

"Because I'm fluent in body language for a living, and that's your *I don't want to deal with this* pose." He pulled out his wallet to pay for his drink. "I've got Carlos ready to go."

Peyton tapped her foot. She'd spent the last two months trying not to think about the messy state her family was in. She'd spent the last few weeks dodging Big E's calls and attempts to meet. She was finally on a better footing with her sisters; she didn't need to add an interfering, brand-new grandfather to the mix. Given what she'd learned about Big E, however, she shouldn't be surprised that he'd turned up this way.

What the heck? The evening was a loss, anyway. Might as well bite whatever bullet he'd have in his six-shooter and get this over with.

"I'll stay," Peyton said finally. "I have to deal with this, with *him*, at some point, and a public place is probably best." Not that she would make a scene. If there was one thing Peyton was known for, it was her utter and complete control over her emotions.

"All right." Matteo gave a curt nod. "I'll keep an eye on you from—" He broke off as she and Matteo spotted Big E back at Peyton's table, waving them over.

"Perfect." Peyton offered a satisfied smirk and slipped her arm through Matteo's. "You can join us." She tugged him with her. "Exactly what should I call you?" she asked Elias as she slipped into her chair.

"*Grandpa* works." Big E's smile broke across his face and lit up his eyes. "Or Big E. Whichever you feel comfortable with."

"You know what? I don't want to intrude

on a family—" Matteo spoke up, but Big E was already motioning to their server for another chair.

Big E cleared his throat. "You two stay here. I'm going to grab myself another drink. Sit, Matteo."

"Yes, sir." He lowered himself into the chair beside Peyton.

"You're not getting away that easily." Peyton eyed Matteo, shifted closer to the wall and picked up her wineglass, still half-full. "I need a buffer, and you are it. Even better, you seem to speak Big E."

"Buffering isn't usually part of the job." Seemingly unfazed, he glanced around casually.

"It is now. Look." She lowered her voice. "I don't have time to fill you in on all the family drama, but what he said is true. His son was my sisters' and my biological father. We were all adopted by my stepfather when we were young. The truth about our real dad only came out a couple of months ago. The day of my sister Lily's wedding. And poof. Instant grandfather." *Instant Blackwells.*

"Must have been a difficult thing to learn

for all of you. Especially with your sister starting a new life."

Guilt had her stiffening her spine. "Yeah, well." She swallowed hard. "Long story short, in the end Lily didn't get married and instead she ran off to Montana of all places. To Big E's ranch. She's getting married this Christmas. For real this time. To a different groom."

Matteo smothered a laugh. Big E returned to his seat. "I appreciate the invitation to join you," he said to Big E.

"My pleasure." Big E set his whiskey down. "Peyton? Another glass of wine?"

"Why not." When Matteo raised an eyebrow at her, she looked away. It wasn't every day Big E walked into her life.

Because Peyton had already ordered, they held her food back for when Matteo and Big E were served. In the meantime, she embraced the bread basket and dunked a chunk of freshly baked sourdough into the plate of balsamic-and-pepper-kissed olive oil. She had plans to devour the entire loaf and mentally penciled in an extra half hour on the treadmill in the morning to pay for it.

"Lily sends you her best," Big E said after the silence stretched to the point of discomfort.

Peyton shook her head. "Starting our relationship off with a lie isn't a good first step, Big E. She's not really talking to me, and you know it."

"Well, it's not entirely a lie." He had the good sense to look contrite. "She told me to have a good trip."

"Is she…" Peyton's chest tightened. She hated that she had to ask a practical stranger about her sister, but all of the conversations with her sisters of late had been so cursory. "Is she doing all right?"

"She's doing fine. I wish you girls would get over this hang-up about secrets already. I don't like you being at odds with each other. You know, Rudy told me the five of you used to be tighter than peas in an overstuffed pod."

"Things change," Peyton said. Especially when keeping secrets from those you loved was involved.

"Sure they do. But family's always the most important thing. I'd think you of all people would realize that, Peyton."

"Me of all people?" She reached for her wine and suddenly rethought Matteo's presence. If the conversation continued in this direction, whatever good opinion he did have of her would vanish by the time the tiramisu was served. And for some reason, she didn't like the idea of him thinking the worst of her.

"You did what was best for your family," Big E said. "You helped give your sisters the father they needed."

"I was seven," Peyton told him, desperate to change the subject. "I didn't exactly have a choice." But he was right. Rudy had been—still was, even now that their mother was gone—a wonderful father. The stabilizing force they'd all needed. And for that, Peyton wouldn't apologize. "What exactly are you doing here, Big E?"

"Well." Big E sat back as his and Matteo's salads were served along with an antipasto platter. "A grandfather can only take leaving multiple voice mails for so long. I even tried to make an appointment with you through your assistant, but the nice young man told me you'd instructed him not to take my calls anymore."

"I've been busy." Peyton broke off another chunk of bread. She always overcarbed when she had to deal with emotional issues.

"Can never be too busy for family," Big E pronounced. "That's been a lesson hard learned, let me tell you, but I'll live by it every day now. As I'm not easily put off, I decided to take matters into my own hands. Have to say, it's been a while since I've tailed someone in a car."

Peyton's hand froze halfway to her mouth. "You've been following me?"

"Gray sedan?" Matteo rattled off the plate number and continued eating as if he hadn't just had the mystery of the evening solved.

"Good eye." Big E nodded in wary appreciation. "I thought maybe you were trying to shake me." His eyes—the same color as Peyton's—narrowed. "Why would you be keeping a watch for possible tails?"

"No reason," Peyton replied quickly. Too quickly. "This looks good." She plucked a couple of olives and thin-sliced prosciutto off the platter in the center of the table.

"Seems I'm not going to get a straight answer out of my granddaughter about anything." Big E watched her for a long moment. "Matteo?"

"I'm not at liberty to say, sir." Matteo didn't come close to looking flustered. Or intimidated. "If Peyton wants you to know, she'll tell you."

"Smart man, staying loyal." Big E nodded in approval and finished his salad. "I like you, son."

Matteo seemed to purposely avoid Peyton's irritated glare. "Would you excuse me for a moment?" she asked. "I'd like to send something out to Carlos for dinner."

Matteo pushed his chair back and stood up. "I'll come with you."

"I can talk to Rosa on my own, thank you." She plucked up her purse. "Besides, I need to make a stop in the ladies' room. I'll be right back." The need for solitude, the pressure pushing down on her from every aspect of her life, was making it difficult to breathe, let alone carry on a conversation.

After a quick discussion with Rosa, who was only too happy to send out a meal to Carlos in the parking lot across the street, Peyton withdrew into the hallway near the bathroom and pulled out her cell phone. Before she lost her nerve, she skimmed through her contacts list.

Considering how many times she'd dodged Big E's calls over the past couple of months, it would serve her right if Fiona didn't answer now. The knot in her stomach tightened, so she leaned over to try to ease it. Five rings. Six. *Please answer. Please answer. Please—*

"Hi, Peyton."

"Fiona." Peyton forced her name out over the tension in her throat. "Thanks for picking up." Determination broke through the grief. "I need to talk to someone. I know you all are still mad at me—"

"We aren't mad anymore, Peyton." Fiona's tone softened. "We're just...confused. We can't understand how you never told us the truth. When we were kids, sure, but we haven't been kids for a long time."

Peyton squeezed her eyes shut. She hadn't told them because her mother had made her promise. Because, after all the years that had passed, what good would it do? Thomas Blackwell wasn't coming back. She'd had a hard enough time accepting that herself; why subject her sisters to the same heartache? Rudy had been there every day since he'd walked into their life, and he had never once, not once, disappointed them.

"I don't know how many more times I can say I'm sorry." She breathed deeply and shoved the mixed emotions down deep into that place she never let herself access. "I can't change the past, Fee. For any of us." And she needed to stop wanting to. "And as much as we need to have that conversation, I'm calling about Big E."

"Big E as in our grandfather?" Fiona sounded as surprised as Peyton had felt upon finding her grandfather in the bar where she was having a date.

"If you know of another, I don't want to hear about it." The very idea might give her a migraine. "What can you tell me about him?"

"Not a lot. Only what Lily and Amanda have said. He and his grandsons have that huge ranch—"

"That much I know," Peyton said. She wasn't naive. She'd done her research into Elias Blackwell as soon as Amanda had confirmed he was, indeed, their grandfather. "The Blackwell Ranch has become an important tourist destination for families and group events. And that's on top of the success it's been as a cattle ranch going back generations. It's a family business, with Big E and his grandsons at the helm."

"Our cousins," Fiona added. "I don't understand what you're asking, Peyton. If you know all this—"

"I know about his business. I want to know about *him*."

"Why do you care? You won't even take his calls."

Peyton winced. Apparently she had been a topic of conversation. "Because he's here."

"You mean there? In Silicon Valley?"

"Not only the same town, but in the same restaurant. He followed me to dinner, and I don't know why."

"Well, here's a thought." Fiona paused. "Ask him."

"Fee." Peyton shook her head. "You're not helping."

"Maybe that's because I'm not trying to. You want answers, talk to him."

"Don't hang up on me!" Peyton's voice rose, and she flinched at the surprised expression of a customer passing by to go to the restroom. "Fiona, please. You know I'm not great with all the family stuff."

Fiona went silent for a long moment. "It's funny. You've always used that as an excuse to stay away. It never made sense before, but now it does. Why you left home so early, why you kept getting as far from the rest of us as you could. You know we took bets as to whether you'd make the time to get to Lily's wedding."

Regret and guilt circled her like a shark. "I'd never miss a special occasion like that."

"Yeah, well, there was more to it, wasn't there?" Fiona said. "You kept your distance because you were lying to us."

She was done denying it. She couldn't run from it anymore. Not if she wanted to have a relationship with her sisters again. "I need to fix this, Fiona. With you, with all of you."

"Start by having a conversation with Big E. The rest will work itself out, Peyton. We love you. I love you. We'll get there."

Would they? She couldn't help but think her relationship with her sisters was never going to be the same.

Peyton glanced up as Matteo came into view. He stood there, near the bar, watching her, a disapproving expression on his handsome face. Why did she feel like a naughty toddler who'd been caught with her hand in the cookie jar?

"I need to go," she said reluctantly. Her stalling time had run out.

"All right. How about…how about you call

me tomorrow when you're home from work, okay?"

"Yeah." Hope she hadn't felt in weeks ballooned inside of her. "Yeah, I can do that. Good night, Fee."

"Night, Peyton."

Peyton was still holding her phone seconds after her sister clicked off.

"You done hiding?" Matteo asked when she finally lowered her cell.

"I'm not hiding," Peyton snapped. "I was stalling. There's a difference."

"If you say so. Look." Matteo caught her arm when she walked past him. "I know this is none of my business."

More than anything, she wanted to confirm his statement. But she'd made enough enemies of late. She didn't need to add her bodyguard to the list. His hold on her arm gentled, and she felt herself relax a bit. "I suppose I made it your business by asking you to stay for dinner."

He inclined his head as if in silent agreement. "Your grandfather isn't going anywhere. In fact, he's going out of his way to connect with you. Maybe you can cut him a little slack? Not only did he find out he has five granddaughters he didn't know about, he's also learned he had, maybe still has, a son. I can only imagine how many directions Big E is pulled in. He's come this far to seek you out, Peyton. Is one dinner really going to inconvenience you that much?"

Peyton pressed her lips into a thin line. Faced with the choice between logic and emotion, she'd go with logic every time. She liked her facts, her numbers. Evidence laid out in clear, concise detail. That's how she made most if not all her decisions. Sentimentality and feelings didn't do anything but muddy the picture.

Matteo, ever the observer, no doubt knew this. She didn't particularly like that he did, but what he said made sense. Logically, she reminded herself.

"All right. I'll stop…hiding." She looked down at his hand and waited for him to release her. But when he did, she had the oddest sensation of regret. "Let's get this over with."

When they approached the table again, she saw what Matteo was talking about. In an instant, Big E's expression flashed from concerned to hopeful when he caught sight of them.

He pushed to his feet, napkin in his hand. "I thought maybe you'd made a break for it."

"I'm sorry," Peyton said as Matteo held out her chair once more. "I was talking to Fiona. She, um, she says hello."

"Does she, now? Well, that's good news." He went quiet when their food was served. "I'm glad to hear you and your sisters are mending fences. You know, when you girls all come out to Montana—"

Peyton's fork froze halfway to her mouth. "Who's going to Montana?"

Big E gave her that grin of his. That same grin she bet had earned him a significant fortune. "At some point, all of you girls will. Montana is where the Blackwells belong. We're your family, Peyton. And I don't just mean Lily, who's fit perfectly into ranch life. I mean all the Blackwells, young and old. You'll see for yourself soon."

Peyton opened her mouth but felt Matteo's knee knock against hers. She glanced at him, but he didn't look at her, just concentrated on his linguine with clam sauce, then reached for the refilled bread basket.

Peyton drank some wine, set her glass down and took a steeling breath. "I appreciate the invitation, Big E. But you and I need to be straight with each other."

"All right." Big E slowly, confidently broke off a piece of bread and looked at her, an amused expression on his face.

"While this entire situation seems a bit fluid and…well, unexpected, there is one thing I can absolutely guarantee will never happen." She picked up her fork and stabbed one of the many pumpkin gnocchi she planned to eat. "I will never, *ever* step foot in Montana."

CHAPTER THREE

"CONGRATULATIONS ON THE baby news, Sylvia." Matteo tucked his cell under his chin so he could pour his second cup of coffee of the morning. He was running two minutes ahead of schedule, just enough time to give him a chance to reach out to his ex-wife.

"Gino told you." Sylvia's tone was more dramatic than concerned. "I suppose I should be relieved he's talking to someone since he won't say a word to me or Jiro. The only time he says anything is when he's having a tantrum. It's embarrassing."

"He's just a little boy, Syl." A little boy who was growing more miserable by the day. "You can't expect him to process his emotions and feelings the way either of us would." Still, the idea that Gino had stopped communicating with his stepfather, someone Matteo knew to have genuine affection for his son, was worrying. Another tidbit of information to add to his custody arsenal. "He thinks he's being replaced." Which was what Matteo feared himself. His lawyer had warned him not to let his emotions dictate his actions when it came to Sylvia. The more cordial he could keep his relationship with his ex, the better he'd look in court when he was finally able to sue for full custody.

"I need you to talk to him again," Sylvia said. "Please, Matteo. This situation is starting to get very stressful and that's not what I need right now. I've got a merger with two billion-dollar corporations to deal with, and Jiro's promotion is pending."

"Plus, you're pregnant," Matteo couldn't help but remind her. "All that added stress can't be good for the baby."

"Right. Of course, yes."

Matteo rolled his eyes. Sometimes history was doomed to repeat itself. "What exactly is it you'd like me to say to our son?"

"That everything is going to work out fine. That his new school will be fabulous and—"

"What new school?" Matteo set his coffee mug down with deliberate care.

"Oh. I thought I'd told you. Jiro and I de-

cided a boarding school would be better
suited—"

"Boarding school? Over my dead body."
Matteo couldn't have kept the chill out of his
voice if he'd tried. Suddenly his son's temper
tantrums made sense. The poor kid was scared
to death. "No way are you going to ship him
off from the only family he knows when I'm
right here."

"It's a good school, Matteo. They can help
him with his…difficulties."

"I think we both know who's helped by
shipping him off."

"It's the best school money can—"

"I don't care about money, Sylvia. I'm his
father. I should have a say in his education, not
to mention his living arrangements."

"Well, you're not here, are you, Matteo?"
That clip in her tone reminded him of the day
she'd casually told him she was filing for divorce and taking their then-four-year-old son
to the other side of the world because of her
job.

"Yeah, well, our career paths haven't exactly
gone in the same direction." Not to mention
Tokyo was an obscenely expensive city to live
in. There wasn't any way he could ever afford

to move there. Not that Sylvia would have even thought about that. His ex was many things—successful, driven and wealthy—but she often didn't see anything outside her own bubble. "This wasn't part of our arrangement, Sylvia."

"It's part of it now. If you aren't going to talk to him—"

"I will never not talk to my son," Matteo said with strained patience. "But I also won't convince him to accept something I know will hurt him in the long run. There will be no boarding school, Sylvia. You want to make alternate arrangements to suit your life, fine. Then, you send him home to me. I mean it," he added when she sputtered. "Don't make me take you back to court over this, because I will."

Even as Matteo said it, he could see his bank account draining. But it would be worth every penny he had in the world if it meant he had his son back. "Let me know when you decide." Because he couldn't trust himself to keep things civil, he hung up.

And called his lawyer.

PEYTON RUBBED AT the pain in her stomach, willing her office phone to stop ringing for just five minutes. Usually she thrived on the negotiations phase of an acquisition, but she had to admit, ever since she'd had pumpkin gnocchi with her grandfather two nights ago, her head was not in the game.

When had her office—an office she'd meticulously designed and decorated for maximum productivity—begun to feel like a prison? How could it, with all the glass and brass and bright whites and yellows playing along the windows and walls? It was as if every move she made was being monitored, judged. And not by whoever Matteo had been hired to watch out for. Every time she stepped foot into the bullpen of assistants and employees, she felt like a bug being fried under a magnifying glass. She didn't like it.

She didn't like it one bit.

The number of calls to return was stacking up, her email inbox was overflowing and she was so a zero-inbox kind of person, the three coffees she'd had this morning were sitting sourly in her belly, and her assistant was apparently having a relationship crisis that, if his declarations of this morning could be believed, could trigger the apocalypse.

"If it did, at least I wouldn't have to finish

any of this paperwork." Peyton yanked open her desk drawer and dug around for her antacids. All that was missing from today was…

The knock on her office door had her groaning. Would anyone notice if she banged her head on her desk for the next few hours?

"I know you didn't want to be disturbed." Todd Atkinson poked his head in the door. "But you might want to come see this."

"See what? Why didn't you just buzz me—" She straightened, looked down at her phone and realized she'd left it off the hook. "Never mind," she muttered and ignored her assistant's arched brow as she hung the phone back up.

"A good assistant knows when not to pry," Todd said. "And we both know I am the best."

"You are that," Peyton agreed and exited her office. Hiring Todd had been one of the best moves she'd ever made in her professional life. She'd met him when she'd spoken at a local high-school career day where he'd shown her plans he'd made up for a water treatment system for inner cities and isolated communities. She'd been impressed—with him and the plans—and told him to look her up when he was done with school. He did. The day after graduation, and she'd hired him that afternoon. Three years later, he was carrying a full course load at a local college, working toward his engineering degree and keeping her completely on track. And that treatment system? It was in development with one of their partners and scheduled to be deployed in the next eighteen months. And Todd had the first professional credit to his name.

As the epitome of calm efficiency and organization—second only to herself—it seemed odd that Todd hadn't brought the flower arrangement he gestured to in to her.

Not quite as odd as the flower arrangement itself, however.

"They were left downstairs at main reception," Todd told her.

That now-familiar pang of unease clanged in her already-churning stomach. The flowers themselves were a mishmash of wilted and decaying flora that looked as if someone had ripped them out of a yard. They'd been arranged in an ordinary flowerpot, with a spray of beautiful purple bell-shaped blooms in the middle. "Not exactly breathtaking, are they? Where's the—"

"Step away from the flowers, Peyton."

Peyton barely had time to think as Matteo reached for her arm, pulling her away from her assistant's desk.

"What's going on?" She stumbled, caught her balance and saw the card in Matteo's hand. "Is that for me?"

"It was, yes."

"Let me see."

Todd all but leaped at her, but backed off at Matteo's look. "Oh, you don't need to read—"

"Your instincts were right, Todd," Matteo said.

"Instincts? About what?" Frustration built inside of her. She really didn't have the tolerance for this today. "Someone better tell me what's going on—"

"Something's going on?" The booming, all-too-familiar voice had Peyton clenching her fists. Was the universe conspiring against her?

"Big E, what are you doing here? Who let you up?" She glared at Todd, who shook his head and held up his hands as if surrendering.

"Wasn't me. I just handed off the card to Matteo."

"Peyton, you and I need to have a discussion. If you won't come to me," Big E announced, "then you leave me no other choice."

"You should talk to your grandfather," Matteo urged.

"You must be Elias Blackwell." Todd shifted, seemingly grateful for the distraction, and held out his hand. "I'm Todd."

"The Todd who's been blocking my calls the last couple of days?"

"Uh…" Todd looked over his shoulder at Peyton.

"Okay, everyone stop!" Peyton ordered sharply, then winced when she caught sight of Vilette Wright, president of Electryone Technologies, heading her way. This was not happening. Not now. Her boss rarely came into the office these days. The last time had been when Peyton had been introduced to her protection detail.

"Vilette." Peyton stepped toward her boss. "What are you doing here?" Short and on the stout side, Vilette wore her silver hair razor-cut at her solid jawline, an almost elegant contrast to the jeans, vintage rock T-shirt and well-worn comfort shoes that spoke more of punch lines than elite status.

Vilette had built Electryone from the ground up and focused most of her energy and profit margin on widening the female workforce within the tech industry. Every board member and more than sixty percent of the company employees were women. Exactly the way Vilette—and Peyton—liked and wanted it.

"I was told we have a situation." Vilette's voice was firm and left no room for discussion. "Matteo?"

"Todd was right," Matteo told her. "The writing matches, Ms. Wright. The flowers are from the same person who's been threatening Peyton."

"What writing? Let me see—" But Peyton noticed Matteo had put the card in a sealed plastic bag. She froze.

"What does it say?"

Matteo glanced at Big E, who'd moved in behind Vilette. "It says *I know what you did.*"

"What's that supposed to mean?" Peyton locked her jaw, her mind racing for an explanation. "And that's not a threat."

"The flowers are," Matteo said in that cool tone she'd heard in the car the other night. "That's foxglove in the center. It's toxic to humans."

"You're being ridiculous," Peyton snapped. "It's just someone's idea of a joke."

"I'm not laughing," Vilette said. "One of

my VPs is getting threats. It seems you were right, Matteo. She's too visible."

Peyton glared at Matteo. "I beg your pardon?" She was too *what*?

"Excuse me." Big E shifted to face the group, removed his hat and turned his attention toward Peyton's boss. "I'm Elias Blackwell, Peyton's grandfather."

"Pleasure to meet you—" Vilette held out her hand.

"Big E is fine, just fine." He angled a look at Peyton and Matteo, then back to her boss. "Since it seems Peyton isn't willing to share the details, I wonder if you would mind filling me in on what's going on with my granddaughter?"

Peyton frowned. Oh, this was not good. This was not good at all. "Vilette, I don't think—" She stopped when both Big E and her boss shot her the same look.

"I think a discussion is exactly what's needed, Big E. We'll move this to my office. I'll have coffee brought in. Todd, would you mind? Matteo, you will join us."

"Ma'am." Matteo nodded. "I'll be in as soon as I speak to the detectives—"

"Detectives?" Peyton practically squeaked.

This was getting out of hand. "Surely the police don't need to be…"

Matteo stepped in front of her so all she could see, all she could feel, was him. When she lifted her chin and looked into his eyes, she found herself swallowing. Hard. Intense didn't come close to describing what she was seeing. But beneath it, in the depths of those eyes, she saw anger. And tempered concern. "Whoever it was sent you poisonous flowers. To your office." He held up the baggie and flipped it around. "The backup delivery address is your home. With your security code to the underground parking lot. The police are not only necessary, they're vital."

"Peyton, please," Todd implored. "I don't want anything to happen to you."

"If you won't do it for yourself, do it for Todd," Vilette cut in. "He could be a target by association. You wouldn't want anything to happen to him. Or anyone else at Electryone for that matter."

Peyton narrowed her eyes. That was a low blow. Hating the anxiety she saw in her assistant's eyes, an assistant she'd come to think of as a little brother, she backed down. "Fine. I should probably talk to these detectives myself."

"If they want to talk to you, I'll make the arrangements," Matteo assured her. "Right now, I don't think they need to see how apathetic you are to the circumstances."

Apa... Peyton gaped at him.

"All right, then. Matteo will contact the police. Todd?" Vilette motioned for them all to follow.

Her office emptied, leaving Peyton with a choice. To follow or remain. And since she didn't put it past Vilette to take this to the next level, she began walking. She glared at Big E, who stood just outside her door, waiting, his arm extended for her to take.

"This is none of your business," she told him, but accepted the courtesy and matched her pace to his. "You need to go back to Montana. The sooner the better."

"I couldn't agree more." Big E drew her closer to his side, and for a moment, she let herself feel the comfort and understanding he was trying to convey.

Before she stepped away and entered her boss's office.

How, Peyton thought a half hour later, Vilette and her grandfather could have struck up such a quick and friendly relationship was beyond her.

She had no doubt she was witnessing Big E's rumored charm on full display, which was why she stepped out: to get away from the sudden camaraderie that she figured would mean something even worse than a bodyguard was about to befall her.

The energy in the offices of Electryone Technologies was positively buzzing, and not from all the electrical devices, experiments and development projects. Marching over to Vilette's office had put Peyton straight in the spotlight, but not in any way she preferred. She scrunched her toes in her shoes, trying to keep a hold of whatever traction she had on her life.

She'd worked hard to get where she was, and she'd sacrificed anything resembling an outside life to do it. Sixty- to eighty-hour weeks, six to seven days a week. Midnight hours spent crunching numbers and finding the right projects to invest in; reading proposal after proposal and result after result to advance technology in various areas of research. Research that could make the world a far easier place to survive in for a good portion of the world that had been left behind. The work was what mattered. It could make such a difference in people's lives.

"Psst."

Peyton spotted one of her fellow VPs heading toward her. Peyton tried to avoid her, but she tugged Peyton into an office and quickly shut the door.

"What's going on?" Belinda Carmichael had been with the company three years longer than Peyton. Though she dressed like a peacock in flamboyant, bright colors and carried herself with the grace of a swan, Belinda was all vulture—perched and waiting to pick up whatever tidbits of information she could. And use to her benefit.

It was no secret Belinda had her eye on Vilette's position when and if Vilette ever retired. Peyton had no doubt Vilette was going to leave this life the way she came into it—kicking and screaming to the very end. "I heard you got flowers," Belinda said. "So, is this about your stalker?"

"I don't have a stalker." Peyton downplayed the flower delivery, but even as she said it, a bubble of anxiety rose in her chest. Matteo had said the flowers were poisonous. How poisonous? If someone had breathed in their fragrance or simply touched…

"It has to be serious. They've given you a bodyguard," Belinda said.

"It's…nothing. Everyone's just being really cautious." Considering the chaos the solution was creating, she'd almost be happier to deal with the one person trying to mess with her head. "Nothing for you to worry about."

"You got another creepy message, didn't you?" Belinda's stage whisper seemed over the top even for a woman who had earned the title of drama queen.

"Belinda—"

"Who's the cowboy?"

"Who?"

"The old guy in the hat and boots. Looks like he was just transported here from the Alamo?"

So much for keeping Big E under wraps. "My grandfather." She wasn't about to get into family details, at least not any more than she had to. "And he's from Montana, not Texas. How are we doing with the Olwen project?"

Belinda's eyes went wide. "Oh, good. Fine. Just waiting on the final design specs. Taking a new solar panel concept out to the masses means we have to get the details one hundred percent right. Just dotting all those t's and crossing my i's."

Peyton didn't manage a full smile at the familiar joke. "We want to keep on track with that. No missed deadlines. That's when rumors get started." And rumors could kill a project launch faster than a lack of funding. They were betting a lot on Olwen, an affordable solar-panel design that could work in the most desolate of countries and communities. Peyton was even pushing for an exploration of how they could be utilized after a major natural disaster like earthquakes or hurricanes. Olwen could be life-changing for so many people.

"Don't worry. I won't crash the ship," Belinda muttered, swung the door open and stepped into the hallway, only to back up to let Todd pass, wheeling one of the company's coffee carts.

"You need any support in there?" he asked with a smile on his face.

"Nope, thanks." Peyton shifted her tone to make sure it sounded light. "Thanks for staying on top of Olwen, Belinda."

"Hey, no problem. Once this deal is done and the project launches, Electryone will be solidly in the big league. And you and I will finally get the credit."

Peyton's forced smile vanished when Belinda focused her attention down the hall. Unlike Belinda, she wasn't in this for the credit; sure, she wanted job security and satisfaction, but she wasn't grabbing hold of an idea just because it could get her closer to the top of Electryone.

If Belinda wanted the credit, she could have it. With three manufacturing companies already vying for the production rights, more than Electryone's stock futures hinged on Olwen: hundreds of potential jobs did as well.

"I wish someone would stalk me so I could have one of him." Belinda sighed. "He's definitely something that would brighten my day. Tell me he's staying in your apartment to guard you."

"That's where I drew the line," Peyton followed Belinda's gaze and noted where Matteo stood with who she assumed were the detectives he'd called. One woman, tall and lean in her jeans and blazer, and a man, older, heavier, but with wise eyes. "We compromised, and he has a coworker keeping an eye on my apartment building at night."

"How do you get any work done with him hanging around?" Belinda asked as if she didn't hear.

"Matteo?" Peyton had to force herself to sound impartial. "Honestly? He's easy to ignore." That could very well be the biggest lie of her life. Given Peyton's past, that was saying something.

Belinda looked as if Peyton had lost her mind. "You seriously need to reevaluate your life choices, Peyton. That's a definite M-A-N man. Imagine coming home to him every night."

Peyton felt her cheeks warm when Matteo glanced at her. Their eyes met, but she looked away before he saw—or read—too much, like the images Belinda's comment conjured. "I don't have to imagine. I mean," she added at Belinda's chuckle, "he's not my type. Not at all."

Belinda patted Peyton's arm as if in sympathy. "No wonder you needed to hire a matchmaker. You clearly don't see what the rest of us do."

Todd approached again. He waved at Peyton to take the escape he was providing. "I'm all caught up on my work, boss, so if there's anything I can help you with? Maybe that report

Vilette asked for yesterday?" He steered Belinda away and when he looked over his shoulder, Peyton mouthed a grateful thank you.

She headed for her office. "Todd saving you again?" Matteo's voice from behind her made her jump. "Sorry," he added when she frowned at him. "Can't imagine why you're skittish."

"I am not skittish." Peyton went to her desk, hoping he would follow. He did. "You really didn't need to call the police," Peyton whispered.

"Agree to disagree." Matteo didn't even flinch. "My job is to protect you, Peyton. Even from things you don't see or think are important."

"Yeah, well." She really wasn't up for a debate. Especially with *him*. "If it were up to me you wouldn't have a job. You weren't my idea."

"And yet, here I am." His lips curved, but there was no humor in his eyes. "Whether I remain isn't up to you. It's up to Ms. Wright, and from what I've seen and heard, she wants to continue having me around. And so long as she keeps signing my checks…"

Right. She was just another job for him, wasn't she? Just another paycheck. Why couldn't she remember that? "You're always there. Here. Everywhere. I feel like I need to put a bell around your neck."

"You can try," he countered. "I get it, Peyton. You're used to being in control. You like your nice, organized little world as tidy and compact as possible. I'm an intruder. But I'm a far nicer one than whoever has you in their sights. Someone who may very well want to hurt you. I have no doubt you'd like to get rid of me, and I bet you think if you're rude or offensive enough I'll quit. But here's something you need to know about me." He moved in, close enough she could feel his breath against her face, feel the warmth of his body radiating against hers. "I don't quit."

"Good to hear, son," Big E said from the open doorway. "Come and join us, please. Let's hear what the detectives had to say."

"This is every nightmare I've ever had rolled into one." Peyton closed her eyes and remained where she was. Personal and professional had collided into a massive fireball about to scorch her world.

"Look on the bright side," Matteo said as he moved around her to follow Big E to Vilette's office. "Nightmares come to an end. I'll leave when the job's done. But not before." That grin was back. "No matter what you try."

CHAPTER FOUR

MATTEO STOOD BESIDE Vilette's ancient school-teacher desk. Big E and Peyton sat across from her in chairs that couldn't possibly be comfortable. While Big E looked strangely giddy at this afternoon's developments, Peyton was acting as if she'd been called into the principal's office and was awaiting punishment.

"Detectives Reno and Gillette assured me they'd have fingerprint analysis back by tomorrow morning," Matteo wrapped up his report of his discussion with the detectives.

"You don't sound optimistic we'll receive any information from that," Vilette observed. She leaned back in her chair, stretched out her legs and reminded Matteo of old Woodstock photos of concertgoers with stars in their eyes. But behind those starry eyes was a mind that was razor-sharp and far ahead of most people Matteo had ever met.

"I would be very surprised if there are any

prints, let alone that they're even in the system." Matteo didn't like admitting it, but he wasn't about to lie, either. "I've already reviewed the security footage from this morning. I gave a copy to the detectives, by the way," he added and had a sudden concern he should have checked with Vilette before doing so. He'd been given control over Peyton's safety, so it had seemed practical and prudent. When Vilette didn't protest, he went on. "Whoever delivered the flowers wasn't from a service. The person was wearing a red hoodie and avoided looking at the cameras. Nothing stood out. Not his clothes, not his walk. His arms and legs were covered, so no birthmarks or tattoos showed. We know he's a white male. And he delivered at a time when the solitary security officer in the lobby went to grab a coffee." Which reminded him, he needed to have a talk with Electryone's head of security to make sure officers varied their routines to avoid another occurrence like that.

"Sounds to me like whoever this is knows the routine around here," Big E interjected. "Or am I misunderstanding what you're saying?"

"No misunderstanding, sir." Matteo nodded.

From across the room he could see Peyton's jaw tense. "I'd like permission to go through all the employee records and client files. Peyton's specifically."

He noted Peyton's spine went steel straight. She looked as if she wanted to start shouting at him.

"What are you looking for exactly?" Vilette seemed to be acknowledging Peyton's pained expression.

Matteo needed to keep the conversation as calm and simple as possible. "His note said he knows what she—what you—" he addressed Peyton now "—did. We need to find out what it is you did that someone took the wrong way. In their mind, anyway," he added when a flush of anger pinked Peyton's cheeks. "I'm not saying you did something bad, Peyton. I'm saying he thinks you did."

"He thinks it so strongly he's taken to threatening you at your place of work," Vilette clarified. "All right. I'll have—"

"Todd," Peyton cut her off. "This is disruptive enough. I don't want anyone from the company other than Todd to be aware of this…" she looked to Matteo and narrowed her eyes "…investigation."

Vilette nodded. "Agreed. We don't want to disturb business any more than necessary, but I'm not going to just let this pass," she stated strongly when Peyton sputtered. "Believe it or not, Peyton, you're what concerns me. Not just because you're vital to this company. You're important to me. And while I rely on you, you're also my friend. I can't run this company without you which, for all we know, could be a reason you've been targeted. I'll have Todd create a dedicated electronic file and jump drive, Matteo. You'll have what you need as soon as possible."

"Thank you."

Peyton scrunched up her mouth. "Is that it?"

"No, actually." Vilette cast a glance at Big E. "Your grandfather and I have been discussing a few things."

"Why?" Peyton asked. "He has nothing to do with this or me. I barely know him. I didn't even know he existed before…" She trailed off at Matteo's disapproving look. "What? I'm telling the truth."

"And the truth sometimes hurts," Big E agreed. "I can't apologize for not being around when I didn't know you and your sisters existed, Peyton. But I can be here now, and I've offered a solution I believe we can all live with."

"What kind of solution?"

"Peyton." Vilette's voice softened, and Matteo had the notion to step out of the way of Peyton's laser-sharp gaze. "Matteo has my utmost trust in all of this. While I will admit when I first hired him I wasn't entirely sure he was necessary, the rest of the board did. I've now come to agree. I have to trust his judgment and his observation that you are far too visible, your routine is too predictable and your focus—"

"My focus?" Peyton asked. "What's wrong with my focus?"

"Nothing. Yet. But I can't take the chance that keeping you here, in the office, even in town for that matter, won't change that. We have too much riding on Olwen for you to be distracted. Therefore, Big E and I have decided that you need to be somewhere farther off the grid. Somewhere unexpected."

Matteo's sympathy kicked in as he saw the color drain from Peyton's cheeks. "No," she whispered and glared at her grandfather, then back at her boss. "No way. You cannot be serious!"

"I can and I am," Vilette said. "You will leave for Montana and the Blackwell Ranch the day after tomorrow. I've already made arrangements for you to use the company jet— that way there will be no public record of your leaving or where you're going. If word gets out, as I'm sure it will, we'll say you're on a much-needed vacation, and that will be the end of the discussion."

Matteo pursed his lips. He wasn't sure anyone would buy Peyton taking even an hour off, let alone days.

"You hate the company jet," Peyton said with something like bitterness in her voice. "It's a pollutant. And unnecessary."

"Which should tell you how strongly I feel about this," Vilette suggested with a thin smile. "Your company car will remain here, at the office. You have to continue to work, of course. I'm not sure I could say or do anything that would prevent that. Take whatever you need to keep up with the Olwen project as well as any other clients you feel can't do without your attention for the next two weeks—"

"Two weeks?" Peyton almost squealed. "I can't be gone that long. We've got the final meeting on the Olwen project the first week of November. Besides, I have…plants."

Matteo rolled his eyes. He'd have expected a better excuse from someone so smart.

"I saw that," Peyton snapped at him.

He dipped his head to hide his grin. "I think sending her to Montana is an excellent idea," Matteo told Vilette and Big E. "I'll call my boss and arrange for one of our best agents to accompany her."

"That won't be necessary," Vilette said. She folded her hands on top of her desk and tilted her chin up so she could smile at him. "You'll be going with her."

Silence roared in his ears. He couldn't possibly have heard that right. "I'm sorry. Can you… Going with her?" Matteo could barely breathe around the knot that tightened in his stomach. "To Montana?" To a cattle ranch? "No. That's not possible. I can't—"

"Too many plants?" Peyton batted her lashes at him and lit a slow-burn fuse on his temper.

"No. I have a son." A son who in the past two days had called him at least a dozen times, crying and pleading with him to stop Sylvia from shipping him off to boarding school. Every conversation had broken Matteo's heart more and given him a good earful of Gino's temper tantrums. There was nothing he could do at this point other than file an emergency motion with the court, but his lawyer reminded him of just how slow custody cases went these days. Especially when the child in question lived outside the country. "I need to stay in touch with him."

"I thought Gino lives in Japan with his mother," Peyton said with a coolness in her eyes he didn't appreciate. "Cell phones work everywhere. Wait. Do they?" She looked to Big E, a flash of horror in her eyes. "Tell me you have cell reception and Wi-Fi out in the middle of nowhere."

"Not to worry," Big E said with a nod. "While we'd prefer visitors to leave their jobs and devices behind, thanks to my forewoman and granddaughter-in-law Katie, along with Hadley, who runs the visitor's portion of the ranch, we are well in the twenty-first century. You'll be able to connect with anyone you need to. Even someone in Japan," he said with a sympathetic look at Matteo, who was beginning to feel a little sick.

The very idea of stepping foot on a ranch— any ranch, let alone an isolated one in the middle of Nowhere, Montana—shot Matteo straight back to a childhood that held zero appeal. "I'm sorry, but I'm afraid—"

Vilette held up her hand, a gesture Matteo had begun to associate with her having made up her mind. "I realize this is an unexpected inconvenience. I'll double what we're paying you," she said. "And include a bonus once the threat against Peyton has been taken care of and she can come back here where she belongs."

Double? The sound of Gino's laughter, laughter he would hear every day of his life should Matteo win full custody, drowned out the cries and fears of Matteo's past. He hated that money was all that stood between him and his son. Money that was being offered to him right here and now. Money he'd earn by walking back into his worst nightmare.

But to have the chance to bring Gino home? Matteo set his jaw against the hope ballooning in his chest. "All right."

"I can't do my job without Todd." Peyton seemed to finally have an argument she believed in. "He's my right hand. What I don't remember or know, he does."

"Do you expect me to ask Todd to take time

off from school to come with you? Peyton."
Vilette shook her head. "I'm disappointed. You
should know better."

"Well, I can't turn up on this ranch place
with a bodyguard. That's hardly under anyone's radar," she argued.

"That's easy to fix. Matteo will go along as
your assistant," Vilette said as Big E nodded
in approval. "Matteo, I'll have Todd give you
a crash course in how to work with and for
Peyton. What it is she'd need help and support
with. Assistant Training 101. That way, Peyton, you'll be prepared for the Olwen meeting."

"That better be a very substantial bonus,"
Matteo said, with what he hoped was a tinge
of humor. Still, he couldn't risk completely
alienating Peyton. A rebellious protectee often
caused more trouble than the threat against
the person.

"Look at him. No one is going to believe
he's my assistant," Peyton muttered. "We
won't blend in at all. Neither one of us will."

"No one's asking you to play Annie Oak-
ley," Vilette said. "As far as anyone who works
and lives on the ranch is concerned, you're
there to get to know the family business and

explore opportunities for Electryone. And maybe relax a little."

Peyton started to respond, then stopped short when Vilette held up one finger.

"I don't think you understand the situation, Peyton. Let me spell it out for you." Vilette clasped her hands together once more and leaned her arms on the table. The woman reminded Matteo of a general leading her troops into battle. "You will either go to Montana with Matteo and hole up until the police find out who is threatening you and why, or you can resign. Right now." Vilette inclined her head. "It's your choice."

Peyton didn't look entirely convinced. In fact, she looked ready to call her boss's bluff. "You can't close this Olwen deal without me. I'm the only one—"

"You're the only one *currently* focused primarily on Olwen," Vilette said. "That can change. I have no doubt Belinda would love the opportunity to get her hands on the project more fully."

Having spent quite a bit of time around the office these past weeks where he'd heard more gossip and gathered enough behind-the-scenes dirt to build his own island, Matteo wasn't surprised in the least when Vilette's suggestion hit its target. Peyton couldn't have looked more sour if Vilette had pushed a lemon into her mouth.

"Peyton." Vilette's tone gentled. "The fact I'm willing to risk Olwen at all should tell you my mind is made up. Deals come and go. Your safety, your well-being, that of any of my employees, is always my top priority. What happens moving forward is now up to you."

Sympathy tugged at Matteo's heart as Peyton's expression went slack. She looked stricken, devastated. And seriously ticked off. It didn't matter what got thrown at her, that fire of determination didn't dim. She was a woman who knew what she wanted, and she'd get there no matter what, even if that meant taking a less desirable road to get there. One more reminder that, no matter how appealing Peyton Harrison was, there could never be anything between them other than professional and mutual respect.

The silence stretched, and Peyton looked at Vilette, a silent plea in her beautiful, sharp eyes. Then she looked to her grandfather, who, despite Big E's obvious affection for his recently discovered granddaughter, didn't so much as blink. When she turned her eyes on Matteo, he wanted nothing more than to remove that expression of betrayal from her face. But he couldn't. Not when he knew that going to Montana—however much he personally hated the idea—was the best solution.

"Fine. I'll go." She pushed to her feet and faced down her grandfather. "And stop smiling like you won the gold medal in barrel racing, Big E. I might be going to Montana, but I'm not going to like it."

Big E watched her leave, then looked back at Matteo and grinned. "That's what they all say."

"YOU CAN STOP laughing anytime, Fiona." Peyton sat curled up in the corner of her sofa, legs tucked in, an oversize wineglass in her hand, and listened to her baby sister cackle on the other end of the phone.

Even though she was irritated, her lips twitched at the sound of her sister's chuckles. Peyton had missed this—the late-night conversations, the endless nonsensical talks she and her sisters had carried on over the years. Being the topic of said conversation, however, put a whole new spin on it.

"Your boss is shipping you off to Montana because she thinks you're overworked?" Fiona snorted. "And Big E helped? Okay, I'm done." She sighed. "I think." She sputtered again. "How bad have you really gotten that your own workaholic boss has taken you to task?"

Peyton winced. She hated lying to Fiona. Again. But no way was she going to tell any of her sisters that her exile was an attempt to protect her from someone who quite possibly meant to do her harm.

Using Vilette as her excuse made things easier and, as Peyton planned to tell Big E in the morning when she and Matteo met him at the airport, a nonnegotiable side-deal. Her sisters had enough to deal with these days; she didn't want them worrying unnecessarily about her.

Besides, after getting the rundown of how many Blackwells there were in Falcon Creek, she didn't want anyone who didn't have to be involved in any way. As far as she was concerned, she, Big E and Matteo were the only ones who knew why she was at the ranch: to hide.

And that, Peyton thought as she downed

the rest of her wine, was what irritated her the most.

"How long will you be at the ranch?" Fiona finally asked.

"Through Halloween, so about two weeks." Peyton examined the skyline from her top-floor apartment overlooking the marina. She'd only just moved in six months ago and, well, honestly? Peyton ducked her head. The place acted more as a pit stop than a home. "Exactly what am I supposed to do on a guest ranch, anyway?"

"I'm so glad you asked!" Fiona gushed. "Lily's been telling me all about it. Besides all the fall activities they've got planned like hayrides, a giant corn maze, and an apple and corn festival, they've got the usual like hiking and trail rides. Lots of outdoor activities from barbecues to—"

"Fiona, stop." Her sister was not helping the situation. In fact, all that information only made her want to call Vilette's bluff. "Does any of that sound like me?"

There was silence for a moment. "You used to like horses when we were kids, remember?"

"Barely." But deep inside, in a place she hadn't let herself acknowledge in a very long time, something broke open. A memory of a day, a day bright with sunshine and a laughing Peyton who, along with her father, her real father, had spent the day riding through a green forest. A day so perfect it hurt her heart to think about it.

"Oh, come on, Pey. You used to have all those horse pictures in your room. You scavenged through Mom's magazines taking everything you could—"

"That was a long time ago." Peyton uncurled from the sofa and returned to the kitchen to refill her wine. There was nothing so personal as horse images hanging on her walls now. Other than the few framed photographs she had of her sisters and her mother and stepfather settled on the hall table, the entire one-bedroom loft apartment looked like a sterile showroom.

"I'm sure when you get bored with your research and reports, Lily will give you a job to do to help with the wedding. Have you talked to her yet? Does she know you're coming?"

"I haven't had a chance to call her." Peyton emptied the bottle. Why was she such a coward? "I'm worried she might tell me not to come."

"She wouldn't do that," Fiona said, but her

tone made Peyton wonder if that was true. "Amanda might have, but Lily won't. You're going to have to face all of us in person at some point, Peyton."

"All the more reason to not reach out until I'm standing in front of her." Peyton knew she had the reputation of not leading with her heart. A reputation that had only been solidified by the revelation she'd kept the identity of their real father a secret. She was tough, probably even cold by some people's standards, but that was her safe place. She knew better than most, certainly better than her sisters, that the more you closed yourself off to people, the less chance you had of getting hurt. And nothing held the propensity for emotional pain—especially self-inflicted pain—like the siblings she'd helped to raise. "I guess I'll see her tomorrow, and whatever happens, happens."

"On the bright side, from what I hear there will be plenty of space for you and your assistant out on that ranch. Let me know what you think about Conner. I'm dying to meet him. I'm hoping to get some time off soon so I can visit before the wedding in December."

It still baffled Peyton how Lily had gone from nearly marrying one of their best childhood friends to settling down in Montana with a cowboy. How did something like that even happen? Then again, unpredictability had pretty much defined Lily since the day she'd been born. That girl had never met a challenge she didn't rise to, before or after a childhood injury had left her with dexterity issues.

After assuring Fiona she'd keep in touch, Peyton hung up and cleaned up the kitchen before she resumed packing. Her soft-sided briefcase was filled to capacity with her laptop, files and various other items she'd convinced herself she couldn't do without. She'd loaded herself up with all the *I'll get to it later* ideas she'd been collecting over the past few years. If she was going to be stuck on a ranch in the middle of nowhere, she might as well make productive use of the time.

She probably should have taken Todd out for dinner, given all he'd done to get her ready and to bring Matteo up to speed on what was expected of an executive assistant. She'd purposely stayed out of both their ways but had kept an ear open just to get an idea of how Matteo was acclimating to his new role.

Much to her disappointment, but not to her surprise, her bodyguard was rolling perfectly with the punches. Funnily enough, he seemed as enamored with the idea of an extended stay in Montana as she was. Having that in common, however, didn't endear him to her. Especially since she hadn't been able to talk him out of the idea. And she'd tried. Multiple times. The last opportunity was only a few hours ago when he'd driven her home and locked her in for the night, leaving behind one of his security officers in a car across the street.

She rinsed out her wineglass, wiped down the barren counters and did a quick emptying of the meager contents of her fridge. Leftover take-out containers had piled up over the past few weeks, turning most of them into unintended science experiments. She took the trash out to the chute and returned to her echoing apartment.

That odd pang she often felt these days struck sharply. At least she'd finally get the chance to have a face-to-face conversation with one of her sisters. So far, she and Fiona had mostly gotten back on the same page, and Georgie had been the only sister to actually answer her email in a way that offered a glimmer of forgiveness. Until she'd also righted things with Lily and Amanda, Peyton wouldn't feel as hopeful they could all move past the recent family revelation.

Climbing the stairs to her loft bedroom and bath, she resigned herself to the fact that for the next few weeks her life was in someone else's hands quite literally.

She couldn't get home and back to work fast enough.

CHAPTER FIVE

"HANG ON, I'M COMING!" Matteo kicked his way free of his covers and cast a surly look at the clock that told him he'd managed a whole two and a half hours of sleep. This was so not how he wanted to start the day. He needed to pick Peyton up at seven thirty so they could get to the airport by eight. More than that, he needed to be alert and ready for anything—not just to protect Peyton, but to deal with what would no doubt be her difficult attitude.

The bell rang again, jangling his fraying temper.

Having lived on the other end of angry raised voices for most of his upbringing, he'd made the decision a long time ago that there was no purpose in losing control. His determination to maintain calm, however, did not extend to a 4:00 a.m. wake-up call in the form of what was certain to be some drunk idiot ringing his doorbell.

After a completely unproductive night spent running background checks on every Electryone employee, the thread maintaining his temper had already been stretched spiderweb thin. Other than a few misdemeanors and traffic violations, he didn't find any reason for an employee to have a grudge against Peyton Harrison.

With his unexpected trip to Montana robbing him of much-needed time, he had two security officers checking Electryone's clients. Maybe, hopefully, a connection would pop there. But for now, he had to strangle someone.

He yanked open the door and glared at the unfamiliar, short, bespectacled man on the threshold. Somewhere in his early thirties, his visitor gave off a vibe of responsibility, and respect. Matteo had made it his career sizing people up at a glance; there was nothing threatening about the stranger, other than the fact that the man's tailored suit probably cost twice as much as Matteo's rent.

"Mr. Rossi." The man's dark hair glistened as he bowed his head slightly. "Please forgive the early-morning intrusion. I am Taro Shinko, personal assistant to Jiro Tadeshi."

"Ah, okay?" Matteo leaned against the door and waited for the punch line. What was his ex-wife's new husband's assistant doing at his apartment? "Nice to meet you."

Taro's mouth quirked in a slight smile. "And you. I have a delivery for you, Mr. Rossi."

"A delivery?" Matteo scrubbed his fingers into his eyes. Was he still dreaming?

Taro held out his arm and stepped back. The familiar little boy who came forward offered an uncertain smile.

"Hi, Dad."

"Gino?" Matteo crouched in front of him, hands reaching for him, skimming up his arms, to capture his sweet face between his palms. "What are you doing here?" He didn't wait for an answer, just swung Gino up and into his arms, ignoring the heavy backpack as it slammed against him. He wrapped his arms tightly around his son, hugging him so fiercely he almost scared himself. The years that had passed since he'd last held him, last felt his heartbeat pound, vanished in the blink of an eye. He tilted his head back to look at his boy, pride, love and relief surging through him. "Are you all right?"

"I'm good."

Gino's huge dark eyes were outlined with thick lashes. His tiny nose wrinkled as he smiled, and the curls in his dark brown hair reminded Matteo of his own when he'd been growing up. He smoothed his hand over his son's hair. His heart filled so full he didn't realize just how empty it had been. "You've gotten so big."

"Mom said she was tired of me whining, so she said you can deal with me for a while." Gino's gap-toothed smile was a stark reminder of just how much Matteo had missed these last few years. "Jiro had Mr. Shinko bring me."

"Mr. Shinko." Matteo released Gino so he could slide to the floor. Matteo held out his hand. "I'm sorry for…" What was he sorry for exactly? He hadn't been given any warning. And if he had been warned, he would have met his son at the airport. "Please. Come in." He moved aside to allow Mr. Shinko entrance.

"I don't want to impose," Mr. Shinko said, but he came in nonetheless.

"There is no imposition. Not after you've flown…how long to bring me my son?" Matteo closed the door and, keeping a hand on Gino's head for fear he might vanish in a puff of imagination, motioned him inside. "Can I get you something to drink? Coffee? Tea? I'm afraid I don't have much more to offer." His brain was a bit fuzzy. He'd cleaned out his kitchen and fridge before he'd gone to bed.

"Coffee would be most appreciated." Mr. Shinko looked to Gino. "Gino, would you mind if your father and I spoke for a few minutes?"

"Nah." Gino's face was flushed and alive. "Dad, where's my room?"

"Last door on the left." Matteo had purposely made sure to always have a place for Gino to call his own if and when he visited. The decorating and furnishings had been chosen with both hope and longing. He'd shown the room to his son during one of their many video chats. Gino didn't have to be told twice. He ran off. "Does he have any luggage?"

"In the car downstairs. I'll have it brought up momentarily." Mr. Shinko followed Matteo into the kitchen, tapping on his cell phone. "Mrs. Tadeshi regrets she was unable to notify you about Gino's delivery herself. A last-minute business trip came up."

Gino's delivery? Matteo gnashed his teeth as he stuck a pod into the coffee machine and pressed Brew. They made it sound as if Matteo had ordered takeout from the corner pizza place. It would be easy, so easy, to speak ill of Sylvia, but the disrespect might trigger something that could work against him in the long run. "I appreciate Jiro sparing you for the journey, Mr. Shinko," he said instead, focusing on the positive. "I'm happy to have my son with me."

"Taro, please. It is nice to be able to put a smile on your son's face. I fear…" Taro trailed off, as if afraid he'd say something inappropriate. "I fear he has not been happy for quite some time. Ah." He sat when Matteo motioned to the small circular table in the kitchen. "I have become quite a fan of the American coffee phenomenon." He closed his eyes and took in a breath. "It is quite intoxicating, is it not?"

"I sure hope so," Matteo said with a chuckle. "It keeps me moving, that's for sure." He waited for the second cup to brew, then placed both filled mugs on the table and sat down. "Why do I feel as if there's more to Gino's visit than a spur-of-the-moment decision?"

"Because you are an observant and attentive parent." Taro nodded approvingly at his coffee. "This is excellent." He set his mug down. "Mr. Tadeshi is very fond of Gino."

"Glad to have that confirmed," Matteo said. "Gino's spoken of him often and with affection. It's made things…easier." As if a custody fight was ever easy. "How bad did Gino get that Sylvia decided to *deliver* him to me?"

Taro smiled. "I have been told by my own parents that boys Gino's age can be a challenge. I believe his refusal to talk was easier to deal with than his temper tantrums. Those seemed to appear out of nowhere in the past few days. As much as my employer loves the boy, he is not, as he has often told Mrs. Tadeshi, his father. It makes disciplining him challenging."

"So, she sent him to me to fix." Matteo smirked. Typical Sylvia. Happy to create the problem, not so willing to deal with the fallout. "I'll take whatever part of my son's life I can get."

The conversation shifted to various topics related to Gino's life: his schooling, extracurricular activities, likes and dislikes. Taro had it all on his phone in a document he forwarded to Matteo's email. Upon finishing his coffee, Taro stood, readjusted his suit jacket and offered his thanks. "This has been most enjoyable, Mr. Rossi. I appreciate the respite before heading back to the airport."

"Matteo, please." Matteo offered his hand and led him back to the door.

"Matteo." Taro nodded. "This has gone much more smoothly than I anticipated. It will be a relief to convey the positive exchange with Mr. and Mrs. Tadeshi."

"Gino's in good hands." And exactly where he should be.

"I will return in three weeks' time—"

"That won't be necessary." Matteo hated to blindside Taro, but that's just how things would be. No way was he going to give up this advantage. "Gino is home now. He's going to stay home. You can tell Sylvia, if she wants our son back, she can see me in court."

"BIG E, WHAT ARE you doing here?" Peyton had no option other than to step back and grant her grandfather access to her apartment. "We were supposed to meet at the airport." She'd been checking her watch every ten minutes for the past few hours. Ever since she'd found herself wide awake and staring at her stark white ceiling.

"Change of plans." Big E clasped his hat in his hands and waited for her to close the door. "I'm afraid I won't be flying back to Montana with you. I've got…alternate transportation arranged for something that needs taking care of."

Peyton didn't know him well, but she'd spent enough time with him to be certain that smile he flashed in her direction held more than humor. He was up to something.

"Well, Matteo will be here in about an hour." She motioned to her bags. "I'm all packed for my trip to purgatory. As you requested." She'd had to invest in some sturdy, cold-weather clothes as the mid-October weather in Montana could be chilly and unpredictable. She'd done more research.

"Could use some coffee if you have any." He cast a weary gaze around her apartment. "Interesting homestead you have. Very…practical."

"That's me. Practical to a fault." She let the snark fall away as he caught sight of one of the photographs of her and her sisters. How could she resent a man when the affection for her and her siblings was so evident? "That was taken the summer after Fiona graduated from high school. We all took a long weekend together in Butterfly Harbor. Up around Monterey." She smiled at the memory. "There's this beautiful Victorian inn on top of the cliffs. Summer sun, amazing food and people." The photograph had been taken by the inn's manager, who had captured the perfect moment when all the Harrison—or was it Blackwell now?—girls were laughing and celebrating. Long before Peyton's betrayal would break them apart.

"You're all so beautiful," Big E said with a throat that sounded tight with emotion. "Sentimentality isn't my strong suit," he said with a quick grin. "One of my biggest regrets is not having found out about Thomas, about you girls, sooner." He set the photograph back down. "Family is all that matters, Peyton. It's all that will ever matter. When you do find yourself cursing me for manipulating you into going to Montana, I hope you'll remember that."

"I'll no doubt have plenty of time to think that over in the coming weeks," Peyton told him and felt her heart soften. "You wanted coffee?" Before she found herself leaning more toward forgiveness than anger, she hurried into the kitchen. No sooner had she set a mug in front of her grandfather than the doorbell rang. She looked at her watch. "He's early."

"Early's on time for some," Big E announced. "He's former military, isn't he? He'd be one who thinks that way."

"Hmm." She was humoring him, she realized. Darn it. She clenched her fist. She was beginning to like her grandfather, and that just wouldn't do!

"Come on in," she said by way of greeting Matteo, who was standing outside her door, hands shoved into his pant pockets. With his slightly untamed mane of blue-black hair and just-as-dark sunglasses perched on his nose, he looked like a federal agent from the movies. When he didn't move, she sighed. "Matteo, I've come to terms with this. If I want to keep my job, this is what I have to do." She loathed the situation, but she hadn't done herself any favors with her reluctant attitude. "Doesn't mean I'm happy about it."

"Good to know. Because I won't be going with you." He reached out his hand and drew a small boy to him. "Gino arrived this morning. We're going to have to make other arrangements."

"Oh." Peyton's heart flipped in her chest. The little boy was beautiful, an almost-identical replica of his father, right down to the dimple in his left cheek. The backpack he wore was almost as big as he was and sagged well below his butt. She found herself wondering what treasures he kept inside. She remembered little girls liked treasures, too, and sometimes kept them hidden away. "Hello, Gino." Remembering how intimidating adults could be for kids, she crouched down so she was at his eye level. "I'm Peyton. Your father's been working for me for a few weeks."

"I know," Gino announced. "He told me. He said you build cool stuff like Tony Stark."

"I help people who build stuff," she corrected, amused that Matteo would compare her to what was clearly one of his son's favorite fictional characters. "Why don't you both come inside?"

"I don't mean to complicate things," Matteo said, his hands resting on his son's shoulders. Gino looked up, first at his father, then at Peyton. "But Gino has to be my first priority. He can't be with me when I'm working a case."

"No, of course he can't." Peyton closed the door and locked her arms around her torso and squeezed. There was such trust in that little boy's eyes when he looked at Matteo. Trust she couldn't remember having for a very long time. She'd come close. Rudy had been an amazing influence on her life and a steady force she could count on. But there had always been something holding her back. Almost as if she'd be betraying her real father by completely accepting and loving Rudy.

"I've already spoken to my boss and she's sending Adam Winchester to the airport to meet you," Matteo went on as if he'd been rehearsing what he was going to say to her. "He's been on nights, so he's up to speed. I've also been in touch with a sister agency out in Montana, who will be on call as soon as the jet lands."

"I'm sure it'll be fine." Unexpected disappointment crashed through her. Somehow the idea of Matteo being with her on this excursion had made the entire prospect less distasteful. Not that she'd ever tell him that. "Gino, I think I have some hot chocolate for you in the kitchen, if that's okay with your dad?"

"Is it, Dad?" Gino's wide eyes went even bigger.

"What's more sugar at this point?" Matteo didn't look half as defeated as he pretended to be. "Yeah, it's fine."

"Go on ahead, Gino," Peyton said. "I'll be right there to fix it."

"'Kay." Thumbs hooked into the shoulder straps of his backpack he swaggered as only a six-year-old could, out of sight.

"What's going on?" Peyton asked. "I thought you said he was with your ex?"

"He was. Now he's here." It was only when he pulled off his sunglasses that she saw the dark circles under his eyes. "If you don't mind, it's been a long morning and I'd rather not re-hash it. As much as I hate to walk away from the money, I need to give him my full atten-tion. He needs me. He's having…issues."

Something in his tone, something she really didn't like, tied a knot in her stomach. "You say that as if you don't think I'd understand."

"Do you?"

Did he have to seem so…shocked? Even if Big E hadn't just lectured her on the impor-tance of putting family first, she'd have agreed with Matteo wholeheartedly. Her reputation might be that of a heartless workaholic, but she knew how fragile—and strong—kids could be. Support, love and a guiding hand was all they really needed.

At the booming voice echoing from the kitchen, Matteo's eyebrows went up. "I thought we were meeting Big E at the airport?"

"It's been a morning for surprises," Peyton mumbled. "He showed up a few minutes before you did and said he, too, has had a change of plans. He's not going with us."

"You must be devastated," Matteo teased.

That he knew her well enough to crack a joke like that both set her stomach to fluttering and her cheeks to flushing.

"Well, don't you two look cozy," Peyton said when they found Gino sitting on a stool beside Big E. "Make a new friend, Big E?"

"As a matter of fact—" Big E eyed them both "—Gino was just telling me how he's come to stay with his father for a while. I take it you think this changes things, Matteo?"

"Uh—" Matteo began.

"What's changing?" Gino tilted his chin up and looked from his father to Big E. "Dad, I thought you said—"

"Give me a few minutes, G, okay?" Matteo brushed a hand on his son's shoulder. "Big E, may I talk to you privately?"

"No need to," Big E boomed. "I already know what you're going to say."

Peyton's radar pinged. "You do?" It had crossed her mind that this was the solution she'd been looking for. If Matteo couldn't go, and Vilette didn't necessarily trust anyone else with her safety at this point—

"Nothing's changed other than your cover story just got stronger," Big E told them. He walked over to the fridge and pulled it open. "No wonder you're so skinny," he grumbled to Peyton. "Ain't nothing in this place but air and ice. Don't worry. A couple of weeks on the ranch and we'll get your blood going." He closed it again. "Guess I'll have to stop for breakfast on my way out of town. Gino, have you heard of Montana?"

"Big E—" Peyton warned.

Gino shrugged. "Don't they have cowboys there? And horses?"

"Among other things," Matteo added in a sour tone that caught Peyton's attention. She'd heard apathy in his tone before. Sarcasm and humor, sure. But this was the first time that disdain clung to his words.

"Other things indeed," Big E confirmed. "There ain't nothing like the big sky of Montana, Gino. Endless blue stretching as far out as any one person could possibly see. Empty land, rolling hills, just as close to perfection as you'll ever find. And this time of year? Beginning of fall? It's the most beautiful place on earth."

"Is that where you live?" Gino shifted onto his knees.

"Lived there my whole life," Big E stated with pride in his tone.

"Wow." Gino's eyes went saucer-wide. "That must be a really long time."

"Gino," Matteo warned. "Mind your manners."

"Yes, sir," Gino said almost dismissively.

"Would you like to see Montana, Gino? You know, I have some great-grandchildren out there I bet you'd be friends with. Granted, they're mostly girls. Got a couple of baby great-grandsons, though. Is that all right with you?"

"I guess." Gino didn't look convinced.

"There's tons of stuff for you to do on the ranch. Animals to tend, adventures to have. You won't be bored."

"Do you have video games?"

"Well, that you'll have to talk with your dad about, Gino." Big E ruffled Gino's hair. "Montana's there to be lived in, not to be ignored in favor of screens."

Peyton shifted uncomfortably when Big E glanced in her direction. She'd seen enough sky in her life. She was happy with her screens.

"I appreciate you trying to salvage this, Big

E," Matteo said. "But I don't think it would be appropriate to bring my son along on a job."

"I have to agree with Matteo," Peyton volunteered. "The job he's doing, it's not exactly...well, safe."

"Finally admitting I'm right?" Matteo asked.

Peyton smirked at him.

"The whole purpose of you going to Montana is so you are safe," Big E said. "And with as many people as are on and around the ranch, not to mention Falcon Creek itself, you'll be surrounded by family and friends and a whole special town, Peyton. Fall's a slow time for guests, with kids being back in school and all, but there's plenty to keep you busy. And Matteo. You won't be safer anywhere else. Neither would Gino."

"I don't know." Matteo still looked unsure. "It doesn't seem professional."

"Again, agreed." Peyton grasped onto the thin thread of hope that Gino might very well give her the out she'd been looking for. "You wouldn't want Matteo's attention divided."

"Man's a former Marine. He can do two things at once. And I promise you, you can trust my grandsons and their kin to keep Gino as close to them as they would their own. After all, you're family now. And by extension, Matteo and Gino are, too."

"Big E," Peyton said with a shake of her head. As adorable as Gino was, as happy as having him here obviously made Matteo, it didn't make sense to haul a six-year-old off to Montana while they were trying to protect her from something dangerous.

Besides, being around Matteo was complicated enough for her. She didn't need to add his son, who might complicate her life. Or her emotions even more. "It's not that simple. What about Gino's mom?"

"Sylvia sent him to me," Matteo answered. "What happens with him now is in my hands."

Was it her imagination or did she hear a hint of defiance in Matteo's voice?

"If Big E says there's enough people around to keep an eye on him so I can do my job—"

"Harvest and cattle time means lots of people around," Big E clarified. "And you know what's a really great day on the ranch, now that Hadley's in charge of social activities?" He looked over at Gino.

"What?" the boy asked.

"Halloween. You should see the party they put on for all the kids in town. There are all kinds of games and fun and prizes and of course trick-or-treating. It's almost as important around the town as Christmas. I bet you'd really like that, wouldn't you, Gino?"

"Dad, can we go? Please?" Gino spun on his stool and nearly toppled off. "It sounds amazing, and I'd really like to make some friends. And I've never had a real Halloween before. In Japan we just dress up. There's no trick-or-treating at all." Gino made it sound as if a major crime had been committed. But it was the friends comment that twisted Peyton's heart. She looked at Matteo, and when their gazes clashed, she forced herself not to look away.

It wasn't that she didn't want father and son to have all the time together they needed. She just didn't want to be involved. She didn't want to be a witness to a relationship like the one she'd lost with her own father. But what was she going to do? Tell them no?

While Gino busied himself sipping his hot chocolate, Matteo lowered his voice. "I really do need the money. With the double pay and the bonus, I might finally have a shot at hiring a top lawyer who'd get me full custody. Especially with the way Sylvia sent him to me. I'll walk away from the job if I have to, but—"

Not agreeing would be tantamount to separating father and son. If not now, then soon. And that was one thing she'd never, ever do. Convinced, Peyton laid her hand on Matteo's arm and squeezed. "You don't have to walk away. We'll make this work. I don't want Gino getting hurt." And she wasn't talking about her stalker. If she could help keep Matteo and Gino together, how could she turn her back on that?

"You're sure?" While his voice was stern, she saw the silent plea in the depths of his eyes. Eyes that made her feel as if she were the only person in his world. Aside from his son. "Because I don't want you realizing later on that this was some kind of mistake you can hold over my head."

"I wouldn't do that." Her reputation must be even worse than she'd imagined. She cleared her throat and pulled her hand back. "All right, Gino. Looks like we're in agreement. Montana, here we come." She walked over to her grandfather as Gino dropped to the floor and ran to hug his dad. "You just can't help yourself, can you?" she said to her grandfather.

"Nope." Big E's smile widened. "Especially when it comes to family."

CHAPTER SIX

"Dad! Dad! Did you see? Look at this here. It's so cool!"

Matteo couldn't help but smile watching Gino bounce from one side of the private plane to the other, pressing his nose against the windows as he looked down into the mountainous range welcoming them to Montana. The wonder filling his son's eyes made the challenging hours following Gino's arrival fade into smoke.

"I see, Gino." He shifted his attention from Gino to Peyton, who had had her head stuck in her laptop since takeoff. "Peyton, did you want to see?"

"Huh?" Her eyes were narrowed behind her glasses when she looked up. With her mussed hair and furrowed brow, she looked like a confused, sexy librarian pulled out of a daydream. He glanced to the window, back to her, and shook his head in amazement when she did the same. Then looked back at her computer. "Yep. Pretty."

It wasn't his place, he reminded himself for the tenth time, to pull her out of her work so she could see at least a fraction of the world around them. It wasn't his place to make sure she took at least more than two seconds to see the vista awaiting them when they landed in twenty minutes. It wasn't his place to...care.

The cockpit door opened, and a woman with dark, tied-back blond hair and a round face emerged. "Big E's arranged for a car once you land. We should be touching down soon."

"Thanks, Donna," Matteo said as Gino shot back across the cabin and landed on his knees on one of the padded bench seats. Donna and her sister Jody were copiloting the flight, which, much to Matteo's dismay, had included an endless supply of sodas and snacks and pretty much anything else they could want or need.

"Hey, Gino," Donna said. "How would you like to sit up in the co-captain's chair for a little while?"

"Really?" Gino spun and dropped into the seat so fast Matteo was surprised the plane didn't shake. "Wow. That would be awesome. Dad, can I?"

"If it's okay with Donna and Jody, sure. Just don't touch anything. I mean it." He used the stern tone he knew would get Gino's attention. "You keep your hands to yourself."

"Yes, sir." Gino's distracted agreement had Matteo crossing his fingers as Donna held out her hand.

"You're really good with him." Peyton's murmured comment was so quiet he wondered if she'd meant to say it out loud.

"Surprised again?"

She shrugged. "I guess. I thought you said you hadn't seen him in years."

"Not in person, no." The truth of that statement dropped like a brick. He looked out the window, losing himself momentarily in the mountains and sky. "I flew out to Japan for his fourth birthday, just after they moved. The trip blew up my savings, but seeing him, being able to spend time with him, made it worth every penny. Ever since then, we've talked at least once a week on video chat, and we play online video games together. I get to at least touch base most days." Resentment he wished he could bank piled up like stones in a wall.

"As happy as I am during those times, nothing comes close to seeing him in person again."

When Peyton didn't respond, he found himself looking back at her. And saw her watching him, chin in her palm, tears glistening in her eyes.

"What?"

She shook her head, blinked as if embarrassed at having been caught expressing her emotions. He had to admit, her expression caught him off guard.

Ever since he'd met her, he'd thought her one of the coolest, most detached individuals he'd ever met. Not unlike his ex-wife, who had frequently gotten so caught up in her work, she'd forgotten anyone else existed, including her own son. The Peyton avoiding his gaze now was a different person. It made him wonder which woman was the real Peyton Harrison.

"You're just really good with your son," she repeated and began shuffling papers. "He likes you. He trusts you. That means, or it will mean, a lot to him when he's older."

"I hope so." He wasn't about to pry into the depths of the Blackwell family issues. They weren't any of his business. But Peyton most definitely was his business. At least for the next few weeks. "You were good with him, too. At your apartment."

She flashed a smile. "I like kids. Always have."

"But you don't have any yourself." The question slipped out of his mouth before he came close to thinking about it. He held up his hands. "Sorry. None of my concern."

"It's okay." She shrugged. "Kids have never been high on my to-do list, I guess. I've always been very focused on business."

"Sure." Where had he heard this before? Sylvia had always had her eye on something beyond him. Something more important to her than marriage. It was a good reminder of the type of woman he was currently protecting. "Like I said, none of my—"

"I helped raise my sisters," she said as she powered down her laptop and put her work away. "My dad, he left when I was seven. Just disappeared one day."

"Thomas Blackwell." He'd been paying close enough attention to glean a few details. "Big E's son."

"The son he apparently didn't know he had. But that's not important."

Wasn't it? Matteo wasn't so sure.

"I was the oldest," she went on. "My mother's little adult," she added with a ghost of a smile. "Having five kids under seven wasn't easy."

Had Matteo taken a sip of his coffee he'd have spit it out. "Five girls under seven?"

"The middle three are triplets—Lily, Georgie and Amanda. Fiona was born a few months after my dad left. We didn't have a lot of money, and Mom needed a ton of help. Our neighbors were great, but I—"

"Stepped up to the challenge." One of the other things he'd noticed about Peyton. She didn't shirk away from anything resembling a problem. She tackled them like a right or left guard protecting the quarterback, or in this case, her family. "I can't imagine a seven-year-old taking care of babies."

"One baby. Three toddlers." Funnily enough, he didn't see a trace of resentment on her face when she talked about her sisters. But he did see affection. Love. And the faintest hint of longing. "When our mom met and married Rudy, well, everything changed. For the better. Mostly."

"Rudy's your stepfather."

"Retired Navy Admiral Rudy Harrison."

Matteo had no doubt his eyes had gotten as big as his son's. "You're kidding me."

"You know him?"

"I know of him. He was, is, one of the good ones. The really good ones," he added. "I've watched some of his commencement addresses from naval graduations. He helped solidify my faith in the service. Reminded me of the honor serving our country is and that I should never, ever take it for granted." Matteo tried not to dwell too much on the past, but there were days—like that day, like the day his son had been born—that left an indelible impression.

"That sounds like Rudy," Peyton said with a soft smile. "He's a good man. An understanding one. And he took amazing care of us and our mom." She hesitated. "She died last year."

"I'm sorry." Matteo meant it. "That must have been rough."

"It was. No rougher for any other family that has to deal with. We weren't as close as I think she'd have liked for us to be."

"Because of Thomas?"

"Yes." There was the closed-off Peyton he knew.

Clearly he'd prodded a little too deeply. "I might not have a lot of experience with family dynamics and relationships, but I'd be happy to listen if you want an objective ear." The plane dipped and angled around, pushing the mountains out of sight.

Her smile was quick and didn't reach her eyes. "Thanks. I'm good. Feels like we're circling for landing."

"Guess so. I'd better go remove Gino from the copilot's chair. Buckle up."

PEYTON WAITED UNTIL Matteo was out of sight before she removed her glasses and pushed her fingers into her eyes so hard she saw stars. How did a simple conversation with a practical stranger churn up emotions she'd kept at bay for most of her thirty-plus years?

It wasn't the conversation, she told herself as she swallowed around her too-tight throat and focused on getting her stuff put back into her case. It was watching Matteo out of the corner of her eye for most of the flight—watching him watch Gino with such obvious joy and pride—that made her heart ache.

Did Thomas Blackwell ever long for the daughters he'd left behind? Had he ever thought about them once he was gone? Tried to see them? Wanted to? There was a time, not so long ago, when Peyton would have given anything to see pride in her biological father's eyes. To know that he was proud not necessarily of what she'd accomplished in her career but of how she'd turned out. Despite of him. Maybe in spite of him.

Sometimes she wished she didn't remember Thomas at all. It would have been better for everyone, certainly easier for Rudy and her mother. She loved Rudy, but despite trying to forgive Susan for the secrets she'd kept, Peyton couldn't withstand the resentment that had built toward her mother. Eventually, the pressure of keeping her promise had driven Peyton away from the family. And made the fallout from Peyton's secret equal a nuclear winter.

"Should just be another few minutes." Matteo returned, Gino a few steps in front of him, and they strapped back in, this time with Gino at the window.

"How was the cockpit?" she asked Gino after having to clear her throat a few times.

"Uh-may-zing! I want to be a pilot like Jody when I grow up. Can I do that, Dad?" Gino looked down as Matteo tightened his son's belt.

"You can do anything you want to, G."

"Cool."

"Matteo?" Peyton couldn't help herself. She kept her voice low, reached over and brushed her fingers over the back of his hand when he took hold of his coffee. "Don't you ever stop being his dad. Whatever else happens, whatever you have to do, don't you ever walk away."

She saw the flare of temper, as if she'd offended him with a deeper, unspoken accusation. But the fire faded when he looked down at their hands touching. With a short nod, he covered her hand with his and squeezed. "I won't."

"ARE WE THERE YET?" Gino's dramatic whine from the back seat reminded Matteo so much of his ex-wife that he found himself gnashing his teeth. "We've been in this car forever."

Matteo glanced at the GPS. They'd passed through Falcon Creek, Montana, a little over twenty minutes before—one of those blink-and-miss-it towns that, despite its size, appeared to display more charm and entertainment value than Matteo honestly expected. It would be worth a trip back to check out the local businesses, maybe find someone who could keep an eye out for strangers, although there would probably be plenty of them. "We should be there soon, G. I bet we're going to be seeing some cattle and horses, so keep your eyes open."

Under his breath, Gino muttered something Matteo probably wouldn't have been thrilled to hear, but he let it pass. The kid was overwhelmed, hungry and tired, and more than a touch cranky. He glanced to the passenger seat, where Peyton was tapping on her phone, eyes scanning constantly over whatever was displayed. Given how she was twisting her mouth, Gino wasn't the only one who could probably do with a time-out.

According to his information, they weren't too far away from Blackwell property. He'd spent the better part of the drive ignoring the dread and unwanted memories of an upbringing he'd struggled so hard to leave behind. It was strange, he thought, as he cast his weary gaze over the expanding sky around them, how it was more beautiful than he'd realized. The second he'd heard Big E talk about the Blackwell Ranch, he had visions of dry, parched earth and air so thick with dust he could barely breathe. Now, driving down the road toward

Peyton's grandfather's homestead, it was like heading directly into a Technicolor world.

Pastures and skies dotted with trees and clouds like someone had plunked down those extra little details that made an already-lush landscape feel more like paradise.

Paradise. Matteo nearly laughed at the description. He'd learned early on that appearances were deceiving. It didn't matter how perfect a place appeared to be, there was always a form of darkness lurking just beneath the facade.

"Aw, man. My battery died." Gino groaned in that put-upon way children had before they went ballistic. "What am I supposed to do now?"

Peyton glanced back. "Right there with you, pal." She jiggled the charging cable she'd plugged into her phone and the car the second she'd closed the door. "My reception just completely disappeared."

Feeling his own patience begin to fray, Matteo pulled over to the side of the road.

"What's going on?" Peyton twisted in her seat. "Is there something wrong with the car?"

"No. There's something wrong with my passengers." He shoved open his door, walked around and opened both Peyton's and Gino's. "Out. Both of you. Leave those." He grabbed Peyton's phone and Gino's handheld gaming device and tossed them back in the car.

"I don't have to pee," Gino said, the confusion on his face evident as he slid out.

"This isn't a pee break," Matteo said when Peyton looked about to respond. "This is a *get your heads out of your devices and look where we are* break." He motioned for them to follow. The wire-fence line wasn't exactly welcoming, but he didn't need it to be.

Peyton started coughing, her impractical heels almost slipping in the gravel and dirt. "What do I smell?"

"Fresh air." Matteo stopped, lifted his head up to the sun and smiled against the rays beating against his skin. "Grass. Maybe a touch of manure. Best get used to all of it."

"Smells like air to me," Gino grumbled. "Can't we just get to wherever we're going, Dad?"

Matteo looked at his seriously cross son and felt his own irritation bubble to the surface. Not at Gino, but at Sylvia, who clearly hadn't done much to show their son how important it was for him to look up once in a while and see the world.

He checked his attitude, giving himself a mental shake. He had to stop blaming Sylvia for whatever shortcomings Gino had. As he was fond of reminding his ex, Gino was just a little boy still figuring out how to maneuver through a world of confusing emotions. Having parents who lived halfway around the world from each other didn't make it any easier.

"Come here, G." Matteo held out his hand, and almost felt relief when Gino did as he was told. Matteo hoisted him into his arms, hitched him against his hip and turned in a slow circle. "Tell me what you see."

"I don't see nothing."

"Then you aren't looking hard enough." For the past few days, Matteo had been dreading this trip, the idea of being out in the middle of nowhere with nothing but land and sky and open spaces to get lost in. When he'd been Gino's age, the world had been terrifyingly huge and unwelcoming. Stifling. "I see a sky that doesn't end. It just goes for as far as you can possibly see. And those clouds racing past? Where are they going?" He pointed to one that reminded him of a wild mustang riding across the land. "I see acres of lush green grass that just begs me to run through it, to see how thick it is, how high it goes. And I see hours spent having fun beneath a full sun or even a full moon."

"I guess I see that." Gino squinted and leaned forward, nearly falling out of Matteo's hold. "I'm not sure that sounds like fun, though."

"You can choose to make anything fun, G. That's what I'm asking you to do. Stop complaining so much. Stop and look around and see what possibilities there are. Can you promise me you'll try to do that while we're here?"

He wasn't talking only to Gino now. He'd glanced over his shoulder to where Peyton stood, stone still, arms wrapped around her torso, razor-sharp hair blowing in the gentle wind. She looked like some kind of outcast, plucked out of one world and dropped into another, one she wasn't entirely convinced would ever accept her.

It was that uncertainty he saw shimmering in her eyes that made him realize her discomfort was about more than being ordered into hiding; it was about facing a family and secrets and changes that scared her.

"You can't look out at that sky and not feel powerful," Matteo said as he carried Gino back toward the car. "We're here. And while Big E is always touting the importance of family and connections, there's something else you might be connected to, Peyton. You come from this land. Your father came from this land. It's in your blood. And I'm betting you can feel that already."

"I wouldn't wager too high on that, if I was you." Still, she offered a weak smile and reached a hand out to Gino's hair, then seemed to think better of it and tucked back into herself. "You're right, though. Sky like this deserves to be seen. I'll try to remember that."

"Then this was worth the stop." He lowered Gino to the ground, then helped him up and into the SUV. "Okay, let's get this show on the road. Blackwell Ranch, here we come."

CHAPTER SEVEN

NEVER IN PEYTON'S wildest imagination could she have conceived of standing beneath so much endless sky. Matteo was right, she thought, as she climbed out of the car parked in front of what the sign said was the main guest house. And wasn't that just flat-out irritating?

The pristine blue dotted with errant, fluffy clouds drifting by seemed almost otherworldly. As far as she could see, up, out, in any direction, even with the smattering of buildings and fence line, the sky seemed to be all there was.

She'd done enough research in the past few days to know the Blackwells were well-off. Very well-off. But there was a difference between fortune estimates and the acres of actual, physical land.

She took it all in, from the horse-filled corrals to the lush, green pastures stretching over the hills like a blanket of velvet dotted with the fiery colors of fallen leaves. A smattering of small cabins filled the landscape, as did a number of outbuildings and a brilliant white farmhouse. Maybe she'd seen too many cowboy movies growing up, but she hadn't considered a working Montana cattle ranch would be so…luxurious, right down to the beautifully maintained garden surrounding the expansive building in front of her.

Huh. Maybe two weeks out here wasn't going to be so difficult after all.

She pressed a hand to her racing heart. It was as if she'd discovered something much larger than herself, something that pressed down and in on her even as it welcomed her into its arms. Was that what Matteo had been feeling? That sensory overload of anything-is-possible that seemed to surround her? He'd been quiet on the drive, as if his thoughts had been moving faster than the SUV. Was it the beauty of this place affecting him?

Or had it been something more?

The front door of the beautiful, two-story guest house sprang open to reveal a trim brunette with an obviously pregnant belly beneath a bright yellow T-shirt. She deposited a basket of shiny red apples on the porch before approaching with a brilliant, welcoming smile on her face.

"You must be Peyton." She held out her hand. "I'm Hadley Blackwell, Ty's wife. Welcome to the Blackwell Ranch. Or I guess I should say welcome to the family."

"Hi." Peyton returned the greeting and tucked her hair behind her ear, a nervous tic she'd never quite managed to kick. The open friendliness seemed genuine. "Nice to meet you, Hadley. Big E sends his regards."

"I'll bet he does." Hadley rolled her eyes. "That man gets into more trouble and mischief than all the Blackwell kids put together. Dot sends her regrets. She was hoping to be here, but she's taking care of some family business out of town. Come on inside. We'll get you checked in and give you the grand tour. Leave your bags for now," she called as she headed back up the porch steps.

Peyton caught Matteo returning her suitcase to the car before he closed the door.

"Dad, look!" Gino darted away from his father, tiny plumes of dust and dirt exploding up over his little sneakers. "Horses! Lots of them!"

Peyton watched Matteo hesitate, the color draining from his face. Instead of turning away from his son, he headed toward Gino and crouched beside him. An arena in the distance boasted a number of people standing on and around the fence observing a variety of horses and presumably their trainers. She could hear the horses huffing and neighing and the audience applauding and cheering the display.

"I bet we can get you on one of those if you want to learn," Matteo said to his son. Peyton hugged her arms tight around her waist. The way Matteo rested a hand on Gino's shoulder, as if reminding him he wasn't alone in the world, misted her eyes. Her stoic, determined bodyguard definitely had a soft side.

"I don't know." Gino's voice wavered. "Those horses are really big."

"Don't worry," Hadley called from the door and waved for them to follow her. "We have horses of all sizes here. Katie will find you the perfect one, Gino."

Matteo and Gino started to move toward the arena, clearly entranced by the horses and activity.

Peyton turned toward the house, finally taking a moment to appreciate the elegant Western architecture. Pumpkins of every shape and size sat on top of one another up and down the edges of the steps, interspersed with pots of bright yellow chrysanthemums, fire-orange gerbera and delicate calla lilies. The oversize wreath on the front door declared fall was welcome, as did the chalkboard sign situated by the basket of apples urging people to help themselves.

It was obvious the buildings, not to mention the land itself, was taken care of very well. Details were pristine. There was pride in this place everywhere she looked, and she felt an immediate sense of peace, despite her anxiety about facing Lily.

"So Big E called a few hours ago to update us about Gino coming with you," Hadley said as she took her place behind what looked like a hand-carved check-in counter. "I understand you need a work space while you're here."

"Not a lot of space. Just…" Peyton tried to stay on point. "Just somewhere to plug in my laptop and cell phone."

"Got it. Fair warning, our Wi-Fi and cell reception can get a bit sketchy, especially when we get storms. Looks like I've got you and Matteo in one of our two-bedroom cabins.

Hmmm." Hadley continued to tap on her computer. "With Gino that probably won't work too great. I've got a beautiful room here in the guest lodge. That way I can put Matteo and Gino in the two-bedroom. Unless—"

"Unless?" Peyton's eyebrow arched. She could just imagine what Hadley Blackwell was probably thinking about Peyton and Matteo's relationship.

Hadley glanced up. "Unless you want to stay with Lily in her one-bedroom cabin next door. She divides her time between here and Conner's place."

"Oh." Her cheeks warmed. "Sorry. It's just... I wanted to avoid any misconceptions when it comes to me and Matteo. We aren't... you know. He's my assistant, and that's all." Oh, yeah. That sounded professional.

"Trust me," Hadley said with a knowing grin. "When it comes to relationship misconceptions—" she actually used air quotes "—I'm your go-to girl. So the room upstairs works okay for you?"

"No." Matteo stepped in through the open screen door, Gino hot on his heels. "The two-bedroom will work fine. Big E said there's a sofa bed."

"Can I sleep on that?" Gino darted forward and gripped the edge of the counter, rising up on his toes to peer over. "That sounds really neat."

Hadley glanced at Peyton, whose face went forest-fire hot. "Can I talk to you for a moment, please, Matteo?" She gripped his arm and led him back onto the porch. "What are you doing?" she demanded in as quiet a tone as she could manage.

"My job," Matteo said, falling right back into that attitude of his that made her wonder if she'd imagined their time together on the side of the road. "I'm here to protect you, remember? I can't do that if I'm in a building across the ranch."

"But won't people think—"

"I don't care what people think, Peyton." There he was again. That brick wall of protection her bosses had hired. "I care about keeping you in sight as much of the time as possible…and safe. We might have come to a different state, but until I've heard from the police back home that you're out of danger, I'm not taking any chances. Now—" he shoved his hands in his pockets and rocked back on his heels "—we can get separate rooms here in the main house or you can stay with me and Gino in the guest cabin. Up to you."

His determination seemed set in concrete. He wasn't going to budge. She could see that on his face. That handsome, infuriating, daydream-inducing face.

"Fine. You win."

He grinned. "Don't worry. I'm sure you'll win something while we're here."

Peyton's mouth twisted. At least now she had a new goal. "Go ahead and make the arrangements you feel are necessary."

He turned to the door, then thought better of it, faced her again. "You know, if you're that concerned about what people think, we could always just tell them the truth."

That she'd received death threats? "Absolutely not." No way was she going to add to her sisters' concerns. And even though Lily was the only other sister in Montana, sibling gossip and information spread like wildfire, from California all the way out to where Georgie currently resided in North Carolina. "I don't want anyone to know why we're really here." Or that she was hiding out. It just seemed so… undignified. She'd rather them think she and Matteo were more than assistant and boss.

"All right, then. Let the rumors start flying." He winked at her and left her speechless on the front porch.

"You two work everything out?" Hadley asked as Peyton followed Matteo back inside.

"Yes, ma'am," Matteo said. "Ms. Harrison and I will share the two-bedroom cabin. She works better in isolation."

Peyton gnashed her teeth. Now he was just making stuff up.

"Miss Harrison." Gino tugged on the hem of her shirt.

"Gino." Peyton crouched in front of him. "I thought we agreed you'd call me Peyton."

"Yes, ma'am. Peyton." He nodded and suddenly looked far older than his six years. "Dad says we're with your family now."

"I suppose that's true." Didn't quite feel true, though. None of this felt real.

"Then, do you know who all these people are?" He pointed to a collection of photographs displayed along the far wall.

"I suppose they're Blackwells." She glanced over to where Matteo was making the final arrangements with Hadley before allowing Gino to tug her closer to the pictures. "I can't say for sure, though. I'm kind of a new member of the family."

"New but welcome nonetheless, cousin." The tall and very handsome cowboy who headed toward them offered a smile as radiant as Hadley's. "I'm Tyler Blackwell, but everyone calls me Ty. It's nice to meet you, Peyton."

"You, too." She hesitated only briefly before taking his offered hand. She recognized his face from the pictures she'd found online. Each of Big E's grandsons had made a name for himself. Ben was an attorney, Ethan a veterinarian, Jon owned his own ranch nearby, and Chance Blackwell—well, everyone who'd ever turned on a radio knew who Chance Blackwell was.

Ty and his wife ran the guest-ranch portion of the business and had been doing gangbuster business for the past two years. What was it about the Blackwell men that they seemed rather, well, for want of a better word, confident? There was no denying, however, that that twinkle in the eye was anything other than genetic, thanks to Big E. "Thanks for making space for us."

"Not a problem. I'm sure Hadley told you, we had some cancellations, which is too bad because we're heading into the holiday season pretty soon. Hello, there." He turned that friendly expression on Gino. "Are you here to check in, too, young man?"

"Yes, sir." Gino gripped Peyton's shirt and scooted behind her, peeking out as if he wasn't quite sure what to think. "My dad works for Miss Peyton."

Miss Peyton. She felt her heart clutch even as she reached back to put a comforting hand on the boy's shoulder.

"Does he?" Ty asked. "Well, that sounds great. Were you asking about who all these people are?"

"Yes, sir." Gino's confirmation sounded more like a squeak.

Peyton took in the photographs featuring people and landscapes from over a number of decades. It gave a sense of history, for sure. A personal touch for the guest-ranch angle, and it made her feel as if she'd stepped a little bit back in time. "Are they all Blackwells?"

"Most," Ty confirmed. "Some are longtime employees. It takes a lot of hands to keep the Blackwell Ranch running. We like to make sure everyone gets their due. This here—" he tapped a finger against a photo of five boys and a beaming, handsome couple "—this is my favorite. My mom and dad, and all five of us Blackwell brothers. This one's me." He poked a finger into his own overly grinning face. "As you can see, I got all the charm in the family."

Peyton peered closer. One taller boy was clearly older than the rest, but the other four... "Are you a twin?" As someone who prided herself on the details, she must have missed that tidbit of information.

"Yes, ma'am. Chance and I arrived together. Well, one of us is a few minutes older. Makes him the baby of the family."

She had no doubt Chance appreciated that moniker as much as Fiona liked it.

The most recent photograph sat front and center of the display, a wedding photo featuring Big E, a dignified-looking woman about his age, surrounded by the five Blackwell boys looking cover-model stunning in their Sunday best.

"That's Dot. Our grandmother," Ty added when she looked closer. "She and Big E got remarried a couple years back. She's off tying off the last loose ends before moving back for good."

"I'm looking forward to meeting her."

Something told Peyton there was no avoiding any of the Blackwells. "I think I'm going to need to make a chart to keep track of everyone." Her family tree had suddenly become a forest.

Ty chuckled. "Don't worry. We won't start quizzing you until you've met everyone. Lily caught on pretty quick. Speaking of Lily, does she know you're here?"

"I'm not sure."

Gino, who had moved on and was exploring on his own, kept his hands behind his back and wandered around reception.

"So, what is it you do exactly, Peyton?" Ty asked. "Lily says you run an electronics company, and Big E suggested there might be business opportunities in the offing."

"Maybe," Peyton said, somewhat relieved to know Lily wasn't pretending as if she didn't exist. "I'm a VP of Electryone Technologies. We hunt out and invest in unique ideas for technology advancements that lessen environmental impact, like wind and solar energy, recycling and sanitation, water treatment systems, stuff like that. Doing our part to get away from the power grid and create more sustainable options. We also do a lot of investing in women-forward companies and businesses, lending capital in exchange for a percentage of the eventual successes."

"Lily said you were a brain," Ty said with a smile and a nod. "You know, Hadley and I have been discussing how we could make the ranch more environmentally friendly. I don't suppose you'd be up for a consult with us? You know, just give us your thoughts as to how we can move the ranch forward?"

Feeling more secure having shifted to a business-related topic, Peyton nodded. "Of course. I'd be happy to." So far everything seemed to be going to plan.

"Great. I'll talk to Hadley about it tonight, and we'll get on your schedule. Looks like she's got your accommodation all set. How about I take you three over to your cabin?"

It was on the tip of her tongue to ask where she might find Lily, but she held back. She might be headstrong and forward thinking when it came to her work, but when it came to her sisters…it seemed she was a borderline coward. "Lead the way."

"Wow, wow, wow, Dad! This place is uh-may-zing!" Gino raced past Matteo into the bedrooms of the cabin Ty had shown them to moments before. He told them to get settled in, then meet him down at the paddock for a tour of the property. "This is like the bestest thing that's ever happened to me!" He was practically pinging off the walls.

Whatever shyness Gino had displayed back at the guest house vanished the second he, Matteo and Peyton were alone. Hadn't Taro said something about his son not being quite so talkative? A headache began to throb behind Matteo's eyes. Instead of pounding back a couple of painkillers, he downed half a bottle of water. Then, with Gino distracted, he hid Gino's gaming system, along with the charger cord on the top shelf of one of the kitchen cabinets.

He found Peyton watching him from her bedroom doorway. Arms folded, brow arched, she just shook her head, then grinned and turned away.

"How about over here at the table for your schoolwork," Matteo suggested and unzipped Gino's backpack to unload the books he'd brought with him from Japan. He flipped through the workbooks and noticed the math and language texts were in both English and

Japanese. Near as Matteo could tell, as he eyed the pages, not much had been done, and what scribbles Gino had made didn't make much sense. "Looks like you have some catching up to do, G."

Gino shrugged.

Matteo might be a bit rusty on the dad stuff, but he knew avoidance when he saw it. Even in a six-year-old. "What's the matter? I thought you said you liked school."

"I like my teacher," Gino said without looking at his father. "She's nice. Most of the time. She stops the other kids from making fun of me."

"What do they make fun of you for?"

"Nothin'."

"Gino…"

"I don't like it there." Gino glared at the floor. "I don't want to go back."

"Hey." Matteo walked over and crouched in front of his son. "Hey, G, you know you can talk to me about anything, right? We'll figure out what to do about school."

"I already told you, I'm not going back. Not there. Not anywhere." Gino's angry eyes caught Matteo off guard, before the little boy turned away and went back to exploring the guest cabin.

Seeing his son needed some space before they discussed this further, Matteo stood, finished rearranging Gino's books on the small table by a window, then knocked on the doorframe to Peyton's room.

"Your bedroom okay?" Matteo stepped inside, and his gaze caught on one of the most organized, well-packed suitcases he'd ever seen in his life. She'd barely left room in there for air. Amused, he did a quick security check. No windows, so that was a plus. Only one way in and out, the door, so he didn't have to worry about anyone getting inside. He'd already done a cursory walk around the cabin, which was semiattached to a single-room cabin next door that was also occupied. He hadn't seen anyone inside, but when he'd looked into the window, he saw what was definitely a lived-in space.

The only point of concern he saw in his future was the shared bathroom between his and Peyton's rooms, generous though it may have been. He could only hope her patience held out where a six-year-old boy and bathrooms was concerned.

"It's fine." She opened the dresser drawers,

then retrieved hangers from the closet. Everything she hung up still had tags on. Even the jeans and long-sleeved shirts that went into the dresser had clearly never been worn before. Did she ever loosen up? Even now, bouncing around the room, she was buttoned-up so tight he was afraid she might snap in two. He watched as she unloaded her shoes, which other than the pair of running sneakers didn't exactly suit the lifestyle of a working ranch. Or a guest one for that matter. "What?"

"I don't see any boots."

"The only boots I own aren't for cowgirling."

Matteo shrugged. "I bet you're going to need some."

"I can assure you, I will never *need* those kinds of boots."

Hi grin widened. He wasn't sure anything entertained him more than irritating Peyton Harrison. "Are you a morning- or evening-shower kind of woman?"

"Am I a what?"

"Just mentally planning out a bathroom schedule for the three of us."

"Oh." She nibbled on her full bottom lip,

tucked her hair behind her ear. "I'd prefer morning. For my hair and…stuff."

"Got it. G and I will take nights. G, let's get you unpacked." Matteo left their conversation there and went to corral his son.

Peyton closed the door behind him and when she eventually emerged, he saw she'd changed into slim black pants, her sneakers, and an oversize T-shirt. Better than he'd expected, Matteo thought as he finished unloading his duffel bag, then changed into jeans and a T-shirt himself.

"There's no TV," Gino said from where he'd flopped down on Matteo's own king-size bed. "I thought there was gonna be stuff to do, Dad."

"What happened to this being the best place ever? There's a whole schedule of events and activities by the front door," Matteo reminded him. "Why don't you go check those out."

"There's a TV in here," Peyton called from the living room.

Gino rolled off the bed and raced out of the room.

Matteo sighed and joined them. Gino was standing in front of a small flat-screen about the size of a computer monitor.

"That's too small," Gino said. "In my room at home I have a big screen. I can't watch anything on that."

"Sounds good to me." Matteo retrieved the remote and set it out of reach.

"Daa-aad!" Gino whined.

"If you don't appreciate what we have, then I see no point in you using it. Peyton, you ready to go?"

"Sure am." If she disapproved of Matteo's handling of the TV situation, she didn't say. "Gino, after you."

"I don't wanna go anywhere. I wanna watch TV." Gino plunked himself on the edge of the sofa and crossed his arms. When he stuck his lower lip out, Matteo saw Peyton roll her eyes.

"Fine," she said calmly. "We'll go without you. I personally can't wait to see the horses. And it's Friday, which apparently means Mexican food for dinner. Coming, Matteo?" She headed to the door.

"Uh…" Matteo looked to his son, who seemed stunned either of them would consider leaving him behind. When Peyton cleared her throat, he got the message loud and clear. "Yep. Right behind you. Why don't you get a jump start on that schoolwork of yours while we're gone, G."

Gino slumped back and glared at them. "I don't like it here anymore."

"And yet here you are." Matteo sighed in the same dramatic fashion as his son. "It's rough to be you. We'll be back in a bit. I'm starving. You hungry, Peyton?" He stepped out behind her and closed the door.

"Don't worry," Peyton murmured and took his arm to lead him away from the cabin. "I give it to the count of twenty, max."

Matteo glanced back as he walked down the path toward the guest house. Sure enough, almost as soon as he turned away, he heard the cabin door slam. "I'm hungry, too," Gino announced when he reached them but refused the hand Matteo offered.

"Then I suggest you get your attitude under control," Matteo said firmly, then glanced uneasily at Peyton. "I'm sorry he's being such a brat."

Peyton shrugged it off. "He's being a six-year-old."

"What do they have to eat?" Gino demanded.

"No idea," Matteo lied. He knew very well

the ranch offered plenty of things with kids in mind. "But whatever it is, we're going to be grateful for it, aren't we?"

Gino glared up at him. It only took a few seconds for Matteo's expression to make an impact. Gino ducked his head and kicked his feet in the dirt. "Yes, sir." Suddenly he broke away and raced ahead toward the paddock and the barn.

"And there was peace in the land," Peyton said under her breath. "He's just tired, Matteo. It's been a long day."

Matteo didn't think so. More likely his ex-wife had let Gino have the run of the house and now the kid had a massive sense of entitlement. No wonder Jiro hadn't had any issues with sending Gino out to Matteo. He was probably grateful for a break. "We need to find something to occupy him for a while," he told Peyton. "So I can get a look at the entire property."

Peyton smirked. "Good luck with that. The Blackwell borders are huge. You couldn't walk it in days."

"Then, I guess I won't walk it." He'd figure out a way to get what he needed. He always did. "Until I'm satisfied all is okay, I

don't want you out of my sight or alone, understood? If I'm not around, stick close to Ty
at the guest house."

"Are you talking to me or your son?" Peyton batted those lashes at him the same way
she had in her boss's office. "FYI, I don't tend
to take orders any better than a six-year-old.
And hiding remote controls and game consoles
doesn't have much effect on me."

"Then, we'll just have to find something
that does, won't we?" He couldn't wait to figure out what other buttons to push with her.

They walked side by side, Peyton's frustration wafting off her in waves while Matteo
memorized every detail his eyes picked up
on. Their cabin was isolated enough to give
him some comfort and did have one landline
phone, probably to communicate with the front
desk. There was a single cabin next door to
theirs, but the others were scattered around
at a far enough distance that he'd hear someone approaching when they were inside. The
path to the main guest house was straightfor-
ward enough; not a lot of places for someone
to hide. Or to watch.

One thing about this part of the country:

lots of open space meant his job was that much easier.

Matteo and Peyton caught up with Gino at the white-fenced corral. Inside the gates, a woman with a long, silver braid down her back held a rope and was clicking her tongue at the glistening palomino galloping around the perimeter. Matteo cringed. He'd forgotten about the sounds of a ranch, sounds that reminded him of days, of years, better forgotten.

Focus on the work, he told himself. Keep his attention on Peyton and making sure she was safe. And keep Gino from getting into mischief. If he focused on those two things, the past wouldn't have time to sneak in and suffocate him.

The crowd they'd seen when they'd first arrived had huddled around a collection of picnic tables offering snacks and drinks. He did a mental count, memorizing faces, looking for anything to be wary of. A married couple and their three kids, all bordering on their grumpy teenage years. An older couple clearly on their second or maybe third honeymoon. Two middle-aged men who seemed determined to get the hang of lassoing one of the nearby sawhorses. From what Hadley had said, all of them would be leaving by Sunday with only a handful of guests between now and Halloween. Perfect.

The fewer people he needed to keep track of, the better.

"There you are." Ty pushed back from the fence and touched the shoulder of a young woman standing next to him. She turned with him, a wide smile on her round face. Beside her, a black-and-white Australian shepherd stood, tail wagging as it looked up adoringly at her mistress. "Katie, this is Lily's sister, Peyton, and her assistant, Matteo Rossi. And that kid peeking out back there is Gino. This is Katie Blackwell. And her faithful friend Hip."

"Hip?" Peyton's brow furrowed.

"Short for Hippolyta," Katie clarified. "But trust me, just leave it at Hip."

Peyton nodded, and it struck Matteo how out of her element his charge was. She was trying, that much was obvious, but the way she was looking around, as if she expected the land to open up and swallow her, made him wonder if Peyton was ever going to be able to relax here.

Matteo glanced back to where Gino had

stepped behind Peyton. "Nice to meet you, Katie."

"Pleasure." Katie pushed up her hat to reveal a freckle-kissed nose and stray strands of strawberry blond hair. "Sorry if I seem distracted. I've been wanting to get my hands on that lady for the better part of two months." She sighed and looked toward the horse, her hand moving to her pregnant belly. "Not going to happen anytime soon. I've been grounded, hence my new assistant, Izzy, out there. Missed out on our cattle move this season, too. First time in over twenty years."

Matteo couldn't relate to the regret. He'd always hated the days it had taken to move cattle from one pasture to another with the changing of the seasons.

"Blackwell babies are coming at us in every direction," Ty joked. "Katie and Hadley are both due around Christmas. Now that's what I call efficient holiday planning."

"At least I'm only having one at a time," Katie said with a smile. "Unlike Ben and Jon. At this rate we're going to double the population of Montana just with Blackwells. So, Peyton, Matteo, do either of you ride?"

"Not anymore."

"I used to."

Matteo and Peyton spoke at the same time, but there was no way to curtail his surprise at Peyton's admission.

"When I was around Gino's age," she explained. "I haven't for a long time, though."

"Well, we'll have to get you both back in the saddle," Katie said. "We've got a trail ride going out on Tuesday morning once the weather shifts. It'll be an easy one, so let me know if you all want to sign up. We'll—well, they'll stop for lunch at the lake before they head back. How about you, Gino? Do you like horses?"

Gino's eyes went wide. "I dunno."

"They look pretty scary, don't they?" Katie nodded with exaggeration. "Maybe if you see them closer up that'll help. You want to come with me?"

Gino looked up at Matteo, who nodded.

"'Kay," Gino said.

"Great. My little girl, Rosie, will be home from school in a bit. I bet maybe she'd like help feeding our animals in the petting zoo. How about you hang out and keep me company while I wait for her? I can tell you all about these horses Izzy's working with." She held out her hand.

"Go on, G. If you want to," Matteo urged.

"Don't worry," Ty assured him as Katie and Gino moved off. He watched as Gino climbed up onto the fence and hooked his arms over the top railing. Katie held a hand against his back, steadying him as she pointed and bent low to talk to him. "Safest place to be on this or any other ranch is with Katie Blackwell. This place wouldn't be standing without her. You guys must be hungry. Help yourself to those snacks. Dinner will hit at six thirty."

"About that tour you mentioned, Ty?" Matteo asked.

"What about it?"

"How much of the place can we see?" Matteo followed Peyton and Ty to the snack table and grabbed a bag of pretzels, an apple and carrots. "I was hoping to get a look at the entire property."

Ty's brow furrowed. "I can show you as much as you'd like. On foot we wouldn't get far, but I've got a truck we can use anytime. Or if you really want the best view, I could saddle up a couple of the horses."

"It's a little late in the day for me to try to manage a saddle," Matteo lied.

"Truck it is, then."

"Peyton, why don't you come with…" He trailed off as he caught sight of a pickup truck heading down the road to the guest house. "Peyton?"

She'd gone still, hand locked around a bag of celery as she stared at a young woman climbing out of the truck. Even from a distance, Matteo saw the resemblance. Not just physically, but there was a similarity in how they stood, how they walked. Matteo knew the instant the woman spotted them. The shift in her body language, the sudden tightness, not to mention the sharp look in all-too-familiar eyes.

"Lily," Peyton whispered.

He heard so much in the one word. Regret. Worry. Fear. Love.

Ty looked between the two women but seemed to think better of commenting. "I'm just going to let Hadley know I'm taking the truck for a bit. We'll need to be back by dinner. I'm in charge of the firepit tonight." He motioned to the stone-and-metal grill nearby.

"Thanks," Matteo said and bit into his apple. Ty headed off to the guest house. "Peyton?"

"Yeah." Peyton set her snacks down and scrubbed her hands down her thighs. "Yeah, sorry. I thought maybe I'd have until tomorrow."

"No time like the present." Considering Lily hadn't moved other than to come around the truck and lean back against the hood, apparently Peyton's sister thought the same thing. "She's family, Peyton." He looked at her from across the table and wished he could fix this for her. Or at the very least make it easier. "Whatever else happens, or has happened, nothing is going to change that."

She gave him a weak smile and nodded. "Right. It's what I came here for."

Among other things, he wanted to add. Instead, he kept silent and watched as Peyton approached her sister.

CHAPTER EIGHT

PEYTON HAD NEVER before paid so much attention to the sound her shoes made as she crunched along in the gravel and dirt. Arms wrapped tightly around herself, she tried to drag her racing thoughts into some kind of order.

The sound of laughter and stomping hooves and the wind rushing in her ears should have been enough of a distraction, enough of a push to keep her fear at bay. It had been weeks since the truth had come out, weeks since her sisters had learned the secret Peyton had kept from them their entire life. Countless days since she'd last seen their faces looking back at her from a computer screen.

This was, Peyton realized, the longest walk of her life. The last time she'd seen Lily or any of her sisters in person had been at Lily's no-go of a wedding to their childhood friend, Danny. Lily had looked so pretty in the hooped wedding dress she'd chosen because it had reminded her of their mother's dress. Lily, the wild daredevil of the Harrison clan, who could easily jump out of a plane or bungee jump off a bridge but had doubts so severe about getting married she'd run off with a cowboy in an antique motor home.

One thing was for sure, Peyton thought with a swell of affection: the Harrison girls were never boring.

Peyton chewed on her lower lip. Or was it Blackwell now? How did both suddenly make her feel as if she was betraying someone?

Her sister didn't move as Peyton approached. Simply stood there, hands resting lightly at her sides, sharp assessing eyes watching Peyton's every move. Her blond hair was tied back, with loose strands catching in the breeze. She wore an oversize T-shirt over her usual jeggings, and on her feet, to Peyton's dismay, a sturdy pair of cowboy boots.

With those bright eyes of hers and the healthy glow of her skin, she looked, Peyton thought as she stopped a few feet away, happy.

"Hadley called and told me there was someone here I should see." Lily's soft voice sounded like music to Peyton's ears. "Have to admit, you were the last person I expected to turn up in Falcon Creek."

Peyton ducked her head, tucked her hair behind her ear and tried to find her smile. "It wasn't all my idea. Big E might have had something to do with it."

"Big E." Lily's mouth scrunched in that way it always did when she was mulling over a problem. "He's really been a bit of a wrecking ball in the family, hasn't he? So, what are you doing here?"

Other than hiding? "I wanted to see you. Had to see you," she added when Lily's brow arched. She had so much she wanted to say, so much she needed to say, but Matteo was right. All that mattered was that they were family, and somehow she needed to find her way back to them. "You're really doing okay, aren't you?"

"You sound surprised."

Peyton frowned. Why did people keep saying that to her? Did she really hold people to such impossible standards they automatically took offense to whatever she said? "I guess maybe I am a little." The admission tugged at her. "Are you…" She trailed off, cleared her throat. "Are you happy, Lily? With Conner? With all this?"

"Is that why you're here?" The friendliness that had been building evaporated. "To talk me out of marrying Conner? Because you can't."

"What? No." The thought honestly hadn't crossed her mind. "I mean it all came as a surprise, of course, but from what Fiona's told me…" She stopped. Nothing good was going to come from her stalling. "I came to apologize, Lily. I owe you, all of you, a real apology." Not something muttered over a cell phone or written in an email.

Lily simply stared at her in silence.

"I'm sorry, Lily," Peyton plunged ahead, all the weeks, all the sleepless nights crowding in on her. "I'm so sorry I didn't tell you all before about Dad. About our real father. About…everything." Tears clogged her throat. "I need you to know it was never malicious. I didn't keep the truth from you to hurt anyone. I did it because…" She struggled to find the right words, words that wouldn't do further damage to their relationship or the memory of their mother. "I did it because one day I came home from school, and Mom was actually happy. Rudy made her happy. From that first day. He made all of you happy." A tear slipped free, and she wiped it away. "I'm sorry I lied all these years, but after a while…" She shook her head. It sounded cold to say that after all these years the truth hadn't seemed to matter. How could it when they'd had a good father who loved and cared for them? "What good would it have done to tell the truth, Lily? Blood or not, Rudy's our father in every way that matters."

"I know that," Lily said. "Now." She winced as if the sun was too bright in her eyes. "Sometimes I wish I'd never gotten that copy of my birth certificate. If I hadn't, we never would have—"

"You never would have found Conner." And seeing the instant, utter contentment on her sister's face, the soft smile that appeared at the mere mention of his name, a contentment all the Harrisons had worried would never be found, made the last few weeks melt away. "Please tell me we can get past this," Peyton pleaded. "I know we haven't all been close these last few years, but I've missed you." She managed a wobbly smile. "I've missed you all so much."

Lily's mouth wobbled, and she pushed off

the truck. Seconds later she threw her arms around Peyton's neck and squeezed tight. "We've missed you, too."

All words, all thoughts dropped away as Peyton wrapped her arms around her sister and held on with all her might. Squeezing her eyes shut, she fought to keep her emotions in check. She forced the tears back and took long, steadying breaths, even as Lily continued to cling.

"We aren't done talking about all this," Lily said firmly, when she stepped back. "There's still a lot I want to know. A lot we all want to know."

"I'll answer whatever questions you have. Promise."

"No more lies." Lily grabbed hold of Peyton's arms and squeezed. Hard. "I mean it, Peyton. Don't you ever lie to us about anything ever again."

Peyton swallowed hard, thinking of the real reason she was here at the Blackwell Ranch: to hide from someone who may very well want to hurt her. But some habits were hard to break—especially habits formed over a lifetime. When it came to her family, when it came to her sisters, she'd do whatever she needed to in order to protect them. Even if that meant breaking a promise.

"I promise," she managed.

The screen door banged open, and Hadley emerged, tears glistening in her eyes. "Good to see you two have worked this out," she said. "Now, how about you continue this conversation inside with some iced tea?"

"Is it me, or did that sound like an order?" Peyton asked as Lily tugged her up the porch steps.

"It's not just you." Lily offered a patient smile. "It's the Blackwell way."

"You SEEING ALL you needed to?"

Matteo didn't miss the guarded suspicion in Tyler Blackwell's voice. As they bumped along the roads outlining the Blackwell property, he'd been making mental notes and, to his relief, accepting that the ranch, while certainly expansive, didn't have a lot of points of open access. He felt fairly safe in thinking Peyton would be fine here.

With the windows open, the fall air billowed in.

"Force of habit," Matteo responded finally. "I spent a lot of time in the service. I just always like to know where I am. What's around me." What's around the people I'm protecting, he added silently.

"So what exactly do you do as Peyton's assistant?"

Matteo wasn't surprised at the question. He had been surprised at how long it took someone to ask the question. "Keep her on track," he recited from the script he and Todd had come up with back in Peyton's office. "Make sure she knows her schedule, remind her of appointments, paperwork that needs to be signed or filed or read. You know." He shrugged. "Stuff."

"Uh-huh." Ty kept his eyes on the road. "Sure. Stuff. You don't mind me saying, you don't strike me as the work-for-someone-else kind of man. And you certainly don't come across as anyone's assistant anything."

"Don't mind you saying it at all." Matteo kept his voice neutral. "Working for Peyton pays well, and right now that's important." There. Not everything he said had to be a lie.

"So, the two of you...there's nothing else going on?"

"No," Matteo said, even as he felt an unexpected pang of regret. He had to admit, the idea of something *else* between him and Peyton held a certain appeal. A very strong appeal. She was a beautiful woman. More compassionate and kind than he'd originally thought. She cared about people, from her real assistant, Todd, to how she'd been with Gino and her grandfather. But she was also driven. Career-focused.

And way out of his league.

"I'm not her type, believe me." He'd seen her type. Smart, established, on-the-move entrepreneurs looking to make their fortunes by changing the world. There wasn't any room in her life for a wayward stray like him. Peyton—the Blackwells—were all about family, and other than Gino, Matteo had none to call his own. "Why do you ask? Don't tell me Big E's got you spying on us."

"Fat chance of that," Ty said with a sour expression. "Not sure how much you know about the Blackwell family situation, but suffice it to say Big E hasn't always endeared himself to his grandsons. Things weren't as easy or friendly as they are now. And, fair warning, they still aren't perfect."

"He's very proud of his family." Matteo had no doubt the Blackwell family situation was complicated, but near as he could tell, family was the one thing Elias Blackwell always put first. And for that Matteo admired him. And envied him. "Must have come as a shock to hear about Peyton and her sisters."

"Not as much as you'd think," Tyler admitted and made a turn up a steep hill. "There's very little about Big E that surprises anyone. One benefit to him finding out he has granddaughters is he isn't quite as focused on his grandsons." His lips twitched. "That old man's managed to wheedle himself into each of our lives, into every aspect of our lives. Feels kind of freeing to have his focus elsewhere for a while. Especially when it comes to the ranch. If it wasn't for Hadley, I doubt he'd have agreed to our plans to open this place to paying guests at all. Not that he gave us much of a choice. We had to find some way to make this stead profitable."

"So Big E has a weak spot for his granddaughters-in-law?"

"Let's just say my wife and sisters-in-law know how to get through to him. Now, was there anything else in particular you wanted to see? Wait, hold up." At the base of the hill he tapped on the breaks. "Wow, that's odd."

He pulled out his cell and pointed across the stream nearby. "Sorry. Give me a sec."

Matteo sat back while Ty made a call, watching as a horse lifted its head from drinking. With glistening, almost-mahogany coloring and an ink-black tail and mane, the horse locked its dark eyes on them as if sizing them up in return. "One of the horses get out?" Matteo asked.

"That's not one of ours," Ty said. "Too bad, too, because he's a looker. Hey, Jon. Yeah, I know." Ty rolled his eyes. "I'm not calling to bug you about the Halloween bash. I already know Grace put it on your calendar. You missing any horses over there on the JB Bar?"

Matteo shifted in his seat. The horse took a step to the side that looked almost painful. "She's hurt." He pushed open the door and dropped to the ground.

"Hold up, Matteo." Ty followed, grabbed his arm before he could start across the stream. "Let's just make sure who she doesn't belong to first. Could be she's just passing through."

"Or she came here looking for help."

Ty looked at him. "Okay, thanks, Jon. No. Just thought I'd check. I've got it covered. See you tomorrow." He clicked off and stepped in front of Matteo. "You didn't just used to ride. You know horses."

"I was raised with them," Matteo admitted, not wanting to dive deeper than that. Even from this distance, he could feel the horse's apprehension. Her desperation. And her curiosity. As if he'd stepped into a time machine, he slipped into the past and old habits. "Doesn't matter who she belongs to. She needs help. Otherwise she'd have moved on."

"I'll take your word for it." Ty nodded and shoved his phone away. "I've got some rope in the truck. We'll see if she'll let us lead her in."

A few minutes later both Ty and Matteo stepped into the rushing stream. Cool water soaked through his sneakers immediately. His palms went damp and clammy. He hadn't been this close to a horse in over a decade. Until now, he hadn't realized he'd missed it. The horse's ears were pinned forward, almost flattened against her head.

"Go steady," Ty said quietly when Matteo almost lost his footing and the horse took a step back. "Okay, I see it now. She's got a sore right front foot. Hey, girl." Ty bent over. "Yes, you are definitely a girl. Aren't you a beauty?" The horse held its head high and snorted. Ty stopped moving. "I don't think she likes me." He held out the rope to Matteo. "You try."

"I don't—"

"It's a rope, not a snake. If you want to help her, we need to get her back to the ranch. I'll call Ethan and have him come out to take a look." He stepped back.

The second the rope was in his grasp, Matteo struggled to breathe. Despite the pristine air and the calming breeze, it felt as if bands of iron had locked around his chest. He stood up straighter, focused on the animal, silently urging her to turn her frantic gaze on him and away from Ty.

His feet were freezing, soaked and turning to ice blocks as he managed to keep his balance and make it across the stream. "Hello, beauty." He felt detached from his voice, as if it wasn't really him speaking. Odd how some things came back. The routine. The tone. The awe he felt when he looked at these animals close-up. "You're not feeling so well, are you?" He wound the rope around his hand and shoved it into the back of his jeans. Holding up both empty hands, he stepped onto the bank and stopped.

He stood there, less than a foot away from

the animal, waiting for the horse's ears to shift and relax. She let out a slow, breathy whinny and nodded her head.

"There you go." Matteo stretched out a hand, waited for the horse to push her nose up into his palm. "Hey, hi there. What brings you this way, beauty?" He stepped forward. The horse tensed, took a shaky step back but then stopped. "You hurt your foot or your leg, didn't you?" Matteo shifted slightly so he could get a look at the horse's coat. There was a long, raw-looking scar along one side of her body, one that arched up her neck. The ragged healing had started a while ago but looked angry. And purposely inflicted. As did the spur scars marring her flanks.

Anger surged, white-hot and fast, but he forced it back, not wanting to scare the horse any more than she already was. "I'm sorry," he whispered as he drew his hand lightly down the horse's side. "You've had it rough, haven't you, girl? I'm so sorry."

He could see the faint outline of her ribs, as if malnourishment was just beginning to set in. But she pushed against his hand again, even as he withdrew the rope and gently slipped it over her head.

"She belongs to someone," Matteo called over his shoulder. "Not a kind someone from what I can tell." When he looked back he saw Ty nodding. "I don't think she'll do well around people on the ranch."

"Ethan's got a couple of empty stalls in his clinic. We'll keep her on her own until we figure out what to do with her. It's a walk back. I can call one of the ranch hands—"

"No." Matteo wrapped the rope around his hand. She'd stood there, waiting for them. Waiting for him. He wasn't going to abandon her now. "I've got her. Just lead the way."

"YOU HAVEN'T SAID how long you're staying for."

Peyton followed Lily back outside after drinking enough iced tea to float a small boat. The afternoon sun was beating down, tempered only by the light autumn breeze that seemed to continually blow. They wandered over to sit at a picnic table where she could watch Gino and Katie, along with a little red-headed girl in pink jeans, a matching shirt and the cutest little pink embossed cowgirl boots she'd ever seen. Both kids were hitched up on the rung of the fence, watching, almost mesmerized, as Katie called out to the trainer and horses.

Guests were milling about, some working on roping techniques, others just lying in the grass under the sun, while two ranch hands worked at getting a campfire blazing in the stone circle.

"I don't have to be back at the office until the first week of November. Gino's excited for Halloween." Peyton found herself relieved she could tell the truth. For that part, at least.

"You're taking that long off work?" Lily didn't just look surprised: she looked baffled. "You know that's like two weeks."

Oh, she knew. "My boss is convinced I need a break from my usual routine. When Big E told her about the ranch, Vilette suggested I make the most of the family connection and see what business opportunities might present themselves."

When Lily didn't look particularly impressed, Peyton clarified. "Electryone doesn't take over anything, Lil. We work to enhance. And Ty's already asked me about consulting with him on ways to make the ranch more energy efficient."

"Leave it to you to turn a family reunion and vacation into a business opportunity."

Was that resentment she heard in her sister's voice?

"There's nothing wrong with liking to work." She'd been so caught up in the fallout from their parental revelation, she'd forgotten how often she'd had to defend her dedication to her job. "It's given me a pretty good life."

"It's given you a lonely life," Lily said.

"You sound like Dad." Peyton tried to make a joke of it even as she felt a little nauseous. Sure, her sisters had teased her over the years about how focused she was on her career, but this time Lily didn't sound amused. "I seem to remember you liked your job as an adventure guide, Lil. And I wouldn't say you took kindly to Dad encouraging you to marry Danny."

"Didn't exactly turn out the way any of us planned, did it?" Lily's lips curved as she tilted her head up and into the sun. "I know Dad's only keeping his word to Mom, to make sure we're taken care of and looked after—"

"How nineteenth-century of him," Peyton muttered.

Lily shrugged. "If I hadn't almost married Danny, I wouldn't have ended up in that RV.

That meant I wouldn't have fallen for Conner, which means I wouldn't have found where I really belong."

"And you belong here, in Montana?" Peyton still couldn't wrap her head around it. "Playing cowgirl and riding off into the sunset with some hunky cowboy? Amanda's phrase," Peyton added when Lily chuckled.

"I won't argue with the last bit, but I'm not playing at anything out here, Peyton. I feel like I'm home. Not just because of Conner and his mom and all the Blackwells, but I'm good with the horses. I like working them, training them. They don't care that I can't work my hands properly or that it takes me longer to do things sometimes. All they know is that I care about them. That's all that matters."

For the first time in maybe forever, Peyton didn't hear the frustration or borderline self-pity that used to accompany Lily's conversations about her dexterity issues. Just thinking about her sister's childhood accident, however, even after all these years, still sent a chill up Peyton's spine. There hadn't been many instances she'd given in to fear, but she had that day. Lily had come out of it okay, but when it came to fidgety things like zippers, eating utensils and sometimes even writing, she needed help. She still did and would for the rest of her life. Not that she'd let any of that ever stop her from doing what she wanted.

"So, you don't miss it?" Peyton asked. "The adventure business?"

"Nope." Lily shrugged off the notion as easy as she would a horsefly. "I don't need to be reminded I'm alive anymore. I've got Conner for that. That said, my job doesn't require me to sit in a cubicle ten hours a day crunching numbers on a computer."

"No." Familiar tension moved up her spine. Why was she the one always being lectured about how her job made other people unhappy. "Your old job meant hours spent on a muddy trail, hiking mountains and racing down rapids. Not exactly safe, was it?"

"No." Lily glanced at her, a quizzical expression in her eyes. "No, it wasn't. We're all opposite ends of the boredom spectrum. You and Georgie with your reports and books and analysis, and me and Fee always looking for adventure and excitement."

"Leaving Amanda to be the practical anchor who balances us all out. Speaking of Amanda, does she have a date for her surgery yet?"

"Next week." Lily winced. "I wish she'd told us all sooner what she was dealing with. Did you have any idea?"

"About the endometriosis? No." Now it was Peyton's time to flinch, even as she reached up to touch the earrings she wore. "Becoming a woman" for the Harrison girls meant another rite of passage, getting your ears pierced with Mom at the mall, but Amanda had been seriously late to that party. It had never occurred to Peyton, until after Amanda had told them about her fertility issues and Peyton had done extensive research, that that late start had been one of the early signs of the disease. "Maybe secrets really do run in our family." Even as she said it, she wished she hadn't. She didn't need to think about the one she was keeping from Lily now: that she wasn't here at the ranch because her boss thought she needed a break. She was here because she was hiding. "From what little she told me, the surgery should go okay. Blake is taking really good care of her."

"He always has," Lily said. "He's a really great guy. He's crazy about Amanda. I got to see that firsthand. Like over-the-moon crazy and so supportive. He'll let us know if she needs anything."

Peyton tried to put herself in Amanda's place. Of all the sisters, Amanda had always wanted a family—not just a family, but a big one. Knowing now that her sister had gone through years of fertility issues and had never said a word was yet more proof Peyton was further out of touch with her sisters than she wanted to admit.

"I'm glad she has him." A pang of envy struck, just hard enough to have Peyton looking to the fence line. Gino jumped down, spotted her and raced over. "What's going on, Gino?"

"Do you know where my dad is?"

"Still out with Ty. Why? Everything okay?"

"Rosie said I can help her feed some of the animals. Can I?"

"Um." Peyton hesitated, wishing Matteo had returned. "What kind of animals?"

"Rosie says she has a pet cow named Splinter! I didn't know you could have a pet cow. And there's a petting zoo with a goat and a rabbit and a hedgehog and…" He scrunched up his face. "I forget what else, but she says they're really cool, and I want to see them. Rosie!"

The little redhead popped up and snapped around to see who'd called to her. Even from a distance Peyton could see her sparkling blue eyes and a grin that would set any heart to tipping. She said something to Katie, who nodded. Then the little girl ran over. "Hi! I'm Rosie Blackwell. That's my Mama K." She pointed at Katie. "Can Gino come to see the animals with me?"

"I suppose?" Peyton glanced nervously at the empty road with no Matteo. She noted Lily's grin. "Just stay in sight, okay? And be gentle," she added to Gino, remembering Matteo's warnings to his son on the plane.

"Hi, Lily! How's Mouse and Pearl?" Rosie asked.

"They're doing great," Lily said. "You and your mom and dad should come out and see them."

"I'll tell them. Come on, Gino. I'll introduce you to Billy and Coconut. Come on, Hip!" Rosie yelled without looking back.

Peyton watched, a little stunned, when the dog at Katie's feet bounded toward Rosie and Gino, all but herding them to a grouping of small outdoor pens. She wasn't entirely sure how to feel about Gino coming to her when Matteo wasn't available. Not that it was a huge surprise. As far as the little boy knew, his dad worked for her. "Who are Mouse and Pearl?" she asked before Lily prodded deeper.

"A horse and burrow I rescued from an auction," Lily said. "They make the cutest couple. Well, maybe the second cutest. Those two look like they're fast friends already." She nodded her head toward Rosie and Gino, who was paying very close attention to whatever Rosie was telling him.

"She's adorable." Rosie also seemed to have made Gino's attitude issues fade away. "Why does she call Katie Mama K?"

"Katie is actually Rosie's aunt." At Peyton's confused look, Lily explained. "Long story short, Rosie's mom was Katie's older sister. She died when Rosie was two. When Chance came back to Falcon Creek a few years ago, he and Katie… Well, they found they had a lot in common," Lily added with a smile. "You know that song he sings, 'Sounds Like Home'?"

"Sure." She'd played that particular ballad on repeat for weeks when it first came out as a single a few years ago.

"He wrote that for Katie. And Rosie."

"I can't believe we're related to Chance Blackwell," Peyton said. "Does that mean we get free concert tickets?"

"Probably," Lily laughed. "But Chance is a regular at the barbecues, and he doesn't go anywhere without his guitar these days."

"Right." Peyton nodded. "So, when do I get to meet Conner?"

"Anytime you want," Lily said. "I can drive you back to the ranch now, in fact."

Torn, Peyton shifted to find Gino. "Matteo might feel better if I kept an eye on Gino, at least for today. Rain check?"

"Sure." It was the way Lily drawled the word, as if it carried an implication, that had Peyton eyeing her sister.

"What?"

"Nothing." Lily's eyes went wide. "It's just nice, I guess. Seeing you with Gino. Thinking about what his father would want. Unexpected, but nice."

"Matteo's a friend," Peyton said and wondered if she should get that tattooed somewhere obvious. "My assistant and my friend," she stated. "There's nothing...else going on."

"Okay."

"I'm serious, Lily. Everything between me and Matteo is strictly professional." Except she did like him. A lot. Far more than she should. More than she wanted to. That meant anything else crossing her mind needed to be compartmentalized immediately. If ever there were two opposites in this world, it was her and Matteo. More importantly, while a lot of women believed they could have it all—marriage, family, career—Peyton knew if she tried it, something would suffer, and she wouldn't want that something to be someone she cared about.

"Oh, I believe you. Anything else would mean you having to look up from your keyboard and monitor once in a while, and we both know you don't do that."

Peyton's cell phone blared as if confirming Lily's comment. Her sister looked at Peyton's phone, offered an arched brow as if challenging her not to answer.

Seeing the name on the screen, however, had Peyton nearly jumping to her feet. "I have to take this."

"Uh-huh." Lily nodded and stood up. "I need to get back, anyway."

"Lily." Peyton could have just met Lily and she would have recognized the disappointment on her sister's face. She also felt it dropping like a dull weight in her chest.

"Just do what you need to do, Peyton. Have a good night."

Peyton answered her phone. "Just a second." Then she held the phone against her chest and watched as Lily climbed into her truck and drove away. She pressed her lips together. She'd talk to Lily tomorrow, apologize for whatever she needed to. "I'm sorry, Mr. Josiah," Peyton said into the phone as she moved out of earshot from the other ranch guests. "I meant to contact you to let you know I'd been called out of town at the last minute, but I'm glad you got in touch…"

CHAPTER NINE

By the time Matteo and Ty returned to the main ranch yard with the injured horse, the sun was about ready to fade for the night. Matteo could see the flames of a firepit flickering and instantly wondered where Peyton and Gino were. The walk had taken longer than even he'd expected, but he'd let the horse set their pace, if for no other reason than to earn a bit more trust with the animal.

Ty circled the truck around in front of them, parked and motioned for Matteo to follow him into the barn that Ethan Blackwell used as his large-animal clinic. "We'll put her in the stall farthest in the back," Ty said as he pushed open the door and turned on the lights. Matteo heard rustling, as if they'd awakened something inside the barn. "That'll be Goldie," Ty said. "She's a two-year-old filly who was abandoned when her owner died. Poor thing is heartbroken, I think. She won't let anyone near her. She's not dangerous," he added as he softened his footfalls. "Just sad."

Matteo couldn't help but look into the stall as he led his own rescue horse into the space. She was another beauty—tan and white with a mane that looked like caught sunbeams. She blinked slowly at him and looked away, backing farther into the corner of her stall. Ty was right. The sorrow wafted off her in waves. "What are you going to do with her?"

"We aren't sure yet. She's not the right temperament for a trail horse. We might have Conner Hannah work with her, or Lily. They've both got that special touch. But for now, every time we even try to lead her out for a walk, she won't have it. She just wants to—"

"Hide." Matteo swallowed around the familiar sense of grief and fear. "Yeah. I'll bet she does." His own horse whinnied as Matteo led her into the stall, then removed the rope. When he closed the latch, he stood there, arms resting on the edge of the sill, to let her know he wasn't leaving her yet. She walked toward him, knocked her nose against his outstretched hand. "You're going to be okay. I promise."

"I'll get her some feed and give Ethan another call so he knows to look at her tomorrow."

"I can do that," Matteo said. "You wanted to go tell Hadley you were back. I can close up here, meet you at the guest house."

"Uh, okay." Ty nodded, gratitude settling in his eyes, and he smiled. "I'd appreciate that. Feed's in the other barn. Maybe check Goldie's food, too?" Ty asked on his way out.

"Not a problem." Matteo ran his hand down the horse's nose. A mixed blessing, for sure, he thought, finding her. He didn't need another distraction, but that seemed to be how his life was running these days. First Gino, now this girl. "How about we get you some food, huh?"

He did a quick run to the other barn, found what he needed and a few minutes later returned and offered the bucket of food to the nearly starving mare. While she ate, Matteo turned his attention to Goldie, who had shifted positions and was in the other corner of her stall now. One that gave her a perfect view of her new roommate. "Hey, Goldie."

Matteo moved slowly, refrained from making any quick movements as he approached the latch so he could check her food bag. Goldie remained still and watched every step he made, though, and she seemed to incline her head in question after he backed out and locked up again. "You're okay here. You know that, right?" He stood there for a moment, meeting her gaze until she blinked away. "You miss your people, don't you, girl? You miss your person. They went and left you."

Goldie sighed.

Matteo squeezed his eyes shut, trying to block out the smell of hay and feed. The sensation of stray bits of both under his feet. How many nights had he hidden in an empty stall, burying himself in the hay to prevent being found so he didn't have to hear all the shouting and fighting. Sleeping fitfully into the early-morning hours as he kept an ear out for booted footsteps that usually meant trouble.

"Matteo?" Peyton's voice broke through the memories and had him looking over his shoulder. "Ty said you were back." She had Gino with her, in front of her, her hands on his son's shoulders. For a moment the world stilled, and he imagined what it would be like to come home to this scene every night. Where Gino and Peyton were waiting for him. "Is everything okay?"

"Yeah." He blinked quickly to get rid of the

past as well as an impossible future. "Yeah, I'm sorry I'm so late. We found a horse while we were out. She's sick, so I walked her back. Gino do okay?"

"He did fine," Peyton said.

Matteo looked at Gino for confirmation. "Miss Peyton let me go to the petting zoo with Rosie. I got to meet Billy the goat and Coconut the rabbit and there's a tiny horse named… um, I forget, but it was really neat. Can I see your horse?"

"She's not mine," Matteo corrected as he headed toward them. "And she's a little skittish. If you are quiet and careful, then yes, you can meet her." He stretched out his hand. "No running, okay, bud?"

Gino nodded and took very large, very deliberate steps beside Matteo. He could feel Peyton behind them, off to one side, as if not wanting to intrude but also wanting to see what had delayed his return. Matteo leaned down and hefted Gino up. The horse's head came up, and she sniffed the air but remained where she was, near her feed bag, which Matteo could tell she'd already been using.

"What's wrong with her?" Gino asked. "What's that mark on her side?"

"I think someone wasn't very nice to her," Matteo whispered. "But we're going to see about making her better. Right now she needs rest and food."

"What's her name?"

"She doesn't have one."

"Everyone needs a name," Gino said.

Matteo agreed. Names were important. They meant something. Better he leave that to Ethan or Ty or whoever might take the animal in. "I'm sure she'll have one soon."

"How about this one over here?" Peyton stepped toward Goldie's stall. Before Matteo could tell her to stop, Goldie approached and met Peyton halfway. "Hi there." Peyton stretched out her hand. "You're awfully pretty, aren't you…" She glanced back at Matteo.

"Goldie," Matteo said, watching as the horse nuzzled Peyton's hand. "Maybe you have a bit of the Blackwell touch yourself."

"The what?" Peyton asked as she petted the horse's muzzle.

"Your sister seems to have it, from what Ty said. Natural way with horses. No doubt all the Blackwell brothers do, too. Ty told me Goldie's avoided almost everyone since she got here."

But she certainly wasn't avoiding Peyton by any stretch. "You said you used to ride."

"That was a very long time ago," she said without looking at them. "My dad, my real dad, Thomas, used to take me out once in a while. Some of my best memories have to do with him and horses."

It was the first time she'd said anything about her real father. What must it be like to know who you came from, even if they hadn't been part of your life for years?

He shifted Gino more securely in his arms. Somehow holding his son made the pain and loneliness from his own childhood fade to where it couldn't hurt him anymore. But it didn't stop the desire to belong to something, to someone, other than himself.

He saw that longing now, when Peyton glanced at the two of them, a soft smile curving her full lips. She seemed...different here. Not quite so buttoned-up and tight. As if the Montana air and atmosphere had loosened something inside of her.

"Let's leave them to get some rest, okay?" Matteo lowered Gino to the ground.

"Can we visit tomorrow?" Gino asked.

"We'll see. She needs to see a doctor first.

Her well-being has to come before anything else."

"Okay." Gino didn't look too pleased with that idea.

Matteo stopped and slipped an arm around Peyton's shoulder. Goldie lifted her head and looked into his eyes for a moment before she let out a huff and moved back into the corner of her stall.

"She looks so lonely," Peyton whispered as he drew her away and out of the clinic.

"Her owner died. Left her all alone."

"That explains that. It's not a good feeling. Being left behind." Peyton tucked her hair behind her ear. "They're serving dinner now up at the dining hall. Are you hungry?"

"Starved," Matteo confirmed as they headed away, but he cast a last look back at the stable where the horses settled for the night.

PEYTON'S EYES SNAPPED OPEN.

The room was pitch-black and smelled of cedar and rain. The world was silent. She sat up, pushed her hair out of her eyes. Montana, she reminded herself. She was in Falcon Creek, Montana. On the Blackwell Ranch. With Matteo and his son.

What had woken her up? Normally she slept like the dead, but now that she thought about it, she'd heard something odd. Something that sounded… She reached up and snapped on the bedside lamp, leaping out of bed. When she pulled open her bedroom door, she looked immediately to the tiny figure sprawled half-in half-out of the blankets on the sofa bed. Gino continued sleeping, mouth open, snoring little-boy snores that would have amused her if she hadn't shivered at the sudden cold.

The front door stood open. And just beyond, standing on the porch, hands braced on the railing, Matteo stood in the moonlight and the autumn rain. His head was bowed as he shifted his feet restlessly.

Barefoot, she padded silently toward him, drawing the door partially closed. "Matteo?"

"Sorry." He answered as if he'd felt her presence. "Did I wake you?"

"It's okay. I thought it was Gino at first." Arms tucked in around herself, she suddenly realized silk pajamas were not Montana-friendly. "I was afraid maybe he'd had a bad dream."

"No." Matteo shook his head, still not looking at her. "That was me." He took a deep breath. "Go back to bed, Peyton."

"Can't." She checked her watch. Four o'clock. "Once I'm up for the day I'm up. I can't sleep in, even when I want to."

"Sorry," he apologized again. "Nightmares sneak up on me. Today must have brought too much back. I'll get it under control."

"Don't apologize." He wanted her to leave him alone. That much was clear by his clipped tone and his refusal to look at her. But Peyton wasn't one for doing what people wanted. Not when it was obvious they were in pain. "You want to tell me about the dream?"

Now he looked at her, the disbelief and panic in his eyes reminding her so much of Gino her heart stuttered. "It's nothing."

"It's something." Ignoring the cold, she took a seat in one of the two rocking chairs by the door. She curled her legs in, wrapped her arms around them. "Otherwise you wouldn't be standing out here freezing in just pajama bottoms."

It was hard not to notice. That bare back of his was sublime in its definition. The way his hips tapered in and the muscles in his arms tightened as he struggled to find his way out of the hold of the dream. As much as she'd thought about Matteo Rossi—and she'd thought about him a lot over these past few weeks—her fantasies hadn't come close. With that almost too-long dark hair of his and faint scruff on his jaw, he looked like a wounded warrior praying to the moon for guidance.

"You're going to freeze out here yourself," he muttered as he turned to her.

She shrugged. "It'll help me shiver off dinner." She couldn't remember the last time she'd eaten one brownie, let alone two brownies for dessert. And that was after a hearty helping of steak fajitas with homemade tortillas, salsa and guacamole. "You're stalling. You're old enough to know talking about disturbing dreams helps." It always had done that for her.

"They're more like nightmares. Memories are a whole other thing." He braced his hands on the railing, leaned over enough to see inside to Gino.

"He's snoring away," Peyton said with a grin. "He won't hear anything to make you any less his hero."

"I'm no one's hero." The very idea looked distasteful to him.

"Too late. And is that more stalling I hear?"

She cupped a hand behind her ear. "You know I don't give up until I get what I want, so you may as well spill it." Irritation was another great cleansing emotion for helping get rid of the darkness.

"There's nothing to spill. We all have things we wish we could forget."

"Doesn't mean the things were any less terrible or impactful. Case in point." She pointed to the sky. "You're out here in the middle of the night in the rain trying to outrun them."

"Yeah." He leaned back and looked up at the dark clouds. "I am, aren't I? I didn't think it would happen this soon. I thought maybe I could keep it under control." He slammed his hands down hard. "This shouldn't be happening."

"But it is," Peyton said softly. "Matteo, talk to me. We're friends. Or almost friends." She honestly wasn't entirely sure what they were. "I'm here. I won't judge. I won't think any less of you because you need to talk something out."

"You won't report me to Vilette, then, for being unprofessional?"

Peyton waited for the humor to flash in his eyes, but it didn't. Instead, she saw honest doubt reflected back at her. "I wouldn't do that. I wouldn't," she insisted when he let out what she could only define as a divisive snort.

"Even if it meant you could go home and resume your usual routine?"

"I— No." She had been looking for ways to get out of this, to go home. Not just because she wanted her normal life back, but now she knew for certain that Montana was just not her place. "I'd never use something like this against you. Against anyone. I agreed to come here, to let you do your job. I plan to stay until you tell me it's safe to go home." And just like that, any resistance she held about coming to Falcon Creek, Montana, vanished. Not only because it would help her relationship with her sister and she could use a break, but because in the end, it would help Matteo. Fighting against him, resenting him for doing a job he'd taken so he could get his son back was just plain selfish. "Matteo, what was the dream about?"

He took another long breath, shook his head as if his reluctance no longer mattered. "I grew up on a place like this. Well, not as nice as this. I guess compared to here, it would loosely be called a ranch. Out in New Mexico." His gaze caught hers. "It was a home for abandoned boys."

"I see." It was all she could manage around the tightening of her throat.

"No, you don't." There was no bitterness in his voice. Not aimed at her, at least. "Be grateful for that. I wouldn't want you to. I wouldn't want anyone to."

"How old—"

"Four." He seemed anxious to get the details out of the way. "According to my records. I remember the day the social worker brought me there. We drove out in this beat-up truck, dust pluming up from under the tires as we drove. You know those opening scenes of *The Wizard of Oz*, how it's in that sepia, noncolor tone? That's my first real memory. A world without color. I spent the next thirteen years there."

"It wasn't…good." Obviously. She winced. Was she as bad at this as she sounded?

"I would have given my right arm for good. We got the basics, of course. Enough schooling to know how to read and pass tests the case workers would set. Enough food to keep us alive. But mainly we worked, either the cattle or at nearby farms and ranches. The facilitators who ran it, an older married couple and the wife's brother, had their favorites among the boys. I was not one of them."

"For any particular reason?" She needn't have asked. Peyton could see the answer in his obsidian eyes.

"I didn't look like them or sound like them, so I didn't belong in their world." The smile on his face should have been filled with resentment. Instead, it seemed one of acceptance. "One of my earliest life lessons. To never forget how some people saw me. Don't get me wrong. It wasn't all bad. Just…" he seemed to struggle for the right word "…just difficult. I actually learned a lot there. How to hide food in my pockets for later. And that it was warmer to sleep with the horses than in the beds they'd provided. Also, how to sneak books out of the library when we went into town. I'd stay up late reading anything I could get my hands on, including manuals on computers and biographies of soldiers. The older I got, the more I read. Words were my escape. My tether. That's how I found out about the Marines. My caregivers didn't make it easy, but I got out."

"How?"

"Something else I learned—how to hide. I didn't want to be anyone's target in case something bad started to happen. I also didn't like all the shouting and swearing. It freaked me out as a kid, so I'd find other places, quieter places, to be. Fortunately, I grew quickly, and the threat of anything else stopped when I was big enough to fight back. After that, they left me alone."

"I'm so sorry." Peyton's whisper vanished into the night. No child should ever have to go through anything like that. And yet she knew hundreds, thousands, did. "Where did you hide?"

"In the stables. They were off-limits during the night, but I'd made myself a pass-through into one of the stalls. The horses were safe. They didn't see me as anything else than wanting to help them. And in some ways, they protected me. I'd hide under the loose hay until the sun came up and go straight to work. And then, the morning I turned seventeen, I snuck into the office in the house and printed off my file that included my social security number and any other information I thought I'd need. By the time the sun was up, I'd walked out the front door and never looked back. Six months later, after busing it around the country, I joined the service."

The breath of relief he released had her pressing a hand against her hammering heart. "So, the dream you had?" Peyton thought it important he circle back around. "Was it from when you had to hide as a little boy?"

"No." He shook his head. "No. Those memories I can handle. The nightmare is always that I never escape. That I'm still stuck there, trapped. Hungry. Alone." He dropped his head back again. "The hunger was bad enough, along with the fear that came with each new day in those early years. But the loneliness. That was unbearable."

She couldn't imagine it. Even with all that had happened with her father and stepfather, and the disappointment she held for her mother, she'd never been completely alone because she'd had her sisters.

"You've done pretty well since," she managed, knowing whatever else she said was completely useless. She couldn't offer platitudes that held no connection to the life he'd led, nor would her apologies for something she'd had no control over mean anything. What she could do was offer support. Encouragement. Friendship. And… She stopped herself before those thoughts went too far. "You're not alone now, are you?"

"No." And there it was. Relief and acceptance easing the tense lines on his face. "The only times I haven't felt that way were when I was serving with my fellow Marines and when Gino was born. The instant I held him in my hands." He held out his hands now and looked down as if he could see a newborn Gino in his palms. "In that blink of an eye, I knew why I'd made it. Why I'd made a life for myself." His fists closed. "That little boy was and is all that matters to me. And then two years ago, I couldn't do anything to stop Sylvia from taking him away. That was the last time I had the dream. Until tonight."

Until he was back on a ranch. Because of her. Peyton's heart ached for him. He'd come back here to do a job to earn enough money to get his son back. Whatever pessimism she may have felt broke away. She unfolded herself from her chair and, still shivering, went to him, stood in front of him and reached up to cup his face in her hands. And he said he wasn't anyone's hero. "You're a good man, Matteo Rossi."

"I'm a survivor," he said with a tight smile. "Not the same thing."

"Then, you don't see what I do. I see it every time you look at Gino. Every time you put yourself between me and whatever you think will harm me. Whoever you were, whoever they tried to make you into, doesn't come close to who you are now. You have to know that. Somewhere deep inside, you know that."

He tried to shrug off her compliment, tried to pull out of her grasp, but she held on, raised up on tiptoe to make sure he looked into her eyes as she spoke. "You could have surrendered, and no one would have blamed you. You could have given up, because no one should have to fight that hard to exist. That you didn't shows me who you really are. One day, you'll tell Gino what you've told me tonight. And he'll know who you are. Beyond who he sees now. The father who would do anything for him."

His fingers brushed along the exposed skin of her waist, moments before his hands settled.

"Thank you for telling me." She knew she should back away, knew she should release him, but the warmth of him, the depths of his dark eyes drew her in even deeper than she'd been before. "Thank you for trusting me."

He nodded, the question in his eyes. The same question that coursed through her mind as she brushed her mouth against his. The barely there kiss warmed her from the tips of her toes to the top of her head. The feel of his lips, the promise of them had her stretching up and pressing herself into his strength and heat.

All at once, everything she'd never thought she'd feel, everything she'd convinced herself she didn't need, crashed in on her. He drew her closer, his hands still grasping her hips as he returned her kiss with a control and tenderness that had tears burning the backs of her eyes.

"Peyton," he whispered when she pulled herself away and lowered her heels to the porch floor. "What are we doing?"

She looked at him, perhaps seeing him fully for the first time, and felt her heart skip a beat. "I don't know."

And if there was one thing that scared Peyton Harrison, it was the unknown.

MATTEO ROSSI WAS in trouble. Not just any trouble. Nope. His trouble was spelled P-E-Y-T-O-N.

The overnight storm tapered off, and they'd

retreated to their respective rooms, but neither of them had gone back to sleep. He could feel her energy through the walls, that conscious, constant presence he'd been feeling for weeks since he'd begun working for her.

The tousled sheets lay tangled beneath him as he lay there, trying to get reception on his cell phone. He needed something, anything to distract him from the memory of Peyton Harrison kissing him.

Matteo squeezed his eyes shut. He should have stopped it. He'd seen it coming, seen the admiration-tinged sympathy shining in those sparkling green eyes of hers as she'd approached him. Felt the electric charge shoot through his system when she'd laid her hands on his chest, lifted her face to his. He shouldn't have found out what he'd been wanting to know, but he did. He knew, down to the very center of his being, what it felt like to kiss Peyton.

"Yeah, that won't keep you awake at night," he muttered and tossed his phone onto the nightstand. He had a job to do. Protect her. Keep her safe. Keep her away from whoever wanted to hurt her.

His job did not—and should not—include

falling for his charge who was sleeping in the next room.

One night down. Thirteen to go.

If bringing his six-year-old son along on the job was unprofessional, certainly kissing Peyton in the autumn rain was. This had been so much easier before he'd gotten to know her, before he'd fallen into the complicated, fascinating mess that was her family.

It seemed ridiculous to be envious of the situation she found herself in with her grandfather and sisters. But the fact she understood how lucky she was to have those problems made him like her even more. She wasn't the distant, cold businesswoman he'd convinced himself she was.

She had just as many winding roads inside of her as he had in his past. And all of them had led them both to the same place: Falcon Creek, Montana.

From his bed, he could look out the window, see the sun beginning to peek over the mountains. The pink and blue hues in the sky welcoming them on their first full day was something to behold. How long had it been since he'd taken the time to appreciate the sunrise?

How long before he forgot to appreciate it again?

The soft knock on his door had him sitting up. "Yeah?"

Gino poked his head in, his hair mussed to the point of comedic comment, his eyes still droopy with sleep. "I'm up." He didn't look particularly happy about it, a theory proven correct when he came over to the bed and flopped down face-first.

Matteo laughed and reached down to roll him over and tickle him. The sound of his son's laughter made the last two years without him melt into oblivion. This was why he did what he did. This little guy, right here, with his mischievous dark eyes and early-morning smile, while wearing pajamas that were almost too small for him.

"Shh." Matteo finally pushed a finger against his lips before pointing to the wall. "We don't want to wake Peyton."

Gino nodded and crawled up to stretch out beside Matteo. "What are we doing today?"

"I don't know what they have planned for the ranch, but you've got schoolwork to catch up on." He expected resistance. How could schoolwork possibly compete with a stable full of horses, outdoor activities and a ranch that by now must be at least half mud?

"I don't wanna do homework."

"That's too bad because if you don't get caught up, you won't be going on the trail ride Tuesday." Matteo lay back down on the bed and clasped his hands behind his head. "Each of us has a job to do before we can have fun. School is your job, Gino."

"Can I go see your horse instead? And visit Goldie?"

"Not until you're done with your schoolwork." He understood childhood reluctance to learning. No one liked to be told what to study and for how long. But he also knew what it was like to be prevented from studying, period, from filling his brain with information that would make his life better. Gratitude and appreciation were lessons his son needed to learn. When Gino didn't respond, Matteo looked at him. "Gino?"

"I'm no good at it," his son whispered, his eyes filling before he looked away and sniffled. "Kids make fun of me. I get everything wrong. And sometimes the teacher makes me stay after to finish, and then I get in trouble with Mom because I'm late getting home."

Something Mr. Shinto had said about Gino when he'd dropped him off rang in Matteo's head. Something he hadn't quite understood at the time. "Did you ask your mom for help with your schoolwork?"

"Yeah." Gino's chin wobbled. "She said she didn't have time and that I was smart enough to figure it out. Jiro helped a little, but he's always at work, too. He said that was my teacher's job."

Matteo struggled to keep his temper in check. "Well, you know what? You're not with your mom and Jiro anymore. And I love doing schoolwork."

"You do?" Gino's eyes went wide, as if Matteo had just admitted to being a secret superhero.

"I do. I think because..." What was it Peyton had said last night? That his son would understand him better, understand the world better, if he told Gino the truth about his childhood. "I think because when I was your age, the people I lived with didn't want me to be smart. And that's what books and schoolwork do. They make you smart until you figure out what it is you want to do when you're older."

"But what if I'm not smart?" Gino whispered. "What if I'm stupid?"

Anger stabbed him dead center of his chest. "You are not stupid, Gino. You know how I know that?"

"Nuh-uh."

"Because you know that smart boys come to someone when they need help. They talk about it with someone they can trust. Like you're doing now." Like he'd longed to do when he was a little boy. "You can always, always come to me, Gino. I will never, ever think you are stupid."

"So…" Gino bit his lip "…if I asked you to help me with my work—"

"I will always say yes," Matteo said. "And you know what else? The sooner we get through with your work, the more time you'll have to play with Rosie and the animals."

"And your horse?" Gino's eyes brightened.

"And the new horse," Matteo agreed. "But first, you know what I really want?" Other than an IV of coffee. "I think we should find out when and where breakfast is because I'm starving."

"Yeah!" Gino yelled and threw his arms over his head. "Me, too. When do we eat?"

APPARENTLY PEYTON WASN'T as bad at this hiding thing as she thought.

She holed up in her room, in her bed with her laptop whirring and whining, half-listening to Matteo and Gino getting up and dressed. She sat there, tucked under her blankets, biting her thumbnail and wondering what she was going to say when Matteo knocked on her door. She'd kissed him. She shoved a hand into her hair and grimaced.

Heaven help her, she'd kissed her bodyguard.

Not only kissed him but enjoyed it. And wanted to do it again. She'd felt it all the way to her toes, which continued to tingle. It seemed he'd enjoyed it as well, despite their mutual uncertainty about what they did about it now.

"Nothing," she whispered. "You're going to do nothing about it because it isn't going to happen again." Her cheeks flushed, a sign she was lying to herself. Darn it! She didn't want sparks. She didn't want desire or distraction or anything interfering with her perfectly mapped-out life. All she wanted out of a relationship was simple, mutual respect and appreciation. No emotions to get her all tangled up. A simple arrangement was all she needed. She didn't want to know what else was possible. Hearts didn't get broken in simple arrangements gone wrong.

Nope. And since Mr. Josiah wasn't working out, she'd have to find another way to deal with her stepfather's determination to see her happy and settled. Was there a more logical, thought-out solution than Mr. Josiah? It was little more than a signature on a contract.

Except…

Her brow pinched. Except now she did know what she'd be missing with what amounted to simply another business deal. Now she knew what chemistry and attraction provided. And if a single kiss could overload her brain with unwanted information, she could only imagine what…

"Stop it. Just…stop."

Any concern she had about facing Matteo right now vanished with the quiet whoosh of paper sliding under her bedroom door.

Going for breakfast in the dining hall. Will bring you back something unless you join us. Otherwise, don't leave the cabin. M

A moment later, she heard the front door open and close, and the cabin went silent.

The knots in her stomach eased. Alone in the cabin, she made quick work of her morning. She jumped in the shower and, after looking out the window into the gray, drizzly day, donned the brand-new pair of jeans she'd ordered, along with her running shoes and a bright blue turtleneck shirt.

The weather certainly didn't entice her to go out, so she rummaged around in the kitchenette and set a pot of coffee to brewing, made a quick inventory of the minifridge and cabinets, where she found a nice selection of snacks and drinks. She could order breakfast to be delivered to the cabin, but she wasn't typically a breakfast person, so she'd wait and see what Matteo might bring back for her. Otherwise, she could wait for lunch.

Coffee brewed and poured, Peyton settled down with her laptop at the table by the window, across from where Matteo had left Gino's school things. Minutes later, she'd pulled up the Olwen project information and, pen in hand, got to work prepping for the meeting that could launch Electryone into the business stratosphere.

"So, what's the verdict?" Matteo kept one eye on Gino and another on Ethan Blackwell as the vet examined his rescue's front right hoof.

"Well, to start—" Ethan hoisted the horse's hoof higher "—looks like an abscess. I can drain that and start her on antibiotics. We should see some improvement by the end of the week."

"How much will that run me?"

Ethan glanced up, first at Ty, then at Matteo. "Nothing."

"She was found on Blackwell land," Ty said with a nod. "That makes her ours."

"I know how expensive horses can be." Matteo shifted his weight from one foot to the other. "And I know you guys are fine financially, but that doesn't mean I don't want to pay my fair share. I brought her here. She's partially my responsibility. Gino, hey, come away from Goldie, okay? If she's in the back corner of her stall, she wants to be left alone."

Gino huffed what sounded like an impatient breath and rejoined Matteo. "I'm bored."

"I know. Hey, how about you take Peyton her breakfast? It's right over there." He pointed to the paper container containing scrambled eggs, a bagel and homemade huckleberry jam. "I'll be back in a bit, and we can get started with your schoolwork."

Gino looked far from impressed.

"The longer it takes you to make up your mind, the longer it'll take for me to get done here. Remember, no schoolwork, no trail ride."

"But Katie said she found me a horse!"

"So, we shouldn't disappoint her." Even after their discussion this morning, Gino still wasn't on board with his learning. "Or you can wait over there for me, and we'll go back together."

"Fine, I'll do it." Gino stomped over and grabbed Peyton's breakfast.

"And no stomping in mud puddles on your way there," Matteo told him seconds before Gino launched himself into an ankle-deep one outside the clinic door. "Unless you want to learn how to do laundry later today, as well as multiplication." He cringed and returned his attention to the Blackwell brothers, once Gino was out of earshot. "Sorry, guys."

"Nothing to apologize for." Ethan shrugged. "We've all been there. Well, except this one," he said and jabbed a finger at Ty. "He's going to get his first taste this Christmas. Although, it should be a while before his kid is stomping in mud puddles."

"FYI." Ty motioned at Matteo, as Ethan lowered the horse's foot and left the stall to sort through his medical bag. "We've got laundry facilities in the guest house. In the room next to the gym."

"Right. I saw that yesterday," Matteo replied. "I'd been hoping to get in a run this morning, but the treadmill will do for tomorrow." The rain had slowed to a constant drizzle and made his optimistic outlook on the ranch dim a bit. "I take it the trail ride happens rain or shine?"

"Pretty much," Ty confirmed. "But we have a few days for the weather to pass. We can leave later than planned, though, give the ground a little more time to dry, which it should. What are you thinking about those injuries, Ethan?" he asked his brother when Ethan began examining the horse's sides and flanks.

"Barbed-wire scars," Matteo said and earned a surprising neigh and nod of the head from his charge. "Spur scars down below."

"Agreed." Ethan smoothed his fingers over the raw marks. "Not too long ago, by the looks of it. She's also malnourished and dehydrated. I'm going to start her on some fluids, see if we can ease those symptoms. She ate through that entire bag of feed you gave her, Matteo, so that's good news." He patted his hand against her neck. "She hasn't given up."

"No, she hasn't," Matteo agreed. "She's a fighter. Will you look for her owner?"

"I don't see any markings on her," Ty said after examining her ears and the rest of her body. "No brands or identification tags. Tells me whoever had her either didn't know to or didn't care about staying legal. I'd say leave it be and get her back to full strength."

The horse whinnied in agreement.

"Can't argue with a horse," Matteo said. "If it turns out she needs something, though, tell me. Believe me, if I didn't live in an apartment in California, I'd try to find a way to keep her myself." Not to ride. He didn't think she'd ever let anyone on her back again. That was his gut feeling. But to know she was safe.

"She's definitely not a Cali girl," Ty joked. "We've got time to figure it all out, though. Don't worry. I'm off to take a couple of guests to the airport."

After leaving the horse in Ethan's capable

hands, Matteo headed to the cabin, hoping he'd find Gino in a better mood.

"THANKS, LITTLE MAN." Peyton accepted the paper container from a rain-soaked Gino, cringing at the mud spots he'd left on the floor. "How about you go leave those shoes by the door and get a towel for your hair."

He grumbled but did as she said, nearly toppling over when he tugged off his shoes. They landed with a wet plop.

The eggs were cold, but after an initial bite, she found they were tasty. Actual real eggs, not that powdered stuff so many hotels served in their breakfast buffets. She really shouldn't eat the bagel, but she had heard tell of huckleberry jam and how you couldn't leave Montana without trying it. She broke off a chunk of bagel and dipped it into the thick jam and nearly swooned as the slightly sweet mixture hit her tongue. Okay, she thought. That was good.

It didn't take long for the jam and bagel to be eaten. Just in time for her to put on another pot of coffee to brew.

"Dad said he'll be back soon." Gino slipped

into the chair across from her. "What are you doing?"

"Working."

"Oh. My mom works a lot. She says I bug her."

Peyton's initial reaction was to protest, to tell Gino she was sure that wasn't true, but whether or not his mother had told him that, it was clear Gino believed it. "You know what?" She closed her laptop. "I've worked enough this morning. I think your dad said you need to finish your school stuff before you can go riding next week. Maybe you should get started?"

She reached across for the workbooks in front of him. Spelling. Math. Reading comprehension. She flipped through the pages, saw the errant scribbles early in one of the books. Scribbles that didn't entirely make sense. "Where did you leave off?"

Gino shrugged. "Dunno."

"Well, let's find out." She held out her hand, which he took after a moment, and tugged him around and in front of her. She moved her computer aside, flipped open the first page of his spelling book. "Looks like you forgot to finish your spelling list for this assignment." She glanced at the date in the top corner from more than a month ago. "You want to finish it now?"

She reached for a pencil and set it in front of him. "Here. Why don't you show me how you spell *dog*. That's this word right here."

He grabbed the pencil, took an extra beat to find the right grip. He leaned over, then seemed to shy away. "I don't know if it'll be right."

"It doesn't have to be right on your first try, Gino." Peyton smoothed his damp hair back and rested her chin on his shoulder. "That's why it's called learning. If it isn't right, we'll figure it out until it is." It had been so long since she'd sat with a child to help with homework. Most of her sisters had done all right on their own, but Lily had needed help after her accident. Especially when it came to writing and finding a comfortable way to hold a pen or pencil. "How about you try, and we'll see where we are. Come on. *Dog.*"

She could feel the tension in his little body and wished she could find the words to make him less nervous about writing a simple word. Finally, he leaned over and put his pencil over the paper. "There you go," she murmured encouragingly. *"D-O-G."*

He took such care, as if he wanted it to be perfect. When he finished, he stood up like a shot and turned hopeful eyes on her. "I did it!"

Peyton gave him a quick hug and looked down at the paper.

Her stomach dropped, unease clambering in her chest as she ignored the truth and gave him another squeeze. "How about we try the next one? *Cat.* Makes sense. Can't have a dog without a cat."

"Hip has cat friends," Gino said as he went back to work. "Rosie says Hip gets along with all the animals. Even Splinter the Cow."

"I bet Hip gets along with everyone," Peyton agreed, and soon they settled into an easy rhythm, moving down his spelling list.

When he flipped the page, he did so with a little yelp of excitement.

"I'm doing it!"

"Hold on." Peyton flipped the page back. "Let's go over them before we move on. Can you read the words back to me?" She went to the top of the list, only when he did, his smile faded. "Gino?"

"It doesn't look right. It doesn't look the same." He jabbed his finger against the printed text and the word he'd written. "It's supposed to be the same." Tears filled his eyes, and he looked at her as if she could solve all his problems. "I did it wrong, didn't I?"

She drew him back and into his arms. "You know what?"

"I'm stupid."

"You are not." There were a lot of words that did damage, but that was the worst. She wrapped an arm around him and kept him firmly in place when he tried to bolt free. "Gino, you are not stupid. Do you remember what this word is?" She tapped the original text.

"Dog."

"And what letters did you draw?"

"I dunno."

"Yes, you do. We said it before. *D-O-G*, remember?"

"That's what I did. *D-O-G*. But it's not right. It's not right!" He threw the pencil down and broke free of Peyton's hold just as Matteo returned. "I told Dad. It's just like Mom said. I'm stupid. I'm just stupid!" He ran into his father's room and slammed the door.

"What's going on?" She heard the instant disappointment in his voice, the accusation aimed at her at seeing his son upset. She didn't take offense. If anything, the protective instinct for his child endeared him even more to her.

"I might understand why Gino hates school so much." She rose, picked up the workbook and met him halfway.

"Oh?"

"Yeah." She handed him the workbook. "You need to look into getting him tested. I think he has dyslexia."

CHAPTER TEN

"MY EX ISN'T ANSWERING." Matteo clicked off his cell and tossed it onto the table. "It went to voice mail."

"In her defense, Japan is sixteen hours ahead," Peyton said, then held up her hands at his glare. "Sorry. Just sayin'."

Matteo would like to think Sylvia wasn't answering because of the time difference, but it was just as easy to believe she was avoiding his calls. Out of sight, out of mind, and now that Gino wasn't her responsibility... He gave himself a mental slap. He had to stop blaming Sylvia for everything. That said, she had to have seen something was wrong with their son, didn't she? "Okay." He stopped pacing and took a long, deep breath. He blew it out and looked at Peyton. "What did you see that I didn't?"

"This." She tapped a finger on Gino's spelling workbook. "Gino's reluctance to go to school seemed pretty extreme. We worked on his list of spelling words. See here." She stood and circled around to point out the obvious errors. "He's reversed the letters in the word, and some of the letters are backwards. You'll need to get him tested by a professional, but it's early. I'm sure there are easy ways to work with him and help him."

"Taro gave me his school records when he brought Gino to me. Since Gino wasn't going to be starting school right away, I didn't think to look—"

"This isn't your fault, Matteo." Peyton clung to his arm and squeezed, but nothing she did to comfort him broke through. He berated himself for not seeing his son was in trouble. "You've had a lot thrown at you at one time, and now you're dealing with this away from your home base. How about we look at those records together, then do a little research. Hadley mentioned a library in town. Maybe they have some books for both you and Gino."

He nodded, uncertain what else to do at this point. "I want to talk to him first, though. I don't like him throwing that word around." He'd heard it often enough himself growing up. No way was he going to let his son suffer the same humiliation.

"I completely agree," Peyton said. "You go on. I'll start searching online to see what options we have. Also, do you know what school you're going to enroll him in when we get back to California?"

"I haven't had time to look yet."

"No, of course you haven't. I'll compile a list of schools that have dedicated programs for kids who need extra help. In fact..." She walked away, mumbling to herself.

"Thanks." He nodded absently, set the workbook down and headed to his bedroom. "I mean it, Peyton." She settled in behind her laptop and offered him an understanding smile. "It means a lot that you took the time to care."

He rapped his knuckles on the door before pushing it open. "G?" He frowned when he couldn't see his son immediately. As he walked around the made-up bed, he found his son curled up with his back against the mattress, eyes and cheeks damp, his nose red. "Rough morning?"

Gino shrugged, and Matteo recognized the uncertainty. He sat down next to his son, drew his knees in and looked at Gino.

"We're going to get one thing straight right now, okay?"

Gino ducked his chin and when he blinked, two huge tears fell onto his cheeks.

"Gino, are you listening to me?"

Gino nodded, swiping at his eyes and runny nose.

"I don't ever, ever want to hear you call yourself stupid again. Is that understood?"

It wasn't, Matteo thought, what Gino expected to hear. He glanced up, brows knit.

"In fact," Matteo continued, "I don't want you to use that word again at all. It's a horrible word and does a lot of damage. You know that because you feel it in here, don't you?" He poked a gentle finger against Gino's chest.

"But I got the words wrong." His confusion broke Matteo's heart. "Sometimes the letters look right, then they don't. They get all mixed up."

"That's okay. I and some really good teachers can help you figure that out, so you do spell the words correctly. It's called a learning difference. It means you don't learn the same way other people do. But that's okay, Gino. And now we can do something about it, there's nothing wrong with being different."

"I don't want to be different."

"I know." How well he understood that. Matteo put an arm around Gino and drew him close. "I know you don't, but we don't always get to decide what sets us apart from others. This is a little bit scary for me, too, Gino. Because I want you to have the absolute best life you can, and now I need to figure out how to make that happen."

"Does that mean…" Gino frowned again and turned trusting eyes up to him. "Does that mean you can fix me?"

Matteo caught his son's chin in his fingers. "There is nothing to fix. I know it's hard, but I really need you to try to stop feeling and thinking that you're broken. There are so many people who have the same difficulties you do. And there are so many people out there who can help us. We're going to find them." He jerked a thumb toward the door. "Peyton's out there right now looking stuff up on the internet. That's pretty cool, right?"

"Yeah. She's nice." Gino snuggled against him. "She didn't get mad and yell at me or leave me alone to figure it out even when I got it wrong."

Anger thrummed deep inside Matteo. "Have other people made you feel that way?"

"Yeah. The kids at school. And sometimes... Mom."

"And that's why you stopped doing your work at home?"

"Yeah."

"And why you got in trouble in school?"

Gino's head shot up, his eyes wide. "Did Mr. Shinto tell you?"

No, Matteo thought. *You just did.* "I bet it was a lot easier doing something wrong and getting sent to the principal's office than doing work you didn't understand."

Another shrug. "I guess."

"Well." Matteo gathered him close and held on. "You don't ever have to worry about that with me. Not ever. That's a promise. And I always keep my promises."

"Does this mean I get to go on the trail ride?"

"How about we maybe do a little more homework before I say yes. Right or wrong, I want you to get in the routine of doing your school assignments. Like I said this morning, school is your job. We just need to find a way to make it a little easier for you."

"Okay." Gino gave him a slight smile.

Matteo got to his feet and helped Gino up. Together, they returned to the living room. Peyton glanced up from her computer.

"Everything all right?"

"It will be," Matteo assured her. "Gino and I are going to do some more schoolwork."

Peyton nodded, and when Gino walked over to her, she handed him his books. "I'm glad you're feeling better, Gino."

"I am."

She cupped his face in her hand. "Your dad's a smart man. And you—" she kissed his forehead "—are a very smart boy. You know how I know? Because you listen to your father."

Her smile from across the room made Matteo's heart sing. "Gino, how about we work over here." Matteo pointed to the sofa. "And let Peyton get back to her business."

Gino did as he was told, leaving Matteo to approach Peyton himself. "Thank you."

"My pleasure." She handed him a few sheets of paper she'd printed off on her portable printer. "These are exercises I found on the internet that are used to help diagnose dyslexia. It's just alphabet and number tests."

"I also made a list of storybooks for his age and thought maybe we could head to the library this week. In the meantime—"

"In the meantime, you've done enough." Matteo crouched down and grabbed hold of her hand. "I appreciate all this, but you have Electryone and the Olwen project to deal with. We've got this."

"Oh." She blinked, frowned, then seemed to force a smile. "Sure. I just thought I'd... Never mind. You're right." Her smile seemed tight and a bit regretful. But this wasn't about Peyton. This was about his son. "Gino's your responsibility, not mine."

"Thanks." Papers and pencils in hand, he joined his son on the sofa, and after earning another smile from Gino, they got to work.

BY TUESDAY MORNING, the rain had vanished, and the sun was shining once again. The trail ride was definitely on and, after a few days of mostly being cooped up inside, it didn't take much convincing to get Peyton to shut down her computer and see what Falcon Creek had to offer.

It might, however, take a little extra effort to get her on a horse.

Katie and her assistant forewoman, Izzy, were lining up the trail horses nearby, checking saddles and pointing to Peyton, Matteo and Gino. Ty had already checked in with them and was making the final lunch-delivery arrangements with Hadley before they headed out. Peyton sank her hands deeper into her poofy red jacket and tried to remember how much she used to love to ride.

"They can smell fear," Matteo murmured in her ear.

Peyton yelped and spun, her sneakers slipping and sliding in the mud.

"Whoops. Got ya." Matteo grabbed her arms and kept her from losing her balance. "Sorry. Didn't realize you were so lost in thought."

"Neither did I." Peyton stood there, caught in his hold, and looked up into the eyes that ever ceased to fascinate her. He'd cowboyed up, as he'd called it this morning, and was wearing jeans, a long-sleeved dark blue flannel shirt and a hat he'd borrowed from the bunkhouse.

Never in her life would Peyton have thought a cowboy hat could have made him more attractive, but looking at him, those amazing eyes of his glinting from beneath the dark brim, the way his hair was begging to be touched, had her thinking all kinds of things a woman should never, ever think about her bodyguard.

But she had been thinking those things. Even before the hat.

She'd been thinking about them a lot.

They'd fallen into a bit of a rhythm the past few days, her, Matteo and Gino, with their walks down to the dining hall, stopping to check in on Matteo's horse—who still didn't have a name—and Goldie, who continued her affectionate attachment to Peyton.

Ty had even taken advantage of Peyton's influence and asked her to lead Goldie out of her stall with tempting apples and carrots so he could clean out the space.

It had felt good, Peyton thought, to help. First with Gino, now with Goldie. The fact Gino no longer fought his father when Matteo suggested practicing his letters and numbers felt like a triumph.

"How's your project going?" Matteo asked, stepping back and releasing her.

"Good. Fine." Peyton tucked her hair behind her ear. "I finally settled on a company for the solar-panel construction. Shot Vilette an email this morning." The response had been short, precise, and essentially told Peyton she was officially out of work to do before the final signing meeting with Olwen's creators as soon as she got back.

"So, that's why you agreed to come out and play?"

"I guess." Peyton managed a laugh. "I wouldn't be a very good example to Gino if all I did was work, right?"

Matteo's eyes sparkled. "I appreciate you thought about that."

"All right, here we go!" Katie Blackwell stepped away from the horses and headed over to her, Matteo and Gino. "I think we're good. We're just waiting on two more people... Ah. There they are now."

Peyton turned in time to see Lily's truck pull up beside the guest lodge. Her sister climbed out, then held out her hand to a tall, very handsome, very cowboy-looking cowboy. After stopping to speak briefly with Hadley and Ty, they headed their way.

"Hope you don't mind us crashing the party," Lily said. "We got done early this morning, and since Katie's out of riding commission these days—"

"Yeah, yeah." Katie's cranky muttering was tempered by how her hand gently brushed against her belly.

Lily grinned. "Conner, this is my sister, Peyton. Peyton, your soon-to-be-brother-in-law, Conner Hannah."

"Hi." Peyton made sure to make the first move, holding out her hand. "It's nice to finally meet you."

"You, too." Conner returned the greeting, then tipped his hat. "Have to admit, you're about exactly what I imagined, given Lily's description." He turned his attention to Matteo. "Conner Hannah."

"Oh, sorry. Matteo Rossi," Peyton said. "My assistant." The lie was almost easy to tell now. "And this is his son, Gino."

Matteo reached behind him without looking and pried his son around.

"Pleasure."

"I hear you both used to ride," Conner said.

"It's been a while," Matteo admitted and cast an uneasy look to the horses. "This will be Gino's first time, though. He's been looking forward to it for days."

"Then, let's get you up and into the saddle." Katie reached out her hand. "I'll give him the basics, run him through a few things. Conner will ride next to him as a precaution, if that's okay with you?" She asked Matteo, who nodded.

"That's fine. Thanks. Gino, you mind Miss Katie, all right? You mind whatever she or Mr. Conner has to say."

"Uh-huh." Gino's shoes squelched in the mud as he walked off.

"So, you're Peyton's assistant?" Lily rocked back on her heels, still clinging to Conner's hand. "What happened to Todd?"

Peyton started. She didn't realize Lily knew her real assistant's name.

"School," Matteo said before Peyton could. "He couldn't take time away and Vilette was adamant about Peyton having time off."

"You're here to make sure she relaxes?" Lily cast a knowing look at Peyton, who glared back. "Good to know. If you find out how to make that happen, believe me, that'll be priceless information. Heard you found a horse wandering the property the other day. Ethan said he thought she'd been abused."

"Looks that way," Matteo said. "We looked

in on her this morning. She's doing better, I think."

"We've dealt with a number of traumatized animals," Conner said. "Happy to work with her if you decide you want to keep her."

"I haven't gotten that far yet. But thanks," Matteo said.

"Hey!" Katie yelled as she strapped Gino into his saddle. "You guys need to saddle up already. Sun's climbing. Lily, you and Conner have Starbuck and Apollo." She pointed to the two painted horses at the far end of the barn. "Peyton, we're giving you Spock. He's easygoing and knows this trail better than I do. Matteo, that's Bones. He's all yours. Need help?"

"Yes—" Peyton stopped when Matteo's hand brushed against her back.

"We've got it. I'd rather she stay with Gino," he said under his breath, and Peyton nodded. "And remember what I said. They smell fear."

"I'm not afraid," she said and had to be pushed forward toward Spock, who was a deep, dark brown and reminded her of her favorite imported chocolate. "Just…cautious. It's been a long time since—"

"If I can do this, you can."

Odd, she thought, how she could almost see

his past in his gaze. A past he'd accepted and moved beyond rather than wallowed in. So much about Matteo was admirable. Appealing. Attractive. And not just because of how he looked; she hadn't met a lot of men like him—maybe, she thought, because her father was right. She didn't take the time to look up and see what was going on around her. But she was looking up now.

And saw Matteo Rossi.

She smiled, shielded her eyes. "It's just like riding a bike, right?"

"Sure." Matteo grinned. "A bike with a mind of its own, but if that makes you feel better..."

"Ha ha. Not helping."

Peyton hesitated, catching sight of Lily and Conner up at the front of the group. Conner reached down and tucked Lily's hair behind her ear. Lily beamed up at him before reaching for the saddle horn.

Peyton instinctively made a step toward her sister to help. Lily didn't have enough strength in one hand to pull herself up and into the saddle. Peyton stopped when Conner placed his hand around Lily's, steadying her balance and her grip as she mounted the horse. Peyton's heart swelled. The ease with which they worked together, the way they looked at each other, as if they were sharing secrets only the two of them knew, erased any doubt she might have had about Lily being in Montana. It was impossible to miss the absolute adoration she saw shining on Conner's face as he moved on to his own horse.

"Hey, you stalling again?" Matteo's teasing jolted Peyton back to reality. She climbed the three-step platform, but before she pushed her foot into the stirrup, she took a second to meet her charge. "Hi there, Spock." She held out her hand, then drew her palm gently down the side of the horse's neck. "It's nice to meet you."

"Please don't tell me you are expecting an answer."

Peyton would have glared at Matteo, but the teasing tone in his voice had her smiling instead. "He might. You never know. I'll be fine. Go on. Unless you're stalling."

"Kettle, meet pot." But he moved to his own horse, climbed his own platform, and after only a slight hesitation, hoisted himself into the saddle as if he'd been doing it every day of his life. She saw it, the flash of momentary panic in his eyes, as if he'd just realized what he'd done.

Matteo's hands seemed to tremble as he grasped the reins, but when he lifted his gaze to meet hers, it was steady. "Your turn."

"Right. Hear that, Spock?"

Spock gave her a look that didn't exactly bolster her confidence. She pushed her foot into the stirrup, grabbed the horn and hoisted her other leg up and over. As if the saddle and her body had muscle memory, she settled right in.

"You good?" Matteo said from behind her.

"So far." Spock took a step back, then forward. She draped the reins loosely into her hands, squeezed her knees into Spock's flanks and leaned over. "We're going to do just fine, you and me, right, boy?" She petted him again, then looked to where Gino was beaming at Katie.

Unable to resist the expression of pure joy on the little boy's face, she pulled out her cell phone and took a picture. Spock took exception to the faint click and let out an odd sound.

"Whoops." Katie looked back as Spock did a little unexpected dance away from the fence. "Should have warned you he doesn't like cell phones." She hurried over, held out her hand. "I'll hold onto it until you get back."

"Go on," Matteo urged when Peyton hesitated. "Bet you can't go a day without it."

"That sounds like a challenge." She loved the way his lips curved into a smile.

"Can be. Want to make it interesting?"

"Name your stakes."

"You go a full twelve hours without using your cell phone for anything, and I'll deliver every meal to you at the cabin for as long as we're here. Whenever, whatever you want, I'll get it."

"Aren't you already her assistant?" Katie asked with a confused frown.

"Assistant, not servant," Matteo clarified, still grinning at Peyton. "Sound good?"

"And if I lose?"

"No work for the rest of our stay. None. Nada. You just enjoy the ranch."

"No…" She actually balked.

"Better make up your mind. We're heading out." Matteo jerked his chin toward the front of the pack.

"You can do it," Katie urged. "Meal delivery alone is worth it."

"Fine." Peyton held out her phone to Katie.

"Nope." Matteo moved Bones up until he was next to her. "You have to do it on your own, with your phone with you. Is it okay with Spock if the phone's off?"

"Yeah," Katie said, shielding her eyes even beneath her hat. "Guess that does make it a bit more of a challenge, doesn't it."

"Wouldn't want it to be easy, now, would I?"

Peyton scrunched her face and, with one hand, turned off her phone and shoved it into her pocket. "All right. You have a deal." And with that, she kicked her feet and set Spock to falling in line.

CHAPTER ELEVEN

"WHAT ON EARTH am I going to do for a week without my computer or cell?"

Matteo hadn't been able to wipe the smile off his face for the past five hours, ever since Peyton had succumbed to her cell-phone addiction and pulled it out to snap pictures during their lunch at the lake.

"Deprogram yourself?" Matteo suggested as he waved Gino inside the cabin after supper at the dining hall. The kid was already yawning wide enough he could very well drown in the shower he needed. Little boy dirty, covered in mud and grime and sweat from head to toe.

And looking as happy as Matteo had ever seen him.

"Don't blame me for you losing the bet," Matteo told Peyton when she aimed a particularly irritated glare in his direction. "You made the choice to use your phone."

"But I was taking pictures of you and your

son," she tried to argue again. "That should be an exception."

Matteo's brow arched. "It would have been if that's all you'd done." He waved a finger in the phone's direction, where it was shoved in her pocket. "You checked your email and voice mails. Don't try to deny it. It's my job to see everything, remember?"

"I won't forget it again." She collapsed on the sofa, patted a hand on her stomach. "I've eaten more today than in the past month. Why does riding a horse make you so hungry?"

"Because you're spending a lot of mental energy keeping your animal focused."

"Fat lot of good that did," Peyton scoffed. "Did you see the way Spock dumped me? He just dropped to the ground and let me roll right off."

"Oh, I saw." Matteo had a front-row seat for her horse's sudden desire to take a rest. He'd jumped off Bones before she'd even hit the ground, then cursed himself for not insisting either she or Gino wear a helmet for their ride. "You heard what Ty said, though. The high grass was tickling her belly. She just wanted a scratch."

"Well, it was just rude." She didn't sound

nearly as irritated as she was pretending to be. "I suppose you want your bed, little man, huh?"

Gino shrugged.

"He's not going to bed without a shower." Matteo set his hat down and dived for his son, flipped him over and carried him, feet up, into the bathroom. "You stink, Gino. Let's get you cleaned up."

"Conner said stinking means you've had a good day on the ranch," Gino declared when he caught his breath from laughing and Matteo righted him.

Matteo bit back a retort that would have had his son asking questions he wasn't ready to answer. It had taken him years to get the stench of ranch work out of his nose. Early on in his Marine training, he'd signed up for every cleaning crew, anything that would have him inhaling the nose-curling smell of ammonia and bleach.

"Doesn't mean you carry it with you into the next day. Strip. Clothes by the door. I'll bring in your PJs." He reached over Gino's head and turned on the shower. "Gino?"

"Huh?"

"This means you get in, stand under the water and wash yourself off."

Gino rolled his eyes. "I know."

"Just making sure." His son had emerged from the bathroom last night with suspiciously dry hair. "Make it quick. Peyton and I need to clean up, too. And use soap."

He closed the door behind him, and found Peyton looking at her cell phone again. Without glancing at him, she held up a hand. "Relax. It's not email. I'm sending you the pictures I took today." She flipped her phone around to show him. "Thought maybe you'd like them. That's my favorite."

He took her phone. She'd got a great shot of him and Gino, backs to the camera, with the sun hitting just right to cast them into shadow. They were standing by the lake, hand in hand, Gino's face in profile—his smile was one of pure joy.

"I like this one, too, though. I call this the Enabling Shot." Matteo with Gino jumping on his back and Matteo laughing over his shoulder. "You knew I had my phone and still practically posed for it."

Matteo shrugged. "Just wanted to make you aware of your problem."

"It's not a problem, it's a necessity. Speaking of which, I need to send one email to Vilette. Just one. To let her know I won't be checking in every day for the rest of the trip."

Matteo shook his head.

"I can't just not check in, Matteo. There's a lot riding on the Olwen deal. I have to know if there are any issues cropping up."

"Fine. I'll amend the bet to a half hour in the morning before breakfast. And you can leave it on to screen calls, but only answer if it's an emergency or one of your sisters."

"My hero." Peyton grabbed the phone back and began to dial. "You going in the shower after Gino?"

"Unless you want to go first."

"I can wait," she said. "Any idea what's on the agenda for tomorrow?"

"We can check the calendar of events when you're done." He already had his eye on the pumpkin-carving party tomorrow afternoon. One thing this unexpected trip was providing him was a lot of firsts with Gino. "You want wine?"

"I'd love a glass of wine."

"I think I saw a bottle in the fridge. Go

make your call." He pulled his own cell out and set it on the counter as she stepped outside.

When the water abruptly turned off in the bathroom, Matteo frowned. He walked back and knocked on the door. "Gino? You wash your hair?"

"Um. Maybe?"

"Want to try that again?" Matteo shook his head. What was it with this kid and showers? When he was that age, he'd have killed to have one every night.

"All right." The muttered response was almost drowned out by the water going back on. Satisfied, Matteo returned to the wine and glasses, caught the vibrating of his phone and the display on the screen. "This is Rossi. Detective Gillette, how's the investigation going?"

"Well, until today it wasn't going anywhere." The professional, firm female voice on the other end of the call sounded very optimistic. "One of your coworkers reached out to us this morning after he found something with Electryone's client list."

"Oh?" Matteo glanced toward the door, wondering if his sequestered time with Peyton and his son would soon be coming to an end.

"You asked him to look into everyone Peyton's had professional contact with in the past few months. I'm not sure if he overreached, but he came across Peyton's account with Mr. Emery Josiah. I believe he's a professional matchmaker?"

Matteo cringed. "Um, yeah." He pinched the bridge of his nose. "She signed up with him a while back." Darn it! Peyton was going to strangle him when she found out he was poking around her personal life, however inadvertently. Unless... "Is there something there?"

"Maybe. Three weeks ago, Mr. Josiah's assistant reported a break-in at their office. Her laptop and a few others were stolen. A few days later, their tech guy found malware in their system which, even after they changed password access, gave whoever it was an in. The city's cybercrime investigative unit was able to backtrace the malware and see what files were accessed."

Obviously Peyton's name came up; otherwise the detective wouldn't be calling. "Peyton's?"

"Among others, but it looks as if hers was the only one that got a deep dive. I thought it might be worth mentioning in case you wanted to let Ms. Harrison know. If for no other reason than to speak with Mr. Josiah and verify what information was obtained."

"Yeah, I will." So, someone knew enough about Peyton to be aware that not only had she signed on with a matchmaker, they knew which one she'd used? That couldn't be a coincidence. "Is there anything else? My background checks on Electryone employees haven't turned up anything."

"Right, I got your email," Detective Gillette confirmed. "Reno and I concur—we aren't finding anything concerning there. Doesn't mean we'll stop looking."

"Okay, great." He snapped his fingers. "Oh, one more thing. When was the last time Peyton's data was accessed?"

"A little over forty-eight hours ago. Right before the entire system was reset and cleaned. Those laptops are useless now, at least as a way to get into Josiah's system. They're keeping the trace on them active, but when last checked, they hadn't been used to access the internet. Guy probably realized he'd worn out his welcome and destroyed them."

"Sure." That uneasy knot he'd hoped he'd left behind in California tightened. "I'll let you know if Peyton has any more information that might be helpful. Thanks for calling."

"You bet."

The bathroom door opened as Matteo hung up. Gino came out, a towel wrapped around him like a toga. "Daaaaad. You said you'd bring me my pajamas." Gino stood there in the sitting room, looking seriously grumpy.

"Sorry. Right. Coming up." He patted his son's head as he passed just to confirm he'd washed properly. "Get dressed in here so I can hurry up with my shower, okay?"

Gino nodded. "Can I play with my video game before I go to bed?"

"How about we find you something on TV instead?" Matteo didn't want to charge that video system up unless he absolutely had to. After Gino was in his PJs and Matteo tossed the dirty clothes in the laundry bag in his closet, he found an old cartoon network featuring Matteo's personal favorite crime-solving pooch and hit the shower and changed for bed.

When he emerged, he found Peyton curled up on the sofa next to Gino, a glass of wine in her hand, watching cartoons.

"What did Vilette say?" Matteo asked, scrubbing his damp hair with a towel.

"She said you getting me off my laptop and phone for the rest of the trip might earn you another bonus." She toasted him with the wine. "Congratulations. My turn?"

"Yeah. It's all yours." He backed up against the wall as she passed. "When you get out, we need to talk about something."

"Oh?" Her eyes sparked a bit as her lips curved.

"About the reason we're really here." He hated seeing the humor fade from her face.

"How about you tell me now so I don't over-think and obsess about it in the shower?"

Matteo looked back at Gino, who had that dazed *I'm lost in the story* look in his eyes.

"Okay." He took her arm and pulled her into his bedroom. "I spoke with one of the detectives on your case."

She touched a hand to his chest. "Tell me they've figured out who it is and that we can go home."

"Afraid not." He shouldn't feel quite so good about that, should he? If he was smart, he'd be as anxious as she was to get back to real life, so Gino could get used to his home and school, now that he'd filed for full custody of his son. He could feel the warmth of her touch through his shirt—a shirt he'd purposely worn to avoid any repeat of the other night's kiss when he'd had to admit he saw Peyton as far more than a client he was protecting. "When was the last time you spoke with Mr. Josiah?"

Whatever she'd been expecting, it wasn't that. "The day we got here. He called to let me know he didn't appreciate me taking off unexpectedly when he'd already lined up another three dates."

"He didn't say anything else? Nothing about his system getting hacked?"

Her eyes went cold, and in an instant, he saw the woman he'd met all those weeks ago. Cool, detached. Controlled. "No. He didn't mention anything about that. But that might have been because I offered to double his fee if he'd keep me on as a client."

"He threatened to drop you?"

"Yep." Her fingers gripped his shirt. "Did the hack have something to do with me? It must have—otherwise you wouldn't be telling me all this."

"I'm not one for coincidences. The system's been reset—"

"I know all about reset systems. If they got in once, they can get in again." She pushed away, began to pace. "If whoever it is read my profile, the questionnaire I filled out, they know about me. A lot about me." She stuck her thumb in her mouth, began to chew on her nail. "There were a lot of personal questions I had to answer."

What kind of questions, he wanted to know, then backtracked. None of that was his business. "I have no doubt Mr. Josiah forgot about all that when you threw more money at him."

"Money solves a lot of problems, doesn't it?"

"Actually," Matteo said, and that earned one of her glares, "I've found it ends up creating more problems than it solves. But moving on..."

"Moving on is exactly what I'm going to do." She started to move away, then pivoted back. "Tell me you'll suspend the bet and let me make one more phone call, please."

"Only if you're going to fire Mr. Josiah." Matteo struggled to keep a straight face.

"Fire, sue. Tomato, tomahto. Stay tuned."

WHO KNEW A simple evening spent on the sofa munching on popcorn, sipping wine and watching goofy, nostalgic cartoons could cheer her up?

Peyton looked down at Gino, who had conked out shortly after bowl number two of popcorn and around the same time the old lighthouse keeper was revealed as the latest episode's villain. The little boy's head was in her lap, and he'd stretched out, his feet on his father's. Soon, Gino's mouth was open, and he was snoring, little puffs of air that made Peyton grin.

"He's so cute when he's asleep." She drew her fingers through Gino's hair, felt her cheeks warm when she glanced up and found Matteo watching her. "What?"

He shrugged one shoulder. "You continue to surprise me. A few weeks ago I wouldn't have thought you had a way with children. But you do."

"Like I said before, I like kids." Despite how difficult it was at times to have four younger siblings, she wouldn't have traded her life with them for the world.

"But you don't want any of your own."

She eyed the nearly empty bottle on the table. This conversation was going to require more wine.

"Sorry." He shifted Gino's feet and leaned down to scoop up his son. "None of my business. I'm going to put him in my bed for now. How about another round?"

Of wine or popcorn? She decided to go for both as Matteo disappeared into his bedroom. She clicked off the TV and set the air popper to popping as she uncorked another bottle and topped off their glasses.

"Kid's going to snore like a buzz saw in another few years. Thanks." Matteo toasted her with his glass when he joined her in the kitchenette. "Extra butter this time." He retrieved a stick from the fridge and set it in the microwave to melt.

"Your arteries," she said with a shrug. "About your question."

"That was out of line." He seemed to be avoiding her gaze, and she wasn't sure why. "Sorry."

"No, it's fine. I love kids. I suppose for a long time I felt as if I'd already raised my family, but the truth is, while I was definitely a big part of my sisters' lives, Rudy and my mother did all the heavy lifting. It wasn't their fault I felt responsible."

"And maybe a little guilty?"

She let out a long breath. "Wow. You just cut right to it, don't you?" Suddenly extra butter on the popcorn didn't seem like a bad idea. "Okay, maybe a little. Or a lot. Turns out lies of omission are more damaging than the ones you flat-out tell. For a lot of years, I overcompensated, trying to make up for the fact that our real father wasn't around, even though they didn't know that. I think I felt I owed it to him as much as to them." She sipped her wine, plucked a kernel out of the bowl. "It's difficult, knowing one of your parents chose to walk away from you, from the family, and never looked back."

"You can't be certain of that." Matteo covered her hand with his.

"No, I can't." She kept her gaze locked on their hands. "But I do know what it feels like to be left behind, and while he might not have left me alone, he still left. And that hurts." She pressed her other hand to his. "It's a difficult lesson to learn when you're seven. That the people you love can hurt you so much. It's easier not to get invested at all." She drizzled the butter over the freshly popped popcorn and carried the bowl back to the sofa, this time setting it between them as he joined her.

"Relationships are meant to be messy, Peyton. That's what makes them so rewarding."

"Is that what yours was with your ex-wife? Messy?" She expected pushback, defensiveness. Irritation. Instead, he gave a brief hesitation before he answered.

"Complicated and messy," he confirmed. "I met Sylvia right after I got out of the service. There was a lot of attraction, obviously, and it was such an escape from what the years before had been. She was smart and driven and, well, to be honest, we had absolutely nothing in common. Whatever affection we had for each other was already dwindling when she got pregnant. Marriage just made sense. She had a good job. I'd only started in private security, so I was still finding my footing. Then her job got more and more demanding, and she got more ambitious. It wasn't long before Gino and I were little more than a pit stop in her life. She barely saw him those first two years. Next thing I know, she's offered a job in Japan, and she wants a divorce. Gino was only three. It didn't sit right with me to fight for custody then. Something I regret now. Three months later she's on a plane with our son, and I—"

"You were left alone." Her heart broke for

him. Not over Sylvia. She didn't hear any affection in his voice when he talked about his ex-wife. But the love he projected for his son? There was no mistaking that devotion, even if she hadn't been witness to it the past few days. "Again," she murmured, thinking of his childhood, "I'm so sorry."

"Marriages die. Especially marriages that were doomed from day one," Matteo said with a sad smirk. "And kids get abandoned. That's what's been the worst thing about him being so far away these last few years. I never wanted him to feel as if any of this was my choice. But he's here now. And I'm going to do everything to make sure he stays here."

"Will she fight you for custody?"

"She already is." Matteo drank some more wine. "I haven't been in a good financial position to fight the way I need to." He rubbed his thumb and index finger together. "And she has enough money to keep me in court until Gino's of age. Good custody lawyers are expensive. And so are good schools, which she can afford to keep him in, and I can't."

Peyton bit her lip, reached for a handful of popcorn.

"What?" he asked, ducking his head to look into her eyes. "What's that face?"

"Well." She'd been waiting for the right time to spring this on him. "You know me. When I see a problem I like to tackle it head-on and…"

"Spit it out, Peyton." Matteo's eyes sharpened.

"When I was doing research about dyslexia, I might have emailed a friend of mine who's the dean of a school Electryone's invested in over the years. It's a private academy with a dedicated education department for kids with learning differences. They're one of the best in the country, with a diverse student body and faculty. We helped create education software with them a few years back, and she remembered me and said she can get Gino in once you're back in California."

When he didn't respond, she cringed, pressed on. "I know I'm not his mother or responsible for him in any way. You're his father, and it should be your decision, obviously, but it's an option, and if you have one that helps you with the custody case…"

"How much?"

"Ah, well." Bolstered, Peyton set her glass down and shifted to face him. "Here's where we get into negotiations. The scholarships have already been set for the next school year, but I was thinking—"

"How much?"

She blurted out the cost per year and watched the color drain from his face. "I know! It's a lot, but—"

"A lot? That's a couple months' salary for me." He shook his head. "Look, I appreciate you checking into this, but I'd have to work night and day to put him in that school, and I would never see him, which is what's led to him coming out to Montana with me in the first place. I can't swing it."

"I can. Could." She'd already done the math. She made good money. Really good money. All it was doing now was accumulating and earning interest. This was something she could do, something good. More importantly, she *wanted* to do it.

"You could what?"

"I could swing it. I can pay Gino's tuition. That way you don't have to change your hours, and you can spend as much time with him as you need. Win-win."

"No. Absolutely not."

"No? Oh, come on, Matteo, you can't say no

to this." She reached across to take his hand but found his ice-cold beneath hers. "It's the perfect solution."

"For you, maybe. Not for me. And not for Gino. This isn't something you can just wave your magic wallet around and fix, Peyton. So again, thank you. But no." He pulled his hand free, finished his wine and stood up.

"But—" Magic wallet? Where had that come from?

"Money doesn't solve everything, Peyton. It might make custody fights easier for some—"

"Exactly! It would be leveling the playing field. She wouldn't be able to use your inability to provide for Gino against you." The instant she said it, she realized she'd gone too far. "Wait, Matteo, I didn't mean that the way it sounded."

"Didn't you?" The question was asked as calmly as a windless night, but it made her heart shiver. "I can provide for my son, Peyton. Maybe not as financially fancy as Sylvia and her new husband can, but I can certainly give him the love and attention he's been missing."

"You're being naive if you think that'll be enough to win in court," Peyton tried again.

"That's all I was trying to say." She just wanted him to have every weapon available at his disposal in his fight to keep his son.

"Okay, so let's end this conversation now, before either of us says something we'll regret."

She already regretted it. She continued to regret what she'd let slip even as she cleaned up and popped out the sofa bed for Matteo to deposit a sleeping Gino into.

"Matteo, I'm sorry," she whispered when he headed to his room and they'd turned out the lights. "I didn't mean to offend you."

"I know you didn't." In the pale moonlight streaming through the front windows, she saw him look back at her. "Good night, Peyton."

"YOU WON AGAIN!" Gino whined the next afternoon as he trudged over to retrieve the horseshoes from around the pole. "It's not fair. I'm too little."

"We'll get those muscles of yours built up soon." Peyton waved him back, glancing quickly over at the fence line where Matteo stood watching the horses. He wasn't ignoring her. Not exactly. But he was keeping his distance. "Want to play another round?"

Gino didn't look thrilled at the idea. "Is there something else we can try? Like roping?"

"Roping, yeah, sure." Peyton looked toward the activity shack, where they kept the activity supplies. "Let's see what we can find for that."

Matteo shifted, his gaze following them as she and Gino pulled open the door and began searching through the ropes, saddles, boxes of beanbags and other toys and games.

"Found it!" Gino came up from a bottom shelf, two long ropes in his hands. "I don't know, though." He scrunched his nose. "Maybe I'm too little for this, too?"

"Let's try outside." She turned toward the door only to bump straight into Matteo. "Oh, hi."

"Hi." He peered around her toward his son. "What are you doing?"

"We're going to learn to rope!" Gino announced and stalked past them. "Outside, though. Where we have room."

Peyton offered Matteo a smile. "I don't suppose you know how to rope anything?"

"I used to." He shrugged. "Guess I can find out if I remember."

"I'll leave you to it, then."

"What?" He caught her arm when she tried to pass. "Peyton…"

"You should have some time with your son, Matteo. This is something you can teach him. Something he'll remember. I'll just get in the way." It hurt to say it, more than she expected, but she knew it was the truth. "I'll see you both back in the cabin."

She hurried out, waving to Gino as she passed.

"Where's Peyton going, Dad?" Gino asked his father.

"Nowhere," Matteo said. Before Peyton could turn around, she felt something drop over her head, cinch around her waist and stop her. She faltered, nearly pitching forward as she was tugged back. "Got her."

Gino's laughter danced against her ears as Peyton righted herself. "What on earth?" She tugged at the rope around her waist, then froze when she saw Matteo striding toward her, wrapping the rope up as he drew her in.

"We aren't letting you get away that easily." His voice was low, determined, and sent a chill racing down her spine that had her surrendering to her captor. "I guess I haven't lost it."

"No," Peyton chuckled. "You definitely

haven't." She pulled the rope off and over her head, then dropped it over Gino when he raced over. Beaming up at her, the little boy threw his arms around her waist and squeezed. "All right," she sighed, unable to ignore father and son. "Let the lassoing lessons begin."

"YOU WERE RIGHT."

Considering the past two days Matteo and Peyton had conversed only about ranch happenings, Gino, the injured horse that was rapidly on the mend, or the weather, he needed clarification. "About what exactly?"

He scanned the schedule of events and didn't see anything that would interest Gino, who had begun every morning with an alphabet exercise. Peyton had found a bunch of them on the internet. He'd foregone Gino's workbooks; they only stressed his son out. He'd rather Gino remain excited and positive about the things he was learning instead of what he might be getting wrong.

"About these." Peyton pointed at her severely abused running shoes. "I need boots. Before these disintegrate."

"All right."

"I thought maybe we could head into town

today? Stop at the library? I've heard there's a bakery, too."

Matteo's eyebrow arched. "You're hungry?"

"No. They serve coffee as well." She turned hopeful eyes on him. "Gino? You want to go into town with us?"

"Can't." Gino scribbled letters on his paper. "Rosie doesn't have school today, and she's going to help Katie around the ranch. I want to help, too."

"Oh." Peyton looked suddenly uneasy at her suggestion. "All right, then. I guess I can go on my own."

"No," Matteo said. "You won't. Or have you forgotten why we came here in the first place?"

"We've been in Falcon Creek a week," Peyton said under her breath. "Nothing's happened. No one's shown up looking for me."

"That we know of," Matteo explained. "Going into town seems like a good way to verify that. Come on, G. We'll walk you over. I want to check on the horse, anyway."

"Can't we give her a name already, Dad?" Gino whined. "It's been forever, and we keep calling her *the horse*."

"He's not wrong," Peyton piled on. "Although, it does seem to be a good way to make sure you don't get emotionally attached to her. Anymore than you already are."

"Much the way someone might hire a matchmaker to find them a husband?" Matteo shot back. "Taking emotions out of it?"

Now she smirked. "Not everything has to be messy and complicated. And I learned my lesson there, didn't I?"

"Remains to be seen."

Gino had come over and was frowning at her, then his dad. "Are you two fighting?"

"No," Peyton said and shot a warning look at Matteo. "No, little man, we're just working some things out. Go get your shoes on."

"All right." Gino didn't look convinced that everything was all right. He stopped at the doorway to his father's bedroom, looked back at them. "I don't like fighting. Makes my stomach hurt. And it hasn't hurt once since I've been here."

"Peyton's right, G." Matteo tried not to feel guilty at the accusing glance he got from his son. "We're just being stu—"

Peyton cleared her throat.

"We're just being silly," he corrected through gritted teeth. "Tell your stomach not to hurt. Everything will be fine."

"'Kay." Doubt marred his little forehead before he retrieved his shoes.

A few minutes later, the trio was heading over to the guest lodge. A few minutes after that, Matteo and Peyton were off to town, the uneasy silence continuing to stretch. He didn't like the tension between them. Not this tension, anyway. He missed the Peyton he'd come to know over the past week—the Peyton he considered a friend.

The idea that money had wiggled and wedged its way between them sat like a festering splinter in his heart. "Okay, enough."

"Huh?" Peyton's head shot up and her eyes went wide. "What? I didn't say anything."

"Exactly." He pulled the car over, shoved it into Park and turned in his seat. "We're both being ridiculous. You made an offer, and I declined. Maybe I should have been better at how to say no."

"Maybe." She shrugged. "Or maybe I should have been better at presenting my case. One that wasn't quite so…saviorlike."

"That wasn't what…" He trailed off at her skeptical look. "I don't think that's what bothered me." Although there was something ego-stomping about a successful woman throwing her money around as a solution to his problems. He'd lived like that with Sylvia for years, and he'd grown to resent her for it. He didn't want to resent Peyton. He liked her. A lot. More than a lot.

He could feel himself flinching even as his emotions circled and tried to grab hold. But he wasn't going to let them. Not now. Not ever. Falling for Peyton Harrison was the worst thing he could do for himself and his son. And yet…sitting here, in this truck, beneath the endless Montana sky, staring at the open land, he could feel it happening. That slow, subtle slide into acceptance and affection and…

"We can't pretend the discussion didn't happen."

"Discussion. Argument. Tomato—"

"Tomahto," he ended for her with a grin he found reflected on her face. "I will try to be more open to your financial and educational suggestions for Gino in the future."

She seemed stunned, but then her face cleared, and she nodded. "And I'll try not to be as much of a sledgehammer with my suggestions. Except…can I say one more thing about the school?"

He couldn't help it. He laughed. "Go ahead."

"Will you at least talk to my friend before you walk away from the offer? If the school can work something out with you, I don't know what, but it might be worth finding out."

He wondered, not for the first time, what his heart was thinking by threatening to beat only for this woman. "You just will not let this go, will you?"

"No. Because it's the perfect place for Gino. And I'm sorry, but I kinda love the kid. I know." She held up her hand. "He's not mine, and I'm trying really hard not to overstep, but you have to admit, you're a little out of your element when it comes to hands-on 24/7 parenting, and I think that's part of what your ex is counting on."

"I'm a fast learner." But she had a point. He had no doubt Sylvia had sent Gino to him to catch him off guard and make him appear the less successful parent. "Though, maybe I could use some help. Let's start with the library and go from there, okay?"

"But—"

"I'm not saying no to meeting with your contact from the school," he explained. "I will think about it. Okay?"

She nodded, the smile he'd missed the past few days reappearing. "Just one more thing."

"What?" This woman was going to be the death of him.

"This."

She moved so fast, so smooth, he didn't have time to register she'd grabbed hold of him and was pressing her mouth against his. Like a lightning strike on the parched prairie, instant fire ignited. She didn't take her time, didn't seem to be testing the waters, but she took what she needed from him and kissed him into oblivion.

When she pulled back just enough to press her forehead against his, his mouth tingled from where her lips had been moments before. "Needed to get that out of my system," she whispered. "It's just been—"

"Building," he murmured. "Yeah. I get that." It was already building again. He needed to get this truck moving again before they both took things too far. Or enjoyed it far too much. "Boots. You need to get boots."

"Yep." She slid back over into her seat and settled in as if she hadn't just been practically in his lap. "Move 'em out, cowboy. I've got shopping to do."

THIS IS WHAT happened when she didn't focus on work: she kissed her bodyguard. No, that wasn't entirely true. She'd goaded him, then kissed him. She'd goaded him until he'd pretty much given in, and then she'd kissed him. All part of her plan.

Not.

What alternate personality had taken over in that truck that had her kissing Matteo Rossi as if it were her last act on earth? Probably the same personality that had her realizing this morning that yes, she did need boots, and she was going to get some.

"How do those feel?" Alice Gardner, one of the owners of Brewster Ranch Supply, stood back to admire the simple but elegant embroidered black leather boots. "They look pretty good."

Peyton walked around, rose up on her toes, rocked back on her heels. "They feel great, actually." The leather was sturdy but also soft and yielding. No severe breaking-in time for these puppies, that was for sure. "Yes, I think these are it." She'd only tried on five other styles, but these felt like butter the second she slid into them. "Consider me a convert. Is it okay if I wear them right now?"

"Absolutely. Keep on shopping. I'll ring you up when you're ready."

"Thanks, Alice." Peyton found herself doing a little boot-scootin'-boogie on her way down the aisle where she found Matteo perusing the kids' boots. "Did you find a pair for Gino?"

"What do you think of these?" They were leather with what looked like flames worked into the leather. "They're different. He'll probably outgrow them in a month."

"He'll love them."

"How'd you do?"

"Excellent. What do you think?" She stepped back and kicked out a foot.

"I think I need to use my camera to take photographic evidence. Maybe use as blackmail material once you're back in the office."

She snort-laughed. "Like anyone would believe it was me." The office. Her happiness dipped. Funny how easily she'd acclimated to not focusing on work. Almost an entire week had passed since she'd been plugged into her computer or cell phone for any significant time, and she didn't miss it. Not one bit.

"Afternoon." Alice's husband, Frank, called out as the door opened and jingled a chime.

"Welcome to Brewster's. Anything I can help you find?"

Peyton didn't hear the answer, just a muffled male voice echoing in her ears as she did another tour around the store. This was definitely one-stop shopping, despite the plethora of smaller shops and stores along the main street. Serving ranchers, tourists and residents alike, Brewster's was a treasure trove of items. She had scribbled down a list of potential Christmas gifts she could get for friends and family. Falcon Creek mementos seemed particularly apropos for her sisters, but for now she focused on her work friends and loaded up on homemade jams, jellies, flavored coffees and candy, enough to make up a number of gift baskets once she was back home.

"I'll probably need another suitcase to get all this home," she joked to Matteo when she dropped another load of items on the counter.

"I can package it up and ship it for you," Alice offered. "No need for you to worry about how to transport it back to California."

"Would you really?" Peyton sagged in relief. "That would be amazing. If that's the case..." She grinned at Matteo, who was shaking his head in mock disbelief. "One more tour around the store. Just a little while longer."

"We aren't punching a clock."

"You all staying for the Halloween bash up at the Blackwell Ranch?" Frank asked as his wife began sorting through Peyton's purchases.

"Hope so," Peyton called as she grabbed another few packages of candy. She was looking forward to the party, where she'd no doubt meet the rest of the Blackwell family, including the Gardners' daughter Grace, who was married to Ethan Blackwell.

She felt something prickle the back of her neck, something that made her jump. She spun around, looking behind her, but there was no one there. But there had been. She could have sworn...

"You're just being paranoid," she muttered to herself and shook off the unease, tried to refocus. "Let's get this list finished."

CHAPTER TWELVE

"Now, IF YOUR boy doesn't like those boots, you bring him in and we'll find something that works," Alice assured Matteo as he paid for not only the boots he found for Gino but also for a pair he bought himself. He hadn't planned to get them—however, seeing as there would be more activities where boots would be far more practical to wear, he surrendered.

He'd found a pair of boots almost identical to ones he remembered seeing when he was a kid. A pair he'd longed to be able to afford in the little town near where he'd been raised. A pair that, at the time, had cost an unimaginable amount of money. They were tan with intricate stitching that reminded him of lines on a map or compass, all leading somewhere and nowhere at the same time.

It was funny, he thought, as he stuffed his sneakers into the bag Alice provided, how he'd assumed being back on a ranch would break him. Instead, he'd found a new strength he hadn't known he possessed. A strength he felt fairly certain came from two sources: his son and Peyton.

Peyton. He blew out a breath. What was he going to do about Peyton? He knew what was behind that kiss. Gratitude, pent-up frustration and…affection…attraction. This was so bad, he thought. Did a woman who outsourced her marital possibilities even believe in love? It didn't matter, couldn't matter, how he felt about her. They were from two vastly different worlds, both in their upbringing and their lifestyles.

Not that he knew what the future held, but if he landed that promotion at work, he could find himself at one of the home offices either in New York or Los Angeles. He'd go wherever the top work would take him; he'd have to, in order to give Gino the best chance he could. Wherever he could put down some roots for him and his son and make a life for both of them. But a life that could include Peyton…

"Afternoon." Frank greeted the man behind Matteo.

"Sorry." Matteo shifted to put his credit card away. "I'm causing a traffic jam."

"No problem. Just these, please." The man placed a backpack, a few bottles of water, a pair of trail boots and a map of the area onto the counter.

"Nice time of year for hiking," Matteo said, admiring the man's watch. He liked antiques, especially ones that looked as if they might have been passed down from family members. Probably because he'd never had anything like that. What would he hand down to Gino? he wondered.

"Should be," the man agreed. His hair was long, unkempt, almost overgrown to the point of obscuring his features, which were hidden behind a dark beard. His clothes were clean but wrinkled, and he looked as if he'd been traveling a lot of miles. He kept his head low as he paid for his purchase and turned away from Matteo without waiting for a bag. Matteo frowned. Something about the guy seemed familiar.

"Have a good day," Alice called after him.

"Seen him in here before?" Matteo asked.

"First time," Frank replied. "Little jittery if you ask me, you know?"

Matteo agreed. He knew. Peyton headed toward him carrying another armload of candy. There was enough to open her own sweetshop. But it was the look on her face that had him moving forward to help. "You all right?"

"Yeah." She shrugged. "Just felt something weird. Like I was being watched. Probably just my mind playing tricks on me."

Matteo wasn't so sure. "I'll be right back." He left his things with Peyton and headed outside just as the man pulled away in a small red pickup. Matteo yanked out his phone and snapped a picture of the model and license plate, but he didn't hold out much hope when he noticed most of the plate was covered— perhaps purposely—in a thick layer of mud. The exhaust spewing from the tailpipes was a shocking contrast to the fresh air he'd been inhaling in recent days.

"Truck like that is on its last legs," an old man sitting on the porch observed. "I'm Pop. You see a sketchy-looking feline around here, that'll be Whiskers." He held out his hand, motioned for Matteo to join him for a game of chess.

"Nice to meet you, Pop." Recognizing a valuable asset when he saw one, he joined him, made an instinctive move with a pawn to queen's knight four. "Have you seen that truck around before?"

"Couple of times over the last day or so. First was early yesterday morning. I remember because I'd just finished my first cup of coffee." He examined the board, looked up at Matteo, made a move. "You staying at the Blackwell Ranch?"

"Yes, sir." Matteo sat forward, countered on the board and earned a look of approval. "Thought we'd come in and pick up some books and stuff for my son. He stayed back to hang out with a friend he's made."

"Let me guess. That'd be little Miss Rosie Blackwell. Girl is full of charm." Pop cackled as Whiskers wandered over and examined Matteo's boots before rubbing its head against his leg. Matteo gave the cat a scratch behind the ears, earning a healthy, grateful purr. "They must be gearing up for that Halloween bash they've got planned."

"I believe so," Matteo confirmed. "We've got pumpkin carving tomorrow." Along with a string of other activities designed to get the ranch in festive shape. "You plan on attending?"

"Son, the entire town will be there, you can

count on it. That Hadley, now she can put on a party like no one's business. And hey, you're distracted now. Got ya." He made another move, shaking his head.

Peyton arrived.

"Shoulda known you'd be one of Big E's new granddaughters. Peyton, is it?"

Matteo smiled as Peyton's cheeks flushed. "My reputation precedes me, it seems. Yes. Hi, Pop." She grinned. "It's a pleasure to meet you. Lily warned me about you. You're a chess shark."

"Shark? Nah," Pop said. He seemed entertained by the notion. "Just something to keep the time passin'. Speaking of passin', nice of you to come out to Falcon Creek and get to know your family. Strong roots here in Montana. You Blackwells, you've made a good place for yourselves in the world."

"So have the Harrisons," Peyton corrected, not willing to abandon the name of the man who had raised her. "No disrespect intended."

"None taken," Pop assured her. "You play better than your man here?"

Matteo sat back in his chair, beamed up at her and reveled in her confusion. "Yeah, honey, do you play better than me?"

"I play well enough to know you left your bishop vulnerable." She made one move that had Pop falling silent. She bent over and whispered in the older man's ear. "Check."

"Well, I'll be," Pop muttered, scrubbing a hand across his chin. "Did not see that coming."

"We'll be seeing you at the bash, Pop." Matteo patted the man's shoulder as he passed, taking both their bags from Peyton to stash in the SUV. "Next stop, library."

"Did you talk to the young guy who just left?" she asked.

"No." He didn't bother pretending he didn't know who she was talking about. Whatever she'd felt back in that store was still written all over her face. "He drove off pretty quick." Matteo didn't believe in coincidences, and he'd talked enough with Hadley to know they weren't expecting a flood of guests until Halloween. Still...it couldn't hurt to check things out.

"I WAS NOT cut out for this." Peyton stood at the end of the hay-filled, restored historic wagon and gnawed on her lower lip. As expected, her boots had been the best purchase she'd made in she couldn't remember how long—her brand-new footwear making the activities she, Gino and Matteo had participated in on the ranch more enjoyable, at least.

But the idea of spending the next few hours being jostled about in a wagon filled with hay...

"You got back on a horse," Lily said from behind her. "You can do this." She planted her hands on Peyton's back and gave her a none-too-gentle sisterly shove. "It's hay, Peyton. Not toxic waste."

"Hay itches." Peyton tugged the sleeves of her yellow sweater down over her hands and climbed up. "When I researched hayrides online, I saw wagons with benches back here." She shuffled through the ankle-deep hay, making her way toward the front—or was it the back?—of the wagon.

"This one's more fun," Lily said. "And more authentic. Besides, the benches hurt your backside after a few bumps."

Deciding to make the best of it, Peyton nestled herself into the corner, reluctantly admitting the hay did provide a nice cushion. She could feel the temperature dropping even now as the sun finished its dip in the sky, casting the ranch in an amazing haze of autumn red, orange and yellow. It was like living in a painted picture that shifted from day to day.

"Is Conner coming?" she asked her sister.

"No." Lily hoisted herself up and plopped down into the hay next to Peyton. "His mom's had a bad day, so he's sticking close to home, hoping to keep her off her feet. Where are your two tagalongs?"

"Helping Hadley with the snacks." Although personally, Peyton didn't think she could eat another bite. One thing was for sure: no one starved on a guest ranch. Sure enough, as she stretched her neck and looked over the edge of the wagon, she saw Matteo and Gino joint-carrying a picnic basket, Ty right behind them. "Are we it for the ride?" she asked Ty as he pulled himself up onto the bench behind the horses and braced one foot on the buckboard.

"We're it," Ty announced.

"Up you go." Matteo hefted Gino into the wagon before jumping up himself. He pulled the gate closed behind him. "Gino..."

Gino had already deposited himself onto Peyton's lap.

"Gino, give Peyton some space. We've got the entire wagon—"

"He's fine." Peyton wrapped her arms around the little boy and drew him closer.

Lily aimed a sly look in her direction, but Peyton purposely ignored her.

"Hadley made caramel corn and apple slices," Gino announced. "And we have root beer and—"

"And enough sugar to keep him awake for a month," Matteo finished as he took a seat near Peyton with enough room between them for Gino should he change his mind.

"All set?" Ty called over his shoulder. "Here we go."

"Tell me again what the purpose of this is?" Peyton asked her sister, who had shifted into the other corner of the wagon and was already looking up at the still-darkening sky.

Lily shook her head, closed her eyes for a moment. "To enjoy yourself, Pey. When was the last time you paused to look up at the stars?"

Peyton grabbed hold of the edge of the wagon as it moved forward and answered without thinking. "With Dad. When I was Gino's age."

"You were seven when Dad…" Lily drew her head up. "You don't mean Rudy, do you?"

Peyton glanced to Matteo for support, but found him staring up at the sky, seemingly uninterested in the sisters' conversation.

"No," Peyton said quietly. "I mean Thomas. He used to point out the constellations and planets to me. He was partial to Orion and Gemini."

"The hunter and the twins." Matteo's observation told her he was paying attention after all.

"Constellations are stars, right, Dad?" Gino leaned forward and out of Peyton's grasp, scooting closer to his father. "Can we see them now?"

"Soon," Matteo said. "It needs to be a bit darker."

"You've never seen stars like you do out here," Ty said over his shoulder. "People who live in the city are always amazed at how dark it can get and how bright the stars are."

Peyton pressed a hand against her chest, trying to touch her suddenly heavy heart. "He was a good man, Lily," she whispered to her sister. "I don't remember a lot about him, but I do remember he loved us. I can still feel that, when I let myself."

Lily leaned her head on Peyton's shoulder,

wrapped her arms around her and squeezed. "Tell me what else you remember about him."

Peyton's eyes filled, at both the memories and the sound of Matteo pointing out different aspects of the sky to his son. And the look of complete wonder and trust on Gino's face.

"Tell me, Peyton," Lily said.

"What do you want to know?"

"Everything," Lily answered without a hint of anger or resentment in her voice. "I want to know everything."

IT WAS TOO QUIET. Yep. That's what her problem was.

It was too darned quiet.

Peyton flopped over in bed and stared at the bedside clock. Two in the morning. She and Matteo and Gino had said good-night soon after getting back from the hayride, and yet here she still lay, hours later, waiting for her mind to stop circling so she could get to sleep.

What was it about the late-night hours that reactivated her brain? All the worry, all the concerns, the responsibilities and regrets all seemed to wake up and tap an irritating dance inside her head.

All these years she'd feared the distance the

truth about their real father would create between her and her sisters, but tonight, for the first time, the subject of Thomas Blackwell had brought her and Lily together. Closer than they'd been in a while. She had the stars and the moon to thank for that. Along with a hayride and Matteo teaching his son the same lessons her own father had taught her.

Matteo. Peyton sighed and squeezed her eyes shut. He was just…everywhere. And when he wasn't, she missed him. Missed him! How was that even possible?

At least at home she could have clicked on the television for background noise. But here? No TV in her room. She was banned from her phone and her laptop and…

It was just too darned quiet.

She grabbed a pillow and dropped it over her face, resisting the urge to scream. Matteo had been strangely quiet and reserved once they got back to the ranch. And why shouldn't he be, considering she'd kissed him again. She'd managed to short circuit her own system doing so. Maybe she'd done the same to him. Still… She took a hot, stuffy breath in. It wasn't exactly something she would regret. Not too much, anyway.

She sat up, shoved her hair out of her face and sighed. She needed—wanted—to be doing something, and while she'd agreed to help Hadley with the bushel of pumpkins that had arrived today for the Halloween party next week, she couldn't very well start hacking now.

She could go next door to the cabin and wake Lily up. Her sister was more than used to Peyton's midnight strolls and need for distraction, but they'd had enough family bonding for one night, and she didn't want to interfere in anyone getting a good night's sleep.

She caught her lower lip in her teeth, glanced longingly at the door. It wouldn't be difficult to creep out and sneak her laptop into her room, then put it back before Matteo got up. Okay, sure, she was reneging on their bet, but it was either that or go mad. Of course, she could have solved the problem today at the library and added books for herself when she'd been gathering up a bunch for Gino. But Gino had been her primary focus. She hadn't even thought about herself.

"A few hours won't hurt," she whispered to herself and slid out of bed. "He'll never know." Her door creaked as she pulled it open. She froze, waiting for Matteo to respond. The man had ears like bat sonar. But when his door remained closed, she breathed easier. With the moonlight streaming in through the windows, she tiptoed around the sofa bed where Gino slept and approached the kitchenette table. She clicked on the small desk lamp she'd brought in from her bedroom.

She'd just unplugged her computer when she heard what sounded like crying coming from behind her. Instinct had her abandoning her laptop. Gino's breathing wasn't quite so even now, and he was thrashing about as if he'd gotten caught up in a nightmare. "No. No, Mama. I don't wanna go. Don't make me go. I wanna stay with Daddy."

"Gino?" Peyton sat on the springy mattress and rested a gentle hand on his shoulder. "Gino, wake up, sweetheart. It's just a dream."

"No, Mama, no." His gut-wrenching sob struck Peyton right in her heart.

"Gino, wake up. Come on." She took hold of his hand, rested her other on his cheek as he blinked awake. "Hey. It's all right, Gino. You're fine. You're safe here with your father."

"Peyton?" He didn't sound convinced she

was real. He scrubbed his hands into his eyes, down his damp cheeks. "It's really you?"

"It is, baby." She tucked him onto her lap the way she used to with Fiona when she had bad dreams. She rocked him, smoothing his hair as he curled into her. Clung to her. "Bad dreams are the worst, aren't they?" Especially when they feature people who are supposed to do what's best for us. "Do you want to tell me about it?"

"I don't want to go to boarding school."

"All right." She nodded.

"Mama and Jiro argued about it. Really loud. Mama said that she made up her mind and that I'd be going. Because she doesn't want me anymore. She's having a new baby."

Peyton squeezed her eyes shut, clinging to Gino as much as he continued to hold on to her. "Just because she's having a new baby doesn't mean she doesn't want you, Gino." She pressed her lips against his temple. "It just means things are going to change."

"I heard her say it." Gino sniffed. "I was s'posed to be asleep, but I heard her and Jiro talking. Don't let them send me away. I want to stay with Daddy."

"I know you do, little man." She took a deep

breath. "And your father's going to do everything he can to make that happen. You know that, right?"

"I guess. Boarding school sounds scary. They put you in a room with other kids. Like all the time. I like my own room. And it's not like home at all. I wouldn't have any of my things, and I wouldn't see Mama or Jiro anymore." He'd started crying again, hiccuping to the point of coughing.

"You're not going to go to boarding school," Peyton whispered. It was so hard, so impossibly hard, not to cast judgment on Matteo's ex-wife. How could she even think about sending a six-year-old off to boarding school? It seemed so...cruel. "You know how I know you're not?"

"No."

"Because neither your father nor I will let that happen." It was a promise she shouldn't make, but she couldn't help herself. Gino's brain, his heart, couldn't take the constant uncertainty of his future. He needed stability. He needed a place for his roots to take shape and begin to grow. He needed his father. Just as she'd had Rudy after her own dad had left; as much as she'd missed Thomas Blackwell, as much as she may have disagreed with her mother's choice to keep him a secret from her sisters, when all was said and done, Rudy had been the steadying force her life had needed. "Do you trust me, Gino?"

She felt him nod against her chest. "Yeah."

"I take that very seriously, Gino. Because I know how hard it is to do." So hard. Sometimes impossibly hard to trust. "So I want you to believe me when I tell you that I'm going to do everything I can to make certain you stay with your father."

"And no boarding school?"

"No boarding school. You will still have to go to school, though." She looked down at him, felt her heart flutter when he gave her a teasing grin.

"I don't have to go to school. You're teaching me good. So's Daddy. I can already do my alphabet."

"And we want you to keep getting better. So, how about we make a deal. You stop worrying about boarding school, and I'll see what I can do about making sure you can stay with your dad."

"And you?" Gino asked, pinching his fingers around her hand. "I wanna stay with you, too."

She snuggled him closer. "I appreciate that, little man." More than her heart could take. "But I'm not your mom. And you and your dad will have great adventures together on your own." Her chest hurt, the regret pressing in on her. She wasn't in a position to promise anything other than what she had. As much as she'd come to love Gino, care about Matteo—and she cared about him a lot—she knew a family, a husband, children, it wasn't in the cards for her. She'd chosen her path a long time ago. She was doing what she loved to do, what she wanted to do. Asking for more, for the impossible, wasn't fair. To anyone.

"You think you can get back to sleep now?"

"Uh-huh." He yawned, but when she went to shift him back into bed, he grabbed hold of her. That lost-little-boy expression spoke to her. She'd known, from the moment he'd appeared with his father on her doorstep, that he was going to slide into her life, into her heart. Now she remembered worrying that Gino would be the one to get hurt when she and Matteo went their separate ways. Little did she know she'd be dealing with fallout, too.

She'd be lying to herself if she didn't admit to fantasizing about a family of her own, but it was one she'd never let herself be a part of. She was too driven. Too selfish. Too…her own person to try to be something she wasn't. She skimmed a hand over Gino's forehead. She couldn't be everything he and Matteo needed. But she could do everything in her power to make sure father and son remained together.

"Would you feel better if I stayed with you until you do?"

He nodded, his fingers loosening as he scooted over to make room for her. She barely had time to stretch out before he rolled toward her again, curling into her as if she was his shelter in the storm. "I love you, Peyton."

"I love you, too, little man." Despite knowing it was the wrong thing, despite fearing she was only setting herself up for heartbreak, she relaxed and waited for him to fall asleep.

She then slipped from the sofa bed, retrieved her laptop and cell phone and got to work digging up contact information for Matteo's ex-wife.

"I'M GOING TO need a shower just from carving pumpkins."

Matteo glanced up from his laptop as Peyton walked in, hands and shirt covered in what he hoped was pumpkin guts. "You know where it is." His gaze flicked back to his screen, but he kept an ear on her.

"I was only joking." She beelined for the kitchen sink and washed up. "Gino's having a ball helping Hadley and her staff carve pumpkins for Halloween. Definitely something for you to keep in mind next year when you have him all to yourself. What are you doing?"

"Reading up on wireless hacking and malware location programs."

"Oh, sexy. You know, Electryone helped develop software security for programs like that. You can email Todd for the information."

"Already did." He managed a quick smile. "You all have that antimalware app on your phones, don't you?"

"Sure do. We don't endorse or work on projects we don't take on ourselves. Why?" She came up behind him. "What's this about?"

He hesitated. He could lie. Maybe he should, but trust worked both ways. She'd trusted him with her safety. He needed to trust her with the truth. He reached back for her hand and drew her around the table. "I'm trying to figure out how someone tracked you to Montana."

Her eyes narrowed, suspicion almost overtaking the flash of fear. Almost. She lowered herself into the chair, dish towel clutched in her lap. "You think someone followed us out here after all?"

"I do. And I'm pretty sure they used your own security program to do it."

"But...the only people who have access to that side of things would work..." She trailed off, her confused eyes easy to read.

"For Electryone. Yes." He nodded. "I've already been in touch with Vilette, and I'm having my people take another run at all Electryone employees. In the meantime, I need you to give me access to your phone."

"Sure." She rose and retrieved her cell from where she'd stashed it next to Gino's now-forgotten video game, rattled off her pass code. "It's my sisters' birthdays. In case you need it again."

He tapped the screens, deactivated the security app she'd installed, then accessed her IP information to delete her locations. The damage was probably already done, but better safe than sorry. "How did you leave things with Mr. Josiah?"

"Ambiguous," she said with a hint of venom

in her voice. "That tends to happen after the topic of a lawsuit is broached."

Considering how razor-sharp her tongue could be, he imagined Mr. Josiah carried a few wounds from the conversation. "I'm going to need you to call him, so he'll give us access to his computer system."

She snorted. "I don't see that happening. He's gone to ground."

"Then, I'll talk to him. I need to see your file."

Her eyes narrowed.

"What?" he asked.

"Just wondering if this is a professional or personal inquiry."

"As in, am I curious about potential competition?" He smiled and took inappropriate pleasure in the flush that crept up her cheeks. Unable to resist the temptation of her full mouth, Matteo stood, walked around, bent down and pressed his lips against hers. That instant heat flared up again, proving the chemistry between them wasn't anywhere close to going dormant. He eventually broke the kiss. "I'm feeling pretty secure about myself these days in that area."

"I'll bet you are," she said with a roll of her

eyes. "Does this whole tracking thing have something to do with you disappearing after lunch this afternoon?"

"I wanted to check on that truck I saw yesterday." He returned to his chair. "The guy from the store. I asked around at a few of the businesses in town if they'd seen him. No luck. I even spoke with the manager at the motel just outside of town, but no one remembers seeing him or the truck after yesterday afternoon."

"Maybe he was just passing through."

"Maybe." But his gut didn't agree. Not by a long shot. "A truck like that, he can camp out in it easy. Doesn't need to find a place to hole up."

"Which also makes finding him more difficult." She frowned. "You know, we still haven't answered the question we had back in California. What is it this guy thinks I've done?"

"Something I plan to ask him when I track him down. From now on, I want you sticking close to the lodge, to Hadley and Ty and Katie. The more people around, the better. And just…"

"Be aware of anyone unfamiliar? Should be easy enough on a guest ranch."

"There's one other thing." He hesitated to mention it, but he needed as many advantages as he could get. "We have to come clean about why you really came out here. I want to talk to the local sheriff, and then we need to tell the Blackwells."

She sighed, sat back in her chair and, for a second, looked as if she was going to pout. "There's really no way to keep this to ourselves?"

"There is. But I don't think you'd forgive yourself if this guy came after you, and Lily or Rosie or someone else on the ranch got hurt somehow. Especially if you could have done something as minor as coming clean to prevent it."

"Not to mention Gino," Peyton said, and he nodded. "All right. We'll tell them. And while you're at it, you might want to think about giving Big E a call and filling him in. Just one thing." She held up her index finger. "Let me tell Lily? She's going to be ticked enough to hear I've lied to her again. I'd rather you stay out of that crossfire. I'll speak to her first thing in the morning."

"Deal."

"THERE YOU GO. Here's another one, Goldie." Peyton shifted another apple free of her jacket pocket and held it out for the horse to gobble. She stroked Goldie's nose, offering a smile of comfort as the animal shifted and tried to nuzzle closer.

"Never thought I'd see the day you surrendered your laptop for a saddle."

Peyton flinched at Lily's comment. They'd reformed a bond the other night on the hayride. She hated the idea of damaging that now. "I haven't. Not permanently." She gave the horse another pat and stepped back. "I lost a bet with Matteo, so I'm technology-free for the rest of my stay." For the most part. Not that Matteo needed to know she'd spent over an hour on the phone this morning with his exwife. He would. Soon enough. It wasn't something she'd be able to keep secret.

"So, I'm a distraction? That's why you had Hadley call me to come over this morning?"

"Yep." She walked over to Matteo's rescue horse and set the last apple she'd taken from breakfast on the ledge of the stall door. "Hadley didn't come down with you?"

"No. She's checking in a last-minute guest."

"Gino and I are going on a shorter trail walk

this morning with some of the day guests. But before we do…" Peyton hedged. "There's something I need to tell you. Something I probably should have told you from the start but…"

"Finally." Lily crossed her arms and leaned against the wood-paneled wall. "I knew you were keeping something from me. Let me guess. Matteo's not your *assistant*."

Peyton's face flushed before she turned around and saw her sister waggling her eyebrows. "No, he's not."

"Note my shocked face." Lily rolled her eyes. "Like anyone believes that. No one has an assistant who looks like that. So, why all the secrecy? Is this about Dad bugging us to get married? You're using Matteo as a decoy? Oh! Did you meet Matteo through that matchmaker dude you've been working with?"

"No, I did not!" The very idea of Matteo joining up with a matchmaking service… She had to struggle not to laugh. "Matteo's my… well, he's my—"

"Spit it out already! The sooner you admit it, the better off we'll all be. He's your boyfriend."

"Bodyguard," Peyton said it at the same

time. "Matteo is my bodyguard. See, there's been this thing going on at work..." And from there, the entire story spilled out like the floodgates had opened. "I know I promised when I got here that I wouldn't lie to you anymore, and I probably shouldn't have." She moved closer until she was standing nose to nose with her little sister. "But I didn't want you, any of you, to worry, but now Matteo thinks—"

"Stop, Peyton." Lily rested her hands on Peyton's shoulders and squeezed. "Just stop and breathe."

"Right." She was normally so controlled, so utterly and completely, that she came across as robotic at times. But around her sisters and those she cared about the most, it was as if her emotions surged to the surface and broke free on their own. "Okay. Breathing." She inhaled slowly. "I guess I thought the faster I got it out the less you'd be ticked at me for lying to you again."

"Well, there is a slight difference between not wanting to tell us there's some scary guy out there looking for you and keeping our paternity a secret." Lily looked amused enough to be joking. Almost. "But just so we're clear."

She leaned closer and frowned. "Are you all right? How dangerous is this guy?"

Peyton shrugged. "Not sure. My boss was convinced it wasn't something to ignore, then Big E stuck his nose in, and Matteo chimed in, so…" She waved her arms in the air. "Here I am."

"While I don't like the idea of anyone coming after you, I'm grateful you came here. I like having you around. You seem different. More relaxed since you got here. Must be that lack of computer time, or…" She arched a brow. "Are you sure Matteo isn't anything more than your bodyguard?"

Peyton's face flushed, negating any protest she might have made.

"I knew it." Lily's face split into a huge grin. "Oh, this is going to make a great video chat tonight when I call Amanda." She tucked her arms around Peyton and led her out of Ethan's clinic and into the fresh air. "Let's back up, start at the beginning. And don't leave a single detail out."

"So, YOU'RE TELLING us that our grandfather's solution to Peyton being stalked was to send her out here to us?" Ben Blackwell leaned back in his desk chair at his law office and aimed a particularly irritated gaze at Matteo. "Without telling us the real reason she's here."

"Pretty much." Matteo wondered if Ben Blackwell had any idea how similar he was to Big E, with maybe a bit haughtier edge than the old man. Matteo had to give the brothers credit, though. When he'd talked to Ty yesterday and asked to meet with Peyton's cousins—three of whom had yet to even meet her—he'd put it together pretty darn quick. Then again, Matteo got the impression mentioning Big E's involvement moved things into top speed.

Ethan and Ty sat on the sofa, silent as ghosts as Jon and Chance stood nearby, tension wafting off them in waves. It was odd, Matteo thought, to see Chance Blackwell, award-winning, bestselling music artist standing in a wood-paneled lawyer's office in the middle of a tiny town in Montana. About as odd as Matteo felt standing there himself.

Theirs was a family history further disrupted by the reveal of Thomas Blackwell and his five grown daughters. Family dynamics, Matteo thought. Both intriguing and…confusing.

"And now you're saying you're pretty sure

whoever has been targeting her followed her to Montana?" Jon said in a slow, deliberate manner.

"I can't prove it. Yet," Matteo admitted. He also had to admit the five brothers together felt a bit intimidating. And for a man who had seen combat duty and protected various high-status clients, he was impressed. "But I've been in the protection business long enough to know not to ignore my gut. It's just by chance we saw him in town the other day. I've given a description to your local sheriff, but I'm not sure what good that'll do."

"Was Louise manning the station's front desk?" Ty asked.

"Yeah." He'd met the middle-aged, silver-haired woman just a few hours ago.

"Then, you did the right thing," Ethan said with a humorless laugh. "By now everyone in Falcon Creek knows what's going on and who to be on the lookout for. He can't keep hidden for long if that's what he's trying to do. Man either has no idea about small towns, or—"

"Or he doesn't care," Ben finished. "The police back in California don't have any idea why Peyton's been targeted?"

"No." And that only added to Matteo's frustration. His call to the detectives this morning had only left everyone with more questions. "Look, I don't want any of you to think I was purposely putting any of you or your families in danger."

"We don't," Ty said. "But this situation does explain a whole lot. Like why you wanted the tour of the property."

"Just wanted to be aware of access points and how the property lines were secured."

"We might want to have the ranch hands do a check to be safe," Ben suggested to Ty, who was already pulling out his cell phone. "Tell them to watch for the truck. The more eyes we have on—"

"Watch." The word turned Matteo's blood to ice. "Watch. That was it. That's what I remember seeing."

"What's he talking about?" Chance asked as Matteo grabbed his case and hauled out his laptop.

"I knew there was something I couldn't connect," Matteo muttered as he powered up and waited to access the file for the security footage from Electryone. "The guy who delivered the flowers to Peyton's office."

"The guy whose face you couldn't see?"

"Yes." Matteo clicked to fast-forward through the tape. Then stopped it, zoomed in. His heart picked up speed as the pieces began to fall into place. "There." He tapped the screen. "Right there. His watch. That's an antique. A distinctive one. And the guy at Brewster's was wearing one just like it."

"Wearing something like that tells me it has sentimental value," Chance said.

"I don't know many stalkers who suffer from sentimentality," Ben chimed in.

"Know that many of them, do you?" Jon asked innocently.

Ben glared. "Still don't have a face to go with the watch, though, do you?"

"No," Matteo agreed. "But it's something else to add to the list."

"You should call Peyton. See if maybe she recognizes it."

"She and Gino went out trail riding a few hours ago," Ty said before Matteo could. He glanced at his watch. "They aren't scheduled to be at the ranch for another hour or so."

"Besides," Matteo added. "She doesn't have her cell phone." And that could be Matteo's one miscalculation in all this. How could he have slipped so badly? Separating her from her phone could put her in direct danger.

"Still couldn't hurt to call someone," Ben suggested.

"I'll phone Hadley," Ty said. "Chance, you call Katie. Find out for sure where Peyton is. And fill them in on the rest. We'll make sure Peyton isn't alone."

"Right." Chance pulled out his cell.

"I should have said something sooner," Matteo confessed. "I could have used all your help."

"You did what you thought was right at the time," Ben told him. "Look, if you want to beat yourself up about it, no skin off my nose, but keep in mind, Big E didn't let on to any of us. And he would have if he thought she was in trouble up here." He pulled out his cell when it rang, turned his back on them to answer it.

"True. Our grandfather's many things," Jon said, "but he'd never put his family in jeopardy. He sent you guys here because he thought it was the safest place for Peyton to be." Jon rested a hand on Matteo's shoulder. "If she wasn't safe before, she definitely is now. You tell us what we need to do to keep her safe, and we're with you."

"That's good to hear."

"You thought we'd say otherwise?" Ethan's arched brow noted irritation. "She's family, Matteo. She's ours. Family you've taken it upon yourself to protect. That goes a long way with us."

"Heads up." Chance held his phone against his chest. "Katie got a call from the trail guide. Gino has an upset stomach, so Peyton and he headed back to the ranch a little over a half hour ago."

"Another reason for me to head over there now," Matteo said, but before he logged off, he sent a screenshot of the video to Peyton via email. "I'll try calling her on the way."

"Hold up." Ben held up his hand as Matteo packed up his laptop, finished talking to whomever had called him. "We're coming, too. That was the sheriff. He just got a call from Ship Haply, who was driving into town earlier. He spotted the guy's truck this morning." He grabbed his jacket and stopped long enough to add, "It was on the way to the ranch."

CHAPTER THIRTEEN

"I'M SORRY I throwed up." Gino rested his cheek against Peyton's shoulder as she carried him to the cabin from the stables. "I didn't mean to get sick."

"These things happen, little man." Peyton hefted him up higher and tried not to admit to herself just how heavy a six-year-old could be. Clearly she needed to up her weight lifting at the gym. "Let's consider pancakes off the menu for a while, though, okay?"

"I told you I could eat four."

Peyton pinched her lips together to stop from laughing. "Yes, you did." Too bad they hadn't stayed down. Seeing Gino be sick over the side of his horse had felt both worrying and unsurprising. She'd spent her childhood growing up with someone in her family having an upset stomach, ankle sprain or acne at any given time. Peyton reached up and pressed her hand against Gino's forehead. "I don't think you have a fever. We'll get you cleaned up, and you can have a nap. I bet you'll be feeling better in no time."

"I feel okay now." He locked his arms around her neck. "Just sleepy."

"Noted." She climbed the porch stairs and had them inside the cabin in record time. "You know the drill." She set him down and turned on the water in the bathroom. "Strip and into the shower. We'll bundle you up, and you can take a nap in your dad's bed, okay?"

"Mm-kay." He sighed and trudged inside.

"And stand under the water," she added, remembering that was one of those details Matteo had begun to specify. "Oh, and don't forget the soap." She ducked into her own room, changed into a T-shirt and kicked off her boots, which, she had to admit, had been a blessing today. "Chalk one up to Matteo being right."

The buzzing from the other room had her walking into the kitchen barefoot. Her phone light was blinking, and when she pulled it off the top of the fridge, she found four missed calls from Matteo. And just as many voice mails. She was about to call him back when he called again.

"Hey. Sorry," she said as a greeting. "We had a bit of a—"

"Yeah, I heard," Matteo said. "Is Gino all right?"

"He's fine. Pancake overdose." She strained to hear. "He's in the shower now, then I'm going to put him down for a nap. What's going on?"

"So, you're back in the cabin. Okay." He sounded so relieved she couldn't help but be confused. "I guess that's good. I'm coming back now, but I need you to check your email."

She hesitated. "Is this some kind of trick?"

"No, it's not a trick," he snapped, then sighed. "Sorry. Just…check your email, okay? Open the picture I sent you."

"Hang on. I need to turn my computer on." She set the phone down and opened her laptop. A few minutes later she clicked on his email. She frowned. This didn't make any sense. She stared at it for countless moments trying to find something that seemed familiar or she could identify…

She heard Matteo calling her name over the phone. "Sorry. I've pulled it up. What am I looking at? I don't see anything—"

"The watch, Peyton. Look at his watch."

Peyton clicked to enlarge the image. Her breath caught in her chest.

"You recognize it, don't you?" Matteo demanded.

Her mind raced, flashing back to a night a few weeks before. The night Big E had shown up at the restaurant on one of her dates. Her date...

"Yes," she breathed, her hand shaking on the touch pad. "Um." Her thoughts spun in and around each other. "His name. What was his name?" She could hear the engine of Matteo's SUV rev up, along with another voice. "Is someone with you?"

"Chance. We're heading back to the ranch now. I need you to tell me—"

"Chance Blackwell is in your car?" She practically squealed as her mind began to clear. "I can't meet him like this! He's—"

"He's your cousin, not made of solid gold. And if you don't tell me what I want to know, I'm going to put him on the phone with you right now."

"Fine. It was my date that night at Toscanini's. Um." She pinched the bridge of her nose, tried to remember. "Shurley. Gabriel Shurley. He was a last-minute matchup from Mr. Josiah. He had a watch like the one in the picture." She heard a creak from the front porch. "You weren't kidding. That was fast." She headed for the door.

"What was fast?" Matteo asked.

"You. You're back already."

"Peyton—"

She pulled open the door. And froze.

"Peyton?" Matteo's voice yelled through the cell.

She met Gabriel's dark gaze, barely recognizing him beneath the beard and too-long hair she now realized he'd combed back for their date. He'd been nicely put together that night. But now? He looked as if he'd been roughing it far longer than probably either she or Matteo suspected. "I need to talk to you." His hands were shoved into deep pockets, but she could see them flex, and she wondered if he had a weapon.

"Gabriel." She spoke into the phone, directly to Matteo. "What are you doing here?"

Gabriel reached out, plucked the phone out of her hand and clicked it off. "I need to talk to you alone. Inside." He slipped her phone into his pocket. "Now."

MATTEO SWORE WHEN the line went dead.

Chance grabbed hold of the side bar as Matteo floored the SUV, all but flying down the road toward the ranch.

"Get on the phone with the sheriff," Matteo

ordered. "Tell him there's a possible hostage situation at the ranch. Cabin number four."

"On it," Chance said.

He never should have left her alone. He should have insisted they go with him into town, but Peyton and Gino had ganged up on him so they could go on that silly trail ride.

The whys and regrets piled on, keeping his emotions, his throat-closing fear barely at bay. Why hadn't he taught Peyton how to defend herself? Panic he'd never once given in to—not even when he'd been growing up on that ranch or serving overseas—threatened to choke him.

Peyton was in trouble. Serious trouble. And all he could think about right now was what would happen if he was too late. He couldn't lose her. Not now. Not when...not when so much was possible.

"You're not going to lose her," Chance said as he hung up with the sheriff.

"Huh?" Matteo swiveled his gaze to Chance.

"You aren't going to lose Peyton. From what I hear, that woman is a quick thinker, clever and tough. She knows you're on the way. Whatever she's dealing with now, she'll handle it. Have faith in that, Matteo. Have faith in the woman you love."

"Love?" Matteo wasn't sure he'd ever squeaked before. "Who said I'm in—"

Chance pulled on his seat belt as if to verify it was still working. "I sing about it for a living, remember? I've also experienced it a few times myself. I recognize it when I see it. And, brother, your feelings for Peyton Harrison Blackwell are written all over you."

"And you think now's a good time for this heart-to-heart?"

"I think now's a good time to talk about anything other than the fear that's going through your head. Now." Chance pushed himself back in his seat. "How about you tell me what your plan is once we get there?"

PEYTON LEANED DOWN and brushed a kiss to Gino's damp temple. He was back to his snuggly, little-boy warmth and burrowed under his father's blankets, already drifting off. She couldn't get her nerves under control. She'd said she'd be quick, and Gabriel hadn't argued, but she didn't want to press her luck. She wasn't, however, going to leave anything to chance.

Before she returned to the living area, she quickly unlocked the bedroom window and lifted it up an inch, just enough so someone would see it was open. If Matteo needed a way in, she'd just given it to him.

She left the room, quietly closing the door behind her.

"Thank you for letting me do that," she said as she joined Gabriel at the table. "He got sick while we were horseback riding. He just needs some sleep to get over it."

Gabriel had chosen one of the chairs, but he hadn't removed his coat. He sat there, hands folded, looking at the picture on her laptop. "It was the watch, wasn't it?" He glanced up as she took the chair across from him.

She'd built up this unknown person in her mind for so long, she wasn't sure what she expected, but it wasn't this calm, almost timid, and very, very serious-looking man.

He ran his index finger over the scratched glass of the watch. "This was my father's. He was an inventor. You know, the kind Hollywood loves to kind of make fun of. Wacky scientist with a lab in the basement." His smile almost reached his eyes. "I haven't taken it off since he died last year."

"I'm sorry," Peyton said quietly. "My mother died last year, too. It's not easy, is it?"

"No." Gabriel shook his head. "No. Especially when…"

"You don't work with a technology investment company, do you?" They might as well get the truth out where they could deal with it. "You put that in your profile because you knew the type of man I was looking for. You stole one of the employee laptops and got into the system to put yourself on file as a match for me. So you could, what? Hurt me for some reason?"

"No." His eyes went wide. "No, see, that's why I'm here. I never wanted to hurt anyone! I just needed to talk to you, to ask why you'd done what you did. How you could have stolen Olwen from my father. From me." He blinked as if tears clouded his vision. "From us."

Peyton didn't move. She barely breathed. "Stole Olwen? But…" She didn't understand. "Crossroads Industries came to us. They presented us with the invention, the technology they developed—"

"My father developed," Gabriel said, cutting her off. "He worked for Crossroads for more than thirty years. Thirty years of his life he devoted himself to finding new energy sources that would be available at a fraction of the cost to customers. Do you know what his favorite word was? *Free.* He thought discoveries in the scientific community should be made available to everyone, to lift everyone up. Instead, Crossroads claimed his research—the work he'd done outside of the office—as their own; every thought he had, every advancement he made, they stole from him even though his employment contract stipulated none of that."

"And you thought, because I made the deal with Crossroads, that I must have been in on that side of things."

"Yes." Gabriel looked at her. "I did think that. Until a few days ago. When her story started to fall apart."

"Whose story?"

"Belinda Carmichael. She said she'd heard from a friend at Crossroads that I was trying to find a lawyer to file a claim of intellectual property theft against the company. She told me Crossroads wasn't who I should be going after, but Electryone, and more specifically the person at Electryone who had pushed Crossroads into the business arrangement."

Belinda, who had been nipping at Peyton's professional heels for the past eighteen months. Ever since… Peyton's face flushed.

Ever since Belinda had brought Crossroads Industries to Peyton and Vilette's attention.

"Hold on. Give me my phone." She held out her hand. Gabriel's eyes narrowed. "You need to give this information to me on the record. Let me record it. Please, Gabriel." She flexed her hand. "I promise I won't make any calls. I just want to record this conversation."

He hesitated, but then finally he pulled her phone out of his pocket and set it on the table. Without moving it, she accessed her apps and hit Record. "Now, I want you to start at the beginning. And tell me everything."

"WHAT DID YOU SEE?" Ben stood with his brothers behind the back of Lily's cabin next door to Matteo and Peyton's.

"They're sitting at the kitchen table talking." Matteo didn't understand it. The quick walk-by he'd done by the window made it seem as if Peyton and Gabriel were sharing high tea. "She doesn't look like she feels threatened. I'm going to go in."

"All right." Ethan and Jon both nodded. "Where do you want us?" Ethan asked.

"Let's have you both by the kitchen window, the other two just outside the door. If I do need you, I'll let you know."

"Exactly how will you be letting us know?" Ben asked.

"Trust me. If I need you, you'll know." He holstered his 9 mm and ran quietly around to the front of the house. Slowly, he clicked the latch on the door handle and pushed it open.

Peyton stood up from her seat, her brow arched, and she waved him into the cabin. "Quiet. You'll wake Gino."

"No, I won't. He's snoring," Matteo said, walking quickly over to place himself between Peyton and Gabriel Shurley, who looked like a spooked rabbit about to bolt. Hardly the picture of obsessive focus he'd anticipated. "One of you want to tell me what's going on?"

"Fraud, theft, possibly industrial espionage." Peyton walked around him, then stopped when she peered out the kitchen window. "Oh, for heaven's sake. Are those the Blackwell brothers lurking out there?" She yanked open the window and leaned out, coming face-to-face with Ben and Ethan. "Everything's all right. He's harmless. Mostly," she said. "Come on in, and I'll explain. Matteo? Put the pot on for coffee, and grab a bottle of whiskey. We're all going to need it."

"ANYONE HAVE ANY QUESTIONS?" Peyton asked the men sitting in the living area of her cabin. This had not been the way she'd intended to meet her long-lost cousins, the Blackwell Brothers, but at least she knew where she stood with them. They'd come to help protect her, no questions asked, the instant they thought she was in trouble.

And that was pretty darn impressive.

"Where to start?" Ben said with a shrug before he held out his mug to Ty, silently asking for a refill. "It's the first time I've been in on a video conference call quite like this. Ms. Wright, I'm assuming this is the first you're hearing about the contested solar panels?"

"You assume correctly," Vilette said from Peyton's laptop screen. Peyton had caught her at home, alone, which was exactly how Peyton wanted it. She didn't want anyone at Electryone getting even the faintest hint of what was about to come down. "Clearly I'm going to be needing to consult with our own attorneys, but I can assure all of you that Electryone will not be going through with the deal as it is currently proposed."

Peyton flinched. "All those jobs will be

lost," she whispered. "Vilette, isn't there anything we can do to salvage this?"

"Possibly. That will depend on whether Mr. Shurley, once we've verified his claims that his father was the real inventor of the Olwen solar-panel system, is amenable to a similar deal with Electryone."

"Possibly," Gabriel said. "I'd want Belinda out—"

"She will be out of Electryone in the next few hours." Vilette cut him off. "And likely arrested by the end of the day. I've already texted our publicity department, and they're drafting a public statement as we speak. Belinda's part in all this will not be swept under any rug, especially any owned by Electryone. We will see this is put right, Mr. Shurley."

"Thank you." He ducked his head, nodded. "I know I didn't go about this properly. I know I shouldn't have let her goad me into trying to scare you into quitting."

Peyton snorted and glanced at Matteo, who grinned. "Fat chance of that happening. Obviously she doesn't know me at all."

"I'm ready to accept whatever charges you or Mr. Josiah want to file against me," Gabriel said. "I got caught up, let my emotions take over, but when I saw her meeting with the higher-ups at Crossroads even after she told me she had nothing to do with the deal, I knew something wasn't right. Thank you, Peyton, for listening to me."

"Next time?" Matteo pushed to his feet. "Maybe make an appointment with her?"

The Blackwell brothers chuckled and began filing out.

"You need an attorney," Ben said to Gabriel before he left. "To deal with the computer theft and hacking charges, not to mention making sure you get what you and your family are owed. I'm not the right one, but I know a few in central California who can help you out and not charge you into the poorhouse." He handed Gabriel his card. "Call my office once you're home, and I'll put you in touch."

"Uh, thank you." Gabriel didn't look entirely sure what to do or say. "What about…" He looked back at Peyton. "What about the sheriff? And charges—"

"I'm not pressing charges," Peyton said and earned a flash of nodding approval from Matteo. "There's no point, and you've already got enough to deal with. Besides," she said as she walked him to the door, "because of you I was able to come out to Montana and deal with my own family issues. And get my first dose of Big Sky Country. I'd say we're even."

"I spent the last of my money on a guest cabin here. I hadn't planned on approaching you so soon." Gabriel slipped Ben's card into his pocket. "Do you mind if I stay?"

"Only if you promise to get some sleep and start making solid plans for the future," Peyton said. "I'm sure the detectives in my case will want to talk to you, and Vilette will need you to make an official statement, but all of that can wait."

"Sure. Whatever you need." He touched a hand to his watch. "I did this for him, you know. I didn't want his life's work to go unnoticed. I didn't want him to be forgotten."

"And he won't be," Peyton assured him, and closed the door behind him.

She sagged back on the door. "Well, that wasn't how I planned to spend the day. Oh, hang on." She held up her hand and returned to the sofa. "Vilette, you still there?"

"I am." Vilette sipped hot liquid out of an octopus coffee mug. "You can consider yourself released from your prison. The jet is ready when you are."

"Oh." Peyton sank onto the sofa. "Well, actually…" She cleared her throat. "I've got a lot of vacation time stored up, and I was thinking maybe I'd take a few days? Maybe celebrate Halloween out here with my family and…" She glanced up at Matteo, who was carrying coffee mugs to the sink. "And friends. If that's all right?"

"It is more than all right." Vilette gave her a slow nod of approval. "I'll take care of Belinda and the fallout. You enjoy your…friends. Matteo?"

"Ma'am?" He popped in behind Peyton.

"I'll wire you your bonuses and pay this afternoon. I'll also be contacting your employer to let them know I'd like to keep them on retainer for any future security needs, with you as our liaison if you wouldn't mind?"

"Wouldn't mind at all, ma'am. Thank you."

"Excellent. If you'll excuse me, I have criminal charges to file against one of my VPs. Have a good rest of your trip, Peyton. See you when you get back."

"Okay." The screen went dark, and Peyton settled against the sofa, reaching out with her bare foot to close her laptop. "I guess that means we are officially free now."

Matteo leaned in and rested his folded arms on the back of the sofa. "I guess we are. What do you want to do?"

She tilted her head up to look at him. Her gaze dropped to his mouth, to those lips of his that seemed to have been made just for her. She reached up, brushed her thumb over his mouth. "I can think of a few things."

"What's going on?" A sleepy Gino was standing in the bedroom doorway, his hair sticking up in mussy tufts, rubbing his eyes. "What did I miss?"

Instead of answering, Matteo walked over and scooped up Gino, holding him in his arms as Peyton joined them. "You have a decision to make, young man."

"I do? 'Bout what?"

"Only the most important decision a six-year-old will ever make."

Peyton caught on to Matteo's train of thought immediately and tugged Gino's too small pajama top down over his tummy. "What on earth are you going to be for Halloween?"

Lily shrugged, "just wouldn't find my secrets useful enough to realize how good a deal you are. How good you are, Matteo. You know I haven't said her me this before. I don't have within the—————————— as with forever."

CHAPTER FOURTEEN

"ARE YOU SURE about this, Lily?" Matteo watched as Peyton's sister smoothed her hand down the nose of the horse he'd come to love. "I don't want to take advantage."

"You aren't," Lily assured him. "Conner and I agree, this lady and Goldie need a good, calm, peaceful environment, and as wonderful as the ranch is, there's a bit too much energy for them here. We'll take good care of them. Promise."

"Of that I have no doubt." He hated to part with the horse, but what was he going to do with her in an apartment in California?

"I hope you know you and Gino are welcome to come back and visit her anytime you want. Seems the least we can do after all you've done for Peyton."

It was how she said it, with that overly lilting, singsong voice that had his ears perking up. "Something on your mind?"

Lily shrugged. "Just wondering if my sister's smart enough to realize how good a man you are. How good you are for her. You know, I haven't seen her go this long without having her nose stuck in a spreadsheet in…well, forever."

"She's feeling free because she's finally taking a vacation," Matteo said. "Nothing to do with me."

"Somehow I think it's more than that."

He had enough of an ego to silently agree. In the days following the revelation her stalker wasn't so much stalking as he was trying to figure out how to explain his side of things, Peyton had been on a tear where ranch activities were concerned. Trail rides, barbecues, games, activities, decorations for Halloween: she was a one-woman whirling dervish. He'd even heard her lamenting the fact that Hadley Blackwell was too good at her job as a resort wedding planner because there was nothing for Peyton to do to help her sister other than assure Lily she would most definitely be back at the ranch for the Christmastime ceremony. "Don't go counting on anything happening between us just yet, Lily. Peyton and I are still…"

What? Figuring things out? Deciding if there was something close to a future together?

He knew what he was leaning toward, what he wanted, but he'd been down this road before with a professionally determined woman.

Would he and Gino ever be enough for Peyton Harrison? If it was just himself he had to worry about, it would be one thing, but with Gino's custody hanging in the balance, not to mention his future, there weren't a lot of chances Matteo was willing to take. Still. It was definitely mood-elevating to consider a future that included Peyton.

"Speaking of my sister, where's she gotten to this morning?"

"She wouldn't tell me," Matteo said. "She and Gino are on a secret shopping trip. Probably something to do with the Halloween bash tonight. They still won't tell me what he's going to be dressed as."

"What are you going as?" Lily teased.

"The scariest thing I could think of." He grinned. "I'm gonna be a cowboy."

Lily laughed. "Oh." She snapped her fingers. "Just one more technicality where the horse is concerned. What's her name?"

"Beauty." No other name suited. No other

name came close. And no other name would do. "Her name is Beauty." He moved closer and held out his hand for the horse to nuzzle. "And she's going to have a wonderful life as a Blackwell."

"COME ON, HURRY UP!" Gino's entire body vibrated as he stomped his feet while Peyton knotted his little black necktie. "The party's already happening!"

"It'll be happening all night, little man. You can be a bit late." How could one small boy cause such havoc in one two-bedroom cabin? He'd been beyond excited from the second he woke up this morning and had only gotten more energetic as the day wore on. Probably, she figured, due to the bottomless bowls of candy Hadley had all around the ranch. Candy corn, marshmallow ghosts, candy-coated apples, cotton-candy spiderwebs… If there was any sugar left in Montana, Peyton would be shocked. Every cabin porch was strewn with twinkling lights, stacks of carved pumpkins and wispy, gauzy ghosts billowing in the October breeze.

"I told Rosie I'd be there now," Gino whined. "Aren't you done yet?"

"Hang on." Peyton reached behind her for the plastic star and clipped it to his belt. She'd convinced him to forego the toy gun he'd had his heart set on and instead talked him into a fluorescent-green water pistol. "And one last thing." She pushed the pair of sunglasses onto his face and watched his face split into a huge grin.

"How do I look?"

"See for yourself." She steered him over to the mirror. "Well?"

"Awesome! It's perfect! Just like you said."

"I happen to be a genius for Halloween costumes." She'd always loved her and her sisters' tradition of dressing up as a group with a common theme. One year they'd donned costumes of mother nature, each representing an element. Another they'd chosen their favorite TV cartoon characters. One of their last Halloweens together they'd each chosen a female scientist—Peyton had gone with Marie Curie despite the less than happy ending the woman had endured. "What's Rosie coming as?"

"A witch." Gino scrunched up his face. "She said it's a witch who wears pink, but I told her I didn't think there was such a thing. She said

I'm wrong and that she'll prove it tonight. Do witches wear pink, Peyton?"

"Witches wear whatever they want to wear," Peyton told him. "I doubt Rosie's often wrong about such things." Talk about a bundle of energy. Katie and Chance's little girl definitely gave Gino competition in that department. "You ready to show your dad?"

"Yeah! Let's go!" he slammed out of the room. "Dad! I'm ready! Come see!" He jumped into a frozen pose that had Peyton snort-laughing as Matteo emerged from his bedroom, cowboy hat, boots, flannel shirt all in place.

What weeks before had been a slight flutter and zinging in her heart had, in the past few days, settled into a constant, buzzing, thrilling hum. There was something about this man—a man who had every reason to run far and fast from anything cowboy, yet here he'd donned the perfect costume to have fun with his son— and it made her heart stand up and take notice.

Matteo stared at Gino, confusion V-ing his brows. "Well, you look pretty professional. Who are you? A character from *Men in Black*? An FBI agent?"

"No." Gino looked stunned that his father didn't see it.

Peyton shook her head, just enough for Matteo to notice. "He's you," she mouthed before Gino caught her.

"I'm Protector Man!" Gino struck another pose. "Like you protect Peyton and all those other people with your job. See? I've got the suit and the gun and everything. I even have a badge!"

"I don't wear—"

Peyton cleared her throat.

"Right." Matteo nodded and walked over to his son, flipped his glasses down his nose. "You look amazing, Gino. I'm very flattered."

"Peyton said you would be. I wanna be just like you when I grow up, Daddy. Peyton said I could, so can I?"

Matteo nodded. Peyton pressed a finger to her trembling lips. He really had no idea how absolutely amazing he was with that boy.

"You can be anything you want to be, G."

"Well, right now I want to be at that party because I'm starving!" Peyton grabbed her own cowboy—or was it cowgirl?—hat, one she'd borrowed from Lily, and boot-scooted over to the door. "Let's see how these Blackwells throw a party."

"I MAY JUST die from the cute." Peyton stuffed another marshmallow ghost into her mouth and tilted her head back to grin at Matteo, hand clasping her hat to her head. "Look how cute they all are!"

Matteo wasn't one to throw the word *cute* around, but he had to admit, glancing at the smorgasbord of costumed children of all ages, *cute* seemed a pretty apt description.

"Look at all those Blackwells over with Gino." Peyton sighed and moved closer to Matteo. "All dressed up like *Wizard of Oz* characters. There's Rosie as Glinda because pink, obviously."

"I think the two Totos are Jon and Lydia's twins. What were their names again?" Matteo was having trouble keeping everyone straight.

"Marshall and Brendan. They're just so… I just want to squeeze their cheeks!"

"Resist," he teased. I see Abby and Gen over there by the ghoul punch. Scarecrow and Tinma—"

"Woman," Peyton corrected him. "And sweet Poppy is Dorothy. Look at her terrific red shoes!"

"Where's the lion?" Matteo craned his neck.

"This is like some weird Halloween bingo game."

"There." Peyton pointed to Ethan's son Eli, who was stealing the show with his golden mane of yarn and a cute black button nose.

They continued making comments and pointing out the various costumes, worn by both kids and parents, grandparents and Falcon Creek residents alike.

"I bet the entire town showed up to this thing." Matteo slipped an arm around Peyton's waist and drew her closer. "Pop said they would."

"Hadley's been working so hard on this. It's nice to see everyone having such a good time."

Strobe lights in orange, yellow and white pulsed and spun into the night sky. The picnic tables had been decked out with lights similar to the ones strung around the porches. Even the fence around the paddock displayed carved pumpkin heads and bushels of red, ripe apples.

Game booths had been set up, too, from bobbing for apples to ring toss onto traffic cones painted to look like giant candy corn. Darts to pop white-balloon ghosts and a fishing pond where frogs were chosen for a jumping contest.

"I like how everything's cheery and fun." Peyton rested her head on Matteo's upper arm. "None of that übercreepy zombie stuff." She shuddered. "That freaks me out."

"Kids get scared enough these days," Matteo agreed. "No need to add the same to holidays. Oh, look. Wonder what those are." He sniffed the air and drew Peyton with him as he checked out the freshly baked handheld pies.

"Oh, good." Hadley handed them each one with a look of relief. She was dressed to the nines as Little Bo Peep, complete with bright red cheeks and ringlet curls. "You two test these out for me. New recipe. I was trying for those English pasties. These are potato and cheese with a little bit of heat from chipotle peppers."

Matteo had a bite, nodding in approval the second the treat hit his tongue. "It's good." He covered his mouth as he laughed. "When do you get to take a break and enjoy yourself?"

"Ah, good question." Hadley pressed her hands into her spine and arched her back. "Junior here is currently doing practice kicks, preparing for his professional soccer career, so... never?"

"You can't have anything else to do," Peyton said, biting into her savory pastry. "And wow, Matteo was right. This is yummy. What can we do to help?"

"Honestly, you don't have to—"

"Hadley," Peyton said in that familiar, no-nonsense tone of hers. "What can we do to help?"

"The punch bowls need refilling, and so do the candy bowls. I've got another two trays of these things in the oven and then there's the dessert table. I think the chocolate fountain—"

"We're on it," Matteo said before she got lost in the details. "Go find Ty and have fun. Get off your feet if you can." He plucked up a nearly empty bowl of apples as Peyton retrieved more bowls and platters to top up from a nearby table.

"You guys are the best. Thanks."

Thanks to Hadley's impeccable organization skills, it didn't take them long to replenish the food and get back to enjoying the party themselves. "I have to admit, this is all pretty great."

"Why are you surprised?" Peyton asked. "Something told me this family knows a thing or two about parties."

"Maybe with a surprise guest?" Matteo

glanced toward the headlights heading along the driveway, jostling and bumping down the road toward the main house. "Is that an RV?"

"A rather ancient-looking one," Peyton said. "I wonder who—"

"It's Great-grandpa!" Rosie squealed before she hiked up her poofy pink gown and ran toward the vehicle. By the time she got there, her oversize crown was tipping precariously to one side. The rest of the kids trailed behind, Gino further away as he clearly was assessing the situation.

"Your cautious little protector," Peyton teased Matteo. "Great-grandpa must mean Big E's back home."

"Wondered what took him so long," Matteo said, then had the good sense to look guilty when Peyton moved in front of him to glare into his eyes.

"Explain, please."

"Uh, it was Ty and Jon's idea. They thought he should know what's been going on since your so-called stalker showed up…"

"Oh, no. No, no, no. Tell me you didn't make Big E aware of what happened."

"Of course we did. Why not? He's the one who sent you out here in the first place."

"Why not?" Peyton groaned. "Because these days Big E's been traveling around with my father!"

"He found Thomas? When?"

"No, not Thomas Blackwell." She flinched as if he'd just reminded her of something she didn't want to address. "Rudy Harrison. The father who raised me. They've been off on a wild-goose chase trying to find Thomas."

"And this is bad because...?"

Peyton sighed. "I guess we really haven't talked a lot about this. But there's not much more to the story. Big E is convinced, and apparently my father is, too, that Thomas is still alive and out there somewhere. He wants us all to reunite in a big family shindig." She rolled her eyes. "After all these years, if Thomas hasn't been seen or found, it's not going to happen."

"Is that what you know?" Matteo asked. "Or are you trying not to get your hopes up?"

All humor faded from her face. "That's... an interesting question."

"I'm full of them." Matteo reached out, stroked a finger down the side of her face. "You have a big heart, Peyton. You don't let a lot of people see it often, but it's there. And it's been broken. Not getting your hopes up about your real dad is one thing you can do to try to protect yourself."

"I wouldn't even know what to say to him if I ever saw him again." She shook her head, the confusion marring her face scraping against his heart.

He took a deep breath, looked up into the pristine night sky, lost himself for a moment in the faint lights of the universe winking at them. "All my life, I dreamed about belonging to someone. Anyone. To know who I came from. My parents. Mom, Dad. Grandparents. Siblings. Cousins." He glanced over to where his son circled Big E as the older man climbed out of the RV, followed by another man who looked a bit shell-shocked by the scene surrounding them. "Don't be afraid of what might be and forget to see what is, Peyton. These people, they're your family. And there are so, so many of us who have never been, will never be, that lucky."

"Matteo." Peyton reached up and caught his face in her hands. "You are lucky. You can be. Maybe we…"

His cell phone vibrated in his back pocket. He held up a finger. "Hold that thought." He pressed his mouth to hers for a long moment before he checked his screen. Knots that had loosened days before tightened in his chest. "It's Sylvia."

"Oh." She frowned. "Are you going to answer it?"

"Yeah. This is the first time she's called me back. Do you... I'm sorry."

"No, don't apologize." She pointed toward the cupcakes as if trying to distract herself. "I haven't tried every flavor yet, and I'm planning to get my fill before I head home the day after tomorrow."

He nodded absently, wanting to answer the call before Sylvia changed her mind and hung up without leaving a message. He moved off toward the cabin and away from the partygoers and noise. "Sylvia. This is a surprise."

"Matteo, hi. Yes, I know. I'm sorry I didn't get back to you sooner." She sounded breathless, a bit anxious, something he'd never known his ex-wife to be.

"Is everything okay? With the baby?"

"Oh, he's fine," Sylvia said. "I'm sorry. I just got the best news and I wanted to... Well, there's this huge deal that came our way a few days ago. Like life-changing, it's-going-to-get-me-my-promotion kind of deal. Major distribution worldwide with serious backing and capital."

"Congratulations." What else was he going to say. "I thought maybe you were calling about Gino. About me calling you the other day to ask if he'd ever been tested for a learning difference." Temper, he reminded himself. Keep it under control.

"Oh, that. Right. Slipped my mind. No, I don't remember his teachers saying anything about it, but here's the real reason I'm calling. This new promotion means I'm going to be doing a lot of traveling. All over the world this time, not just between the States and Japan. Jiro's not crazy about the idea, but it's not something I can pass up. The thing is…and I hope you can tell Gino for me. I'm not going to fight your claim for full custody, Matteo. I think it'll be better for him, for all of us, if he stays with you."

Matteo's head went light. He grabbed hold of the paddock fence to stay on his feet. "Say that again?" The bubble of pressure that had settled in his chest two years before stretched to the point of bursting.

"I'm relinquishing custody to you, effective

immediately. It just makes sense, Matteo. For all of us."

So she kept saying. "Just like that. You aren't going to come out and say goodbye or help him get settled here?"

"I honestly don't know when I'll find the time. You know what? I'll give him a call next week, and we'll video chat. Just like you used to. You do still want full custody, don't you?"

"Certainly." He just wasn't expecting her to give up. And that's exactly what it sounded like she was doing. But why? Why now? What had changed her mind? It couldn't be the new baby. "I'll have my lawyer draw up the documents."

"No need. I had them drawn up and sent copies to you and your lawyer. They should be waiting for you when you get back from Montana."

"Right." He nodded, trying to clear the fog in his brain. "Okay. I'll look them over as soon as I get home. Sylvia?"

"Yeah?"

"Thank you." He didn't know what else to say. "Just...thank you."

"You're welcome. Oh, and do me one favor? Thank Peyton for me? Her stepping in to help make this deal come together changed everything. My bosses are so excited to be working with Electryone, and they're giving me the credit. Next stop, CEO. Talk later. Bye."

The farewell stuck in his throat. He lowered his hand, stared at the screen. "Thank Peyton?"

"Thank Peyton for what?" Peyton ran up behind him, held out a cake pop decorated like a pumpkin. "Eat one of these. They're fab. So, what did she say?"

"Who?" Matteo couldn't quite process everything he'd heard.

"Who?" She hip-bumped him and laughed. "Sylvia. Why did she call?"

Matteo stared into her eyes and looked for even a hint of surprise or curiosity or...confusion. But there wasn't anything like that. Because she already knew. "She gave me full custody of Gino."

Her smile seemed genuine enough, but he thought he also saw relief on her face. "Congratulations, Daddy. I knew it would work out. We should go tell Gino he doesn't have to go to boarding school." She darted away, but he reached out and caught her arm, pulled her back. "What? Don't you want to tell—"

"What did you do, Peyton?"

"Do?" Her eyebrows shot up, but once again, the surprise wasn't there. She was a good liar, except with him. "Do about what?"

"Sylvia said to thank you for helping make this deal of hers happen. What deal?"

Peyton scrunched her nose. "She wasn't supposed to say anything about that. I didn't think she would. I didn't want to share the credit."

"What. Did. You. Do?"

Now the shock appeared as she twisted her arm free. "I did my research. I looked into her. Her business dealings, her résumé and business portfolio. I did an analysis of what she was probably looking to do with her career. Where she wanted to go. I found we had some mutual interests and connections. So, I reached out, and it ended up that there were benefits for both companies, mine and hers, to doing a deal together."

"Why?" It didn't make sense. "Why would you try to help my ex-wife?"

"Because after reading about her, I felt as if I understood her. I hedged my bets in assuming that job was more important to her than keeping custody of your son. I was right."

"You were right." Could she hear herself? "You blackmailed my ex-wife into giving me custody?"

Her gaze sharpened. "It wasn't blackmail. No one mentioned Gino," she snapped. "Or where he'd be better off. It was a business negotiation. It's what I do for a living. I find what works to my company's advantage, and I do what's necessary to get the deal done. Only, in this case, you were the company. I don't understand—"

"No, I can see you don't." Matteo began to pace, shoved his hands into his hair and knocked off his hat. It fell to the ground with a dull plop. "You didn't even give me the chance to fight for him. Instead you just made it all happen."

"I guess this means I won't be getting a thank-you?"

"You want me to thank you for bribing my ex-wife into giving me our son. Tell me something, Peyton. And please, take a moment to think about this." The anger he'd felt toward Sylvia paled in comparison to what raged through him now. "What happens in, say, five or ten years, when Gino's older, and Sylvia, in Sylvia's loose-tongued, callous way, lets slip the fact that she got her fancy new job by giving up her son? That she threw him away in exchange for a payday?"

Peyton's eyes went cold. "Even if she did do that, you have your son with you. He'll be loved, and he'll know he's wanted. He won't be left behind. You won't leave him behind."

The light dawned. Even as he connected the dots, the anger remained. "I am not your father, Peyton. I am not Thomas Blackwell, and you know what? Neither is Sylvia. You can't fix what's wrong with your own life by trying to fix mine."

"That isn't what I was doing." But he could see it in her eyes. The question. The doubt. "I wanted Gino safe. That kid deserves the entire universe, and he was never going to get it with her. She was shipping him off to a boarding school he didn't want to go to that may or may not have clued into the help Gino needs. That light he has inside of him." Her breath caught. "That light inside of him would have gone out, and no one would have been there to see it."

"You didn't even give me the chance to try." He shook his head. "Peyton. You didn't even give me the chance."

"Some risks aren't worth taking," Peyton said.

"Everything's a deal to you, isn't it? A business opportunity. A chance to advance. Tell me, did you talk Ty into those new solar panels? You know, during those days you were hiding out here from a stalker?"

"Gabriel was only stalking me to scare me off my job," she said through tight lips. "And yes, Ty and Hadley let me know this morning they're going to move ahead with the panels once the Olwen deal is...done." She trailed off, as if realizing his question had been rhetorical. "This is done, isn't it?" She whispered, blinking so fast he couldn't see her eyes any longer. "This...whatever it was between us. It's done."

"You went behind my back, Peyton. You could have said something, anything to me about this. We could have found a way to approach Sylvia without you having to buy her off. What if she changes her mind one day about Gino's custody and sues me after all? She's got my..." His what? What was Peyton to him? His girlfriend? The woman he loved? The woman he'd fallen hard and fast for, despite all his reservations. "She's got my client doing my dirty work."

"She won't do that," Peyton said. "She's making her arrangements with you all legal and aboveboard. Presumably she could change her mind at a point down the road, but by then Gino will be happy and used to being with you, and no judge would change that arrangement, surely."

He let out a harsh breath. "You thought of everything, didn't you?"

"Yes." She inched up her chin. "I did. And I won't apologize for making sure your son gets to stay with you, where he's safe and protected and cared for. I am sorry you can't see it for what it was."

"And what was it?"

"Love, Matteo." Her voice broke, but the tears shimmering in her eyes against the moonlight didn't fall. "It was all done for love."

With that, she turned her back on him and walked away.

CHAPTER FIFTEEN

"I WISH YOU were staying longer." Lily gave Peyton a hard hug and rocked her back and forth. "You don't have to go back yet. I thought Vilette gave you more days."

"She did." Peyton offered a tight smile when her sister stepped back. "I need to get things back in order before I resume life at the office." She cast her gaze to the cabin where Matteo stood by the door, arms folded, watching her. "It's just better this way, Lil."

"Better for who?" Lily challenged. "You're both miserable. I don't remember the last time I heard you cry in the night over a boy."

Offended, Peyton balked. "I never did that."

"You did last night. I heard you, Peyton."

Peyton smoothed a hand down the dark, tailored suit pants and matching charcoal blouse she'd donned this morning. She'd gathered all her things from her cabin last night before hiding out in Lily's, pretending to be asleep when her sister returned from the Halloween party. Clearly she hadn't been successful. "Things between me and Matteo are complicated," she said when Lily silently pressed her for more comment. "Please just let this go. I have to keep it together a little while longer at least."

"Going to cry yourself to sleep on the plane home, then?"

"Nah." She patted her bulging briefcase. "I've got work to do."

Lily sighed. "Some things never change. You aren't going to leave him without saying goodbye, are you?"

"I can't talk to Matteo—"

"Not Matteo, Gino." Her sister looked disappointed in her. A look she was becoming all too familiar with. Apparently she was doomed to let everyone she cared about down. "You of all people know how much damage is done by a parent leaving without a goodbye."

"I'm not his mother," Peyton whispered around her too-tight throat. "I shouldn't matter."

"Well, you do." She pointed to where Gino was standing up on the fence rail, cheering on Izzy and two of the horses in the paddock. "We all forgave you for you lying to us all these years, Peyton. But you will never forgive yourself if you walk away from that child without saying goodbye. And neither will I."

"Lily."

Lily backed away toward the RV where Rudy was enjoying his morning cup of coffee. Peyton had seen him earlier when she'd packed and brought her bags to the guest lodge before she left for good. Their conversation had been short and sweet when she'd told Rudy that she loved him to the moon and back, but he was to keep his nose out of her private life from now on. He'd agreed, probably, she suspected, because he'd already moved on to Fiona or Georgie as his next target to see happy and settled.

"One thing you've never been, Peyton Harrison Blackwell," Lily called, "is a coward. Don't disappoint me by turning into one now."

Her sister was right. How could she have even contemplated leaving without talking to Gino one more time? Peyton set her briefcase and suit jacket down, then carefully walked over to the fence where Gino stood. She'd switched back to heels, and had left her muddy cowboy boots for Lily in her cabin.

"Peyton, where have you been?" Gino spun and jumped down, threw himself into her arms. "Did Dad tell you? I'm going to live with him forever and ever. I can still see Mom, but she won't mind me being with Dad. And I won't have to go to boarding school, just like you promised."

Peyton clung to him, tears burning her eyes as she pushed her face into the side of his neck and inhaled that little-boy smell she'd come to love. "That's wonderful news, little man. I'm so happy for you and your dad."

"Where were you at breakfast?" Gino stepped back. "I was going to have pancakes, but then I decided not to because I don't want to ever puke again." He seemed to see her for the first time. "Aren't you going riding with us?"

"No, I'm not." She touched his face. "I'm going home."

"No, you're not. We're leaving tomorrow. Dad said."

"You are. But I'm going home today. I need…" She had to clear her throat. "I need to get back to work. Playtime's over."

All the happiness on his face faded. "But you can't go. We're happy here. And you and Daddy, you like each other. And you both like me. You do like me, don't you, Peyton?" He blinked, and two huge tears plopped onto his round cheeks.

"I don't just like you, Gino. I love you."

"Then, why can't you stay with us?"

"I just can't. Sometimes problems between adults are just too big to get over. I want you to do me a favor, though, okay? I want you to take good care of your dad. I know you don't need me to tell you that because you already do, but just in case." She straightened and spotted Matteo heading their way. "Bye, Gino." She hurried off, ignoring Matteo's voice calling to her.

"Dad, make her stop! No, Dad, she can't go! No!"

She climbed into the SUV, tears blurring her vision as she pulled on her sunglasses.

"You sure you want to do this?" Ty asked as he started the engine. "It's not too late to change your mind."

She looked out to where Matteo held a struggling Gino in his arms. The expression on his face was unreadable. The pain and hurt on Gino's heartbreaking. "I'm afraid it is too late, Ty." She squeezed her eyes shut, and the first tears fell. "Please drive."

MATTEO WASN'T SURE what was worse: a screaming, fit-throwing six-year-old or a sullen, silent boy who was blaming him for Peyton leaving them behind.

It was a question Matteo had asked himself multiple times during the past few days, and he did so again on this first night back in his apartment now that Gino had refused his favorite dinner—pasta rings with mini meatballs. He should count himself lucky the kid didn't chuck them at the wall. It had been that kind of day.

Their morning arrival in California had left Matteo with plenty of hours to fill, which he did by checking out nearby schools, including, much to his personal irritation, the learning academy Peyton had recommended.

She'd been right. It was the perfect school for his son, right down to the dedicated, small-classroom attention for students with learning differences. He'd have to get over the navy blue and burgundy blazers. He couldn't believe he was even considering sending his son to a place like that, but thanks to the bonus and double-time payment from Electryone, not to mention the promotion he'd officially received via email yesterday, a promotion that would mean he could stay in California, he could make it work tuitionwise. At least for a couple of years until Gino was more settled.

He had an appointment with the president of the academy the day after tomorrow, but his initial phone conversation had gone well, so he'd take that as a good sign.

Matteo dumped the dregs of Gino's dinner down the disposal, fixed himself a turkey sandwich before heading to check on his son in his room. He knocked on the door.

Gino didn't answer.

Matteo turned the knob and pushed open the door. "Gino, we need to talk."

"Are you going to send me back now?"

"What?" He stepped inside and sat next to Gino on his bed. "No, I'm not sending you back anywhere. Why would you say that?"

Gino shrugged and tugged on the ears of one of his stuffed animals. "It's what Mom always used to say when I was bad or got angry. That she was going to send me away to boarding school, and she'd never have to see me again."

Bitterness pulsed through his veins. "You never told me she said that."

"I didn't want you to get angry with her. I was afraid you'd change your mind about wanting me, and now I did that anyway and maybe I can go live with Peyton if you don't want to be my dad anymore." Tears trickled down his face.

"Oh, my boy." Matteo pulled Gino into his lap. "You really have had it rougher than I thought, haven't you?" He rocked him gently. "I want you to listen to me, all right? There is nothing, absolutely nothing, you could ever do that would make me not want you. You are all I've thought about since the day you were born. I love you so much it hurts me inside. A good hurt. I'll admit I don't like it when you get angry or stop talking to me or throw a fit that scares the horses."

Gino snorted. "I did do that, didn't I?"

"Yes, you did." He tucked Gino into the crook of his arm. "We're going to work on getting those emotions of yours under control and aimed in the right direction, okay?"

"'Kay. What about Peyton?"

Matteo closed his eyes, feeling his heart break all over again at the mention of her name. "What about her?"

"I miss her, Dad. What did she do wrong that you stopped liking her?"

"I—" Matteo stopped, frowned. "That isn't what happened, Gino."

Gino shrugged. "Then, what did?"

Matteo couldn't believe… Wait. Was that right? When all was said and done, is that what had happened? Had he let his pride, his ego, get in the way of something that could be…that could be a dream come true? Except dreams didn't come true for boys like Matteo. Dreams were nothing more than wishes thrown into the night sky that never gave you the answers you needed.

Except he wasn't that little boy anymore. He'd walked out of that life and into a new one—one that had put him in the path of a woman he knew now he'd loved almost from the start. A woman he'd been too arrogant to let help him. "You know what, G?"

"What?"

"I think you might be the smartest little boy I've ever met."

"I am?" Gino looked up. Clearly, given his expression, he didn't think his father knew very many little boys. "How come?"

"Because you see things I don't. You know what? We've got a plan to make." He stood up, dumped a squealing Gino over his shoulder and headed back into the living room. "And I've got someone I need to talk to."

PEYTON STARED AT her cell phone, trying to feel some regret about the call she'd just made. It hadn't been spur-of-the-moment. She didn't make spur-of-the-moment decisions. She thought things out in meticulous detail. That included skiving off work ever since she'd gotten home over the weekend so she could finally, just a few hours ago, come to the conclusion that this apartment, her life, everything about her, screamed one thing: loneliness.

Her life had been so full these last few weeks. Full of mindless fun and laughter and emotions she hadn't let herself feel since, well, since before her real father had left. All of the pain and anger she'd had about her father leaving had taken off, and at the secrets she'd been forced to keep, all of it had been healed because of one man and his perfect little boy.

Perfect. Peyton laughed to herself. Gino Rossi was far from perfect—instead, he was just like any other child. But he was perfect for his father. And he was perfect for her. Whether Matteo wanted to see her again or not, whether he'd ever see that what she'd done with his ex-wife was done for the best couldn't matter. She'd had it in her power to give Gino every advantage in the world. And so, she had.

The scholarship she'd set up for the boy at the education academy would be specifically for Gino's tuition. "What's Matteo going to do?" Peyton muttered to herself. "Stop talking to me? Cut me out of his life? Too late."

She tossed her phone onto the coffee table. "Nope, still not going to apologize," she muttered. "Boy's where he needs to be. That's all that matters."

But being without them, even for these few days, hurt far more than she thought possible. The take-out container–strewn kitchen was proof of that. Her suitcase was still packed and sitting by the door. She hadn't made her bed in days, and she'd wept her way through a good three seasons' worth of crappy reality television that she swore had begun to rot her brain.

"Time to stop sulking and get back to it."

Except nothing—and that included her job—held much appeal without having someone to share…well, everything with.

With the sun dipping into the horizon, she went to draw the curtains and prepare for another sleepless night. Someone knocking on her door had her stopping in her tracks.

She frowned, turned to the door, hesitating

a second as she wondered whether she should answer it.

The knock came again, only this time she heard a soft, familiar voice on the other side. "Peyton? It's cold out here."

"Gino?" She ran for the door, yanked it open and found a beaming Gino standing on the other side. "What do you mean it's cold? You're inside." She bent down and grabbed hold of him to pull him close. "What are you doing here? How did you get here? Where's your dad?" Matteo never would have let Gino come here alone. She stood up, scanned the hallway in both directions. "Gino, you didn't come here by yourself, did you?"

"I'm a special delivery." Gino held up a crumpled note.

"What's this?" Her cell phone rang. "Darn it. Gino, come inside." She took his hand and pulled him in, retrieved her phone. She didn't bother to glance at the screen when she picked it up. "Yes?"

"Read it." Matteo's voice melted away all the hurt and grief she'd piled onto herself since leaving Montana.

"He didn't come here alone." Relief swept over her. "Thank goodness."

"Read the note, Peyton." He hung up.

She sat on the sofa, tears misting her eyes as Gino came around and sat next to her. "Don't cry, Peyton."

"These are happy tears, little man." She reached out and drew him against her, pressed her lips to the top of his head. "I've missed you."

"You have to read the note."

"Right. The note." Peyton uncrumpled the paper, smoothed it out on her thigh.

You were wrong. Gino doesn't just belong with me. He belongs with us. Forgive me. I love you.

Peyton laughed, the last of the heaviness breaking away from her heart. "Oh, you two." She hugged Gino again and sprinted for the door when Matteo knocked.

She barely had it open before she launched herself into his arms. "I've never been so happy to be wrong in my life." Peyton kissed him, kicking up her feet as he twirled her around. "You were right. I should have talked to you…"

He kissed her silent.

"You risked everything we'd begun to build to give him what he needed," he murmured against her lips. "That's all I ever need to know about you. That you love my son as much as I hope you love me."

"You don't have to hope." She clung to him, then felt tiny hands reach up and grab her hand from behind his father.

"Did it work? Does this mean Peyton's coming home with us?"

"You know what I think would be great?" Peyton said as she stepped back and scooped him up. "I think maybe we should all look for a new place together. Someplace with a home office so I can spend more time with you both."

Matteo's eyes widened. "You'd do that?"

"To be with you? Absolutely. Oh." She bit her lip. "There might be one teeny, tiny thing I did about Gino's schooling you might not be happy about."

Matteo looked at her, looked at his son. "You covered his tuition, didn't you?"

She shrugged. "It's not like you could have been any angrier with me. And he deserves the best. Just like his father does."

"We'll figure it out," Matteo said as she led him and his sweet, smiling son into her apartment. "Together."

EPILOGUE

One week later...
Santa Barbara, CA

THE RAPPING ON the door of the RV brought Big E to his feet. *Who could this be?* he asked himself.

Rudy Harrison, beer bottle in hand, casually leaned back in his chair as the door popped open and Matteo Rossi stepped inside.

"Evening," Matteo said. "You two aren't all that easy to track down, you know that?"

"Ever consider that might be by design, son?" Big E slapped his hand on Matteo's shoulder affectionately and drew the younger man in. "Don't know why you'd be looking for two old codgers like us."

"How did things go with Peyton?" Rudy asked. "You admit to being an overreacting fool?"

Matteo looked at Rudy for a long time before speaking. "With all due respect, sir, I don't think I can answer that truthfully now that you're going to be my father-in-law."

Rudy's face split into a grin so wide Big E swore he saw his back molars.

Big E shook Matteo's hand. "Well, good on you, son. Knew you and Peyton would make a great pair as soon as I saw you two together in that restaurant."

"No taking complete credit," Matteo said, grinning. "But I'll give you some. And I owe you. That's why I made the drive down here to Santa Barbara." He took an envelope from his jacket pocket and set it on the counter. "I called in a few favors, reached out to former intelligence operatives and asked them to do a deep dive for Thomas Blackwell."

"You…did what?" Rudy was on his feet in an instant, but he wasn't fast enough to beat Big E to the envelope.

"Something I learned from your daughter, sir," Matteo said. "Better to ask forgiveness than permission. I know you have your own sources—"

"Naval records didn't get us very far," Rudy said as Big E scanned the information. "Well? What does it say, Elias?"

"Confirms what we thought. That Thomas is still alive. Or was as of a year ago." Big E closed his eyes and, unusually for him, offered a prayer of thanks. "This gives us information his military records didn't, including locations he's been known to work, VA benefits he tried to claim. It's a lot more for us to go on, for our road map, Matteo." Big E offered his hand again. "Thank you."

"I didn't just do it for you," Matteo said. "I did it for Peyton. She loves you, Mr. Harrison. She loves you so much. But she needs closure with Thomas, if it's at all possible. I want that hole in her heart to heal."

"The hole that started to heal thanks to you and Gino," Rudy said.

"I hope so. Well, if you'll excuse me." He pushed open the door.

"Hang on." Big E grabbed his arm. "You drove ninety minutes to an RV park just to drop this off and drive back? Son, that's a bit above and beyond."

"No," Matteo said. "It's not." He smiled and tapped two fingers against his heart. "It's what you do for family."

* * * * *

Get 4 FREE REWARDS!

We'll send you 2 FREE Books plus 2 FREE Mystery Gifts.

Love Inspired books feature uplifting stories where faith helps guide you through life's challenges and discover the promise of a new beginning.

FREE Value Over $20

YES! Please send me 2 FREE Love Inspired Romance novels and my 2 FREE mystery gifts (gifts are worth about $10 retail). After receiving them, if I don't wish to receive any more books, I can return the shipping statement marked "cancel." If I don't cancel, I will receive 6 brand-new novels every month and be billed just $5.24 each for the regular-print edition or $5.99 each for the larger-print edition in the U.S., or $5.74 each for the regular-print edition or $6.24 each for the larger-print edition in Canada. That's a savings of at least 13% off the cover price. It's quite a bargain! Shipping and handling is just 50¢ per book in the U.S. and $1.25 per book in Canada.* I understand that accepting the 2 free books and gifts places me under no obligation to buy anything. I can always return a shipment and cancel at any time. The free books and gifts are mine to keep no matter what I decide.

Choose one: ☐ **Love Inspired Romance Regular-Print** (105/305 IDN GNWC)   ☐ **Love Inspired Romance Larger-Print** (122/322 IDN GNWC)

Name (please print)

Address   Apt. #

City   State/Province   Zip/Postal Code

Email: Please check this box ☐ if you would like to receive newsletters and promotional emails from Harlequin Enterprises ULC and its affiliates. You can unsubscribe anytime.

> Mail to the **Reader Service:**
> **IN U.S.A.:** P.O. Box 1341, Buffalo, NY 14240-8531
> **IN CANADA:** P.O. Box 603, Fort Erie, Ontario L2A 5X3

Want to try 2 free books from another series! Call 1-800-873-8635 or visit www.ReaderService.com.

THE WESTERN HEARTS COLLECTION!

19 FREE BOOKS in all!

COWBOYS. RANCHERS. RODEO REBELS.
Here are their charming love stories in one prized Collection:
51 emotional and heart-filled romances that capture the majesty
and rugged beauty of the American West!

YES! Please send me **The Western Hearts Collection** in Larger Print. This collection begins with 3 FREE books and 2 FREE gifts in the first shipment. Along with my 3 free books, I'll also get the next 4 books from The Western Hearts Collection, in LARGER PRINT, which I may either return and owe nothing, or keep for the low price of $5.45 U.S./$6.23 CDN each plus $2.99 U.S./$7.49 CDN for shipping and handling per shipment*. If I decide to continue, about once a month for 8 months I will get 6 or 7 more books but will only need to pay for 4. That means 2 or 3 books in every shipment will be FREE! If I decide to keep the entire collection, I'll have paid for only 32 books because 19 books are FREE! I understand that accepting the 3 free books and gifts places me under no obligation to buy anything. I can always return a shipment and cancel at any time. My free books and gifts are mine to keep no matter what I decide.

☐ 270 HCN 5354   ☐ 470 HCN 5354

Name (please print)

Address   Apt. #

City   State/Province   Zip/Postal Code

Mail to the Reader Service:
IN U.S.A.: P.O. Box 1341, Buffalo, N.Y. 14240-8531
IN CANADA: P.O. Box 603, Fort Erie, Ontario L2A 5X3

*Terms and prices subject to change without notice. Prices do not include sales taxes, which will be charged (if applicable) based on your state or country of residence. Canadian residents will be charged applicable taxes. Offer not valid in Quebec. All orders subject to approval. Credit or debit balances in a customer's account(s) may be offset by any other outstanding balance owed by or to the customer. Please allow three to four weeks for delivery. Offer available while quantities last. © 2020 Harlequin Enterprises ULC. ® and ™ are trademarks owned by Harlequin Enterprises ULC.

Your Privacy—The Reader Service is committed to protecting your privacy. Our Privacy Policy is available online at www.ReaderService.com or upon request from the Reader Service. We make a portion of our mailing list available to reputable third parties that offer products we believe may interest you. If you prefer that we not exchange your name with third parties, or if you wish to clarify or modify your communication preferences, please visit us at www.ReaderService.com/consumerschoice or write to us at Reader Service Mail Preference Service, P.O. Box 9062, Buffalo, NY 14269. Include your complete name and address.

50BWH20

#351 MONTANA MATCH
The Blackwell Sisters • by Carol Ross
Fiona Harrison's dating app attempts haven't gone according to plan. What better way to make things worse than allowing Simon Clarke to play matchmaker? She's falling for the handsome bartender, but he doesn't see marriage in his own future.

#352 THE COWBOY'S HOLIDAY BRIDE
Wishing Well Springs • by Cathy McDavid
Cash Montgomery is stuck covering his sister's absence from their wedding barn business with event coordinator Phoebe Kellerman. Then come his three former fiancées, all to be wed and each ready to impart their advice about the bride who's right under his nose.

#353 AN ALASKAN FAMILY CHRISTMAS
A Northern Lights Novel • by Beth Carpenter
Confirmed skeptic Natalie Weiss is in Alaska to help a friend, not spend the holidays with a stranger's family in their rustic cabin. Tanner Rockford finds himself drawn to the cynical professor, knowing full well her career will take her away.

#354 MISTLETOE COWBOY
Kansas Cowboys • by Leigh Riker
Ex-con Cody Jones discovers that the love of his life is engaged to someone else. Is there any way the cowboy can turn his life around and convince Willow Bodine to choose him over her successful lawyer fiancé?